LORD EDGWARE DIES

Agatha Christie is known throughout the world as the Queen of Crime. Her seventy-six detective novels and books of stories have been translated into every major language, and her sales are calculated in tens of millions.

She began writing at the end of the First World War, when she created Hercule Poirot, the little Belgian detective with the egg-shaped head and the passion for order – the most popular sleuth in fiction since Sherlock Holmes. Poirot, fluffy Miss Marple and her other detectives have appeared in the films, radio programmes and stage plays based on her books.

Agatha Christie also wrote six romantic novels under the pseudonym Mary Westmacott, several plays and a book of poems; as well, she assisted her archaeologist husband Sir Max Mallowan on many expeditions to the Near East.

Postern of Fate was the last book she wrote before her death in 1976, but in 1975 William Collins published *Curtain: Poirot's Last Case*, which she wrote in the 1940s. The last Miss Marple book (also written in the 1940s) and her autobiography have not yet been published.

AGATHA CHRISTIE

Lord Edgware Dies

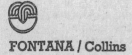

FONTANA / Collins

First published in 1933 by William Collins Sons & Co Ltd
First issued in Fontana Books 1954
Thirteenth Impression July 1976

© 1933 by Agatha Christie

Made and printed in Great Britain by
William Collins Sons & Co Ltd Glasgow

To
Dr. and Mrs. Campbell Thompson

CONTENTS

CHAPTER I

A THEATRICAL PARTY

THE MEMORY of the public is short. Already the intense interest and excitement aroused by the murder of George Alfred St. Vincent Marsh, fourth Baron Edgware, is a thing past and forgotten. Newer sensations have taken its place.

My friend, Hercule Poirot, was never openly mentioned in connection with the case. This, I may say, was entirely in accordance with his own wishes. He did not choose to appear in it. The credit went elsewhere—and that is how he wished it to be. Moreover, from Poirot's own peculiar private point of view, the case was one of his failures. He always swears that it was the chance remark of a stranger in the street that put him on the right track.

However that may be, it was his genius that discovered the truth of the affair. But for Hercule Poirot I doubt if the crime would have been brought home to its perpetrator.

I feel therefore that the time has come for me to set down all I know of the affair in black and white. I know the ins and outs of the case thoroughly and I may also mention that I shall be fulfilling the wishes of a very fascinating lady in so doing.

I have often recalled that day in Poirot's prim neat little sitting-room when, striding up and down a particular strip of carpet, my little friend gave us his masterly and astounding resumé of the case. I am going to begin my narrative where he did on that occasion—at a London theatre in June of last year.

Carlotta Adams was quite the rage in London at that moment. The year before she had given a couple of matinées which had been a wild success. This year she had had a three weeks' season of which this was the last night but one.

Carlotta Adams was an American girl with the most amazing talent for single-handed sketches unhampered by make-up or scenery. She seemed to speak every language with ease. Her sketch of an evening in a foreign hotel was really wonderful. In turn, American tourists, German tourists, middle-class

English families, questionable ladies, impoverished Russian aristocrats and weary discreet waiters all flitted across the scene.

Her sketches went from grave to gay and back again. Her dying Czecho-Slovakian woman in hospital brought a lump to the throat. A minute later we were rocking with laughter as a dentist plied his trade and chatted amiably with his victims.

Her programme closed with what she announced as " Some Imitations."

Here again, she was amazingly clever. Without make-up of any kind, her features seemed to dissolve suddenly and re-form themselves into those of a famous politician, or a well-known actress, or a society beauty. In each character she gave a short typical speech. These speeches, by the way, were remarkably clever. They seemed to hit off every weakness of the subject selected.

One of her last impersonations was Jane Wilkinson—a talented young American actress well known in London. It was really very clever. Inanities slipped off her tongue charged with some powerful emotional appeal so that in spite of yourself you felt that each word was uttered with some potent and fundamental meaning. Her voice, exquisitely toned, with a deep husky note in it, was intoxicating. The restrained gestures, each strangely significant, the slightly swaying body, the impression even, of strong physical beauty —how she did it, I cannot think!

I had always been an admirer of the beautiful Jane Wilkinson. She had thrilled me in her emotional parts, and I had always maintained in face of those who admitted her beauty but declared she was no actress, that she had considerable histrionic powers.

It was a little uncanny to hear that well-known, slightly husky voice with the fatalistic drop in it that had stirred me so often, and to watch that seemingly poignant gesture of the slowly closing and unclosing hand, and the sudden throw back of the head with the hair shaken back from the face that I realised she always gave at the close of a dramatic scene.

Jane Wilkinson was one of those actresses who had left the stage on her marriage only to return to it a couple of years later.

Three years ago she had married the wealthy but slightly

eccentric Lord Edgware. Rumour went that she left him shortly afterwards. At anyrate, eighteen months after the marriage, she was acting for the films in America, and had this season appeared in a successful play in London.

Watching Carlotta Adams' clever but perhaps slightly malicious imitation, it occurred to me to wonder how such imitations were regarded by the subject selected. Were they pleased at the notoriety—at the advertisement it afforded? Or were they annoyed at what was, after all, a deliberate exposing of the tricks of their trade? Was not Carlotta Adams in the position of the rival conjurer who says: " Oh! this is an old trick! Very simple. I'll show you how this one's done!"

I decided that if *I* were the subject in question, I should be very much annoyed. I should, of course, conceal my vexation, but decidedly I should not like it. One would need great broad-mindedness and a distinct sense of humour to appreciate such a merciless exposé.

I had just arrived at these conclusions when the delightful husky laugh from the stage was echoed from behind me.

I turned my head sharply. In the seat immediately behind mine, leaning forward with her lips slightly parted, was the subject of the present imitation—Lady Edgware, better known as Jane Wilkinson.

I realised immediately that my deductions had been all wrong. She was leaning forward, her lips parted, with an expression of delight and excitement in her eyes.

As the " imitation " finished, she applauded loudly, laughing and turning to her companion, a tall extremely good-looking man, of the Greek god type, whose face I recognised as one better known on the screen than on the stage. It was Bryan Martin, the hero of the screen most popular at the moment. He and Jane Wilkinson had been starred together in several screen productions.

" Marvellous, isn't she? " Lady Edgware was saying.

He laughed.

" Jane—you look all excited."

" Well, she really is too wonderful! Heaps better than I thought she'd be."

I did not catch Bryan Martin's amused rejoinder. Carlotta Adams had started on a fresh improvisation.

What happened later is, I shall always think, a very curious coincidence.

After the theatre, Poirot and I went on to supper at the Savoy.

At the very next table to ours were Lady Edgware, Bryan Martin and two other people whom I did not know. I pointed them out to Poirot and, as I was doing so, another couple came and took their places at the table beyond that again. The woman's face was familiar and yet strangely enough, for the moment I could not place it.

Then suddenly I realised that it was Carlotta Adams at whom I was staring! The man I did not know. He was well-groomed, with a cheerful, somewhat vacuous face. Not a type that I admire.

Carlotta Adams was dressed very inconspicuously in black. Hers was not a face to command instant attention or recognition. It was one of those mobile sensitive faces that pre-eminently lend themselves to the art of mimicry. It could take on an alien character easily, but it had no very recognisable character of its own.

I imparted these reflections of mine to Poirot. He listened attentively, his egg-shaped head cocked slightly to one side whilst he darted a sharp glance at the two tables in question.

" So that is Lady Edgware? Yes, I remember—I have seen her act. She is *belle femme*."

" And a fine actress too."

" Possibly."

" You don't seem convinced."

" I think it would depend on the setting, my friend. If she is the centre of the play, if all revolves round her—yes, then she could play her part. I doubt if she could play a small part adequately or even what is called a character part. The play must be written *about* her and *for* her. She appears to me of the type of women who are interested only in themselves." He paused and then added rather unexpectedly: " Such people go through life in great danger."

" Danger?" I said, surprised.

" I have used a word that surprises you, I see, *mon ami*. Yes, danger. Because, you see, a woman like that sees only one thing—herself. Such women see nothing of the dangers and hazards that surround them—the million conflicting interests and relationships of life. No, they see only their own forward path. And so—sooner or later—disaster."

I was interested. I confessed to myself that such a point of view would not have struck me.

" And the other?" I asked.

" Miss Adams?"

His gaze swept to her table.

" Well?" he said, smiling. " What do you want me to say about her?"

" Only how she strikes you."

"*Mon cher*, am I to-night the fortune-teller who reads the palm and tells the character?"

" You could do it better than most," I rejoined.

" It is a very pretty faith that you have in me, Hastings. It touches me. Do you not know, my friend, that each one of us is a dark mystery, a maze of conflicting passions and desires and aptitudes? *Mais oui, c'est vrai*. One makes one's little judgments—but nine times out of ten one is wrong."

" Not Hercule Poirot," I said, smiling.

" Even Hercule Poirot! Oh! I know very well that you have always a little idea that I am conceited, but, indeed, I assure you, I am really a very humble person."

I laughed.

" You—humble!"

" It is so. Except—I confess it—that I am a little proud of my moustaches. Nowhere in London have I observed anything to compare with them."

" You are quite safe," I said dryly. " You won't. So you are not going to risk judgment on Carlotta Adams?"

" *Elle est artiste!*" said Poirot simply. " That covers nearly all, does it not?"

" Anyway, you don't consider that she walks through life in peril?"

" We all do that, my friend," said Poirot gravely. " Misfortune may always be waiting to rush out upon us. But as to your question, Miss Adams, I think, will succeed. She is shrewd and she is something more. You observed without doubt that she is a Jewess?"

I had not. But now that he mentioned it, I saw the faint traces of Semitic ancestry. Poirot nodded.

" It makes for success—that. Though there is still one avenue of danger—since it is of danger we are talking."

" You mean?"

" Love of money. Love of money might lead such a one from the prudent and cautious path."

" It might do that to all of us," I said.

" That is true, but at anyrate you or I would see the danger involved. We could weigh the pros and cons. If you care for money too much, it is only the money you see, everything else is in shadow."

I laughed at his serious manner.

" Esmeralda, the gipsy queen, is in good form," I remarked teasingly.

" The psychology of character is interesting," returned Poirot, unmoved. " One cannot be interested in crime without being interested in psychology. It is not the mere act of killing, it is what lies *behind* it that appeals to the expert. You follow me, Hastings?"

I said that I followed him perfectly.

" I have noticed that when we work on a case together, you are always urging me on to physical action, Hastings. You wish me to measure footprints, to analyse cigarette-ash, to prostrate myself on my stomach for the examination of detail. You never realise that by lying back in an arm-chair with the eyes closed one can come nearer to the solution of any problem. One sees then with the eyes of the mind."

" I don't," I said. " When I lie back in an arm-chair with my eyes closed one thing happens to me and one thing only!"

" I have noticed it!" said Poirot. " It is strange. At such moments the brain should be working feverishly, not sinking into sluggish repose. The mental activity, it is so interesting, so stimulating! The employment of the little grey cells is a mental pleasure. They and they only can be trusted to lead one through fog to the truth. . . ."

I am afraid that I have got into the habit of averting my attention whenever Poirot mentions his little grey cells. I have heard it all so often before.

In this instance my attention wandered to the four people sitting at the next table. When Poirot's monologue drew to a close I remarked with a chuckle:

" You have made a hit, Poirot. The fair Lady Edgware can hardly take her eyes off you."

" Doubtless she has been informed of my identity," said Poirot, trying to look modest and failing.

"I think it is the famous moustaches," I said. "She is carried away by their beauty."

Poirot caressed them surreptitiously.

"It is true that they are unique," he admitted. "Oh, my friend, the 'tooth-brush' as you call it, that you wear—it is a horror—an atrocity—a wilful stunting of the bounties of nature. Abandon it, my friend, I pray of you."

"By Jove," I said, disregarding Poirot's appeal. "The lady's getting up. I believe she's coming to speak to us. Bryan Martin is protesting, but she won't listen to him."

Sure enough, Jane Wilkinson swept impetuously from her seat and came over to our table. Poirot rose to his feet, bowing, and I rose also.

"M. Hercule Poirot, isn't it?" said the soft husky voice.

"At your service."

"M. Poirot, I want to talk to you. I must talk to you."

"But certainly, Madame, will you not sit down?"

"No, no, not here. I want to talk to you privately. We'll go right upstairs to my suite."

Bryan Martin had joined her. He spoke now with a deprecating laugh.

"You must wait a little, Jane. We're in the middle of supper. So is M. Poirot."

But Jane Wilkinson was not so easily turned from her purpose.

"Why, Bryan, what does that matter? We'll have supper sent up to the suite. Speak to them about it, will you? And, Bryan——"

She went after him as he was turning away and appeared to urge some course upon him. He stood out about it, I gathered, shaking his head and frowning. But she spoke even more emphatically and finally with a shrug of the shoulders he gave way.

Once or twice during her speech to him she had glanced at the table where Carlotta Adams sat, and I wondered if what she were suggesting had anything to do with the American girl.

Her point gained, Jane came back, radiant.

"We'll go right up now," she said, and included me in a dazzling smile.

The question of our agreeing or not agreeing to her plan

did not seem to occur to her mind. She swept us off without a shade of apology.

" It's the greatest luck just seeing you here this evening, M. Poirot," she said as she led the way to the lift. " It's wonderful how everything seems to turn out right for me. I'd just been thinking and wondering what on earth I was going to do and I looked up and there you were at the next table, and I said to myself: ' M. Poirot will tell me what to do.' "

She broke off to say " Second Floor " to the lift-boy.

" If I can be of aid to you——" began Poirot.

" I'm sure you can. I've heard you're just the most marvellous man that ever existed. Somebody's got to get me out of the tangle I'm in and I feel you're just the man to do it."

We got out at the second floor and she led the way along the corridor, paused at a door and entered one of the most opulent of the Savoy suites.

Casting her white fur wrap on one chair, and her small jewelled bag on the table, the actress sank on to a chair and exclaimed:

" M. Poirot, somehow or other I've just *got* to get rid of my husband!"

CHAPTER II

A SUPPER PARTY

AFTER A MOMENT'S astonishment Poirot recovered himself!

" But, Madame," he said, his eyes twinkling, " getting rid of husbands is not my speciality."

" Well, of course, I know that."

" It is a lawyer you require."

" That's just where you're wrong. I'm just about sick and tired of lawyers. I've had straight lawyers and crooked lawyers, and not one of them's done me any good. Lawyers just know the law, they don't seem to have any kind of natural sense."

" And you think I have?"

She laughed.

" I've heard that you're the cat's whiskers, M. Poirot."

" *Comment?* The cat's whiskers? I do not understand."

" Well—that you're *It*."

" Madame, I may or may not have brains—as a matter of fact I have—why pretend? But your little affair, it is not my *genre*."

" I don't see why not. It's a problem."

" Oh! a problem!"

" And it's difficult," went on Jane Wilkinson. " I should say you weren't the man to shy at difficulties."

" Let me compliment you on your insight, Madame. But all the same, me, I do not make the investigations for divorce. It is not pretty—*ce métier là*."

" My dear man, I'm not asking you to do spying work. It wouldn't be any good. But I've just got to get rid of the man, and I'm sure you could tell me how to do it."

Poirot paused awhile before replying. When he did, there was a new note in his voice.

" First tell me, Madame, why you are so anxious to ' get rid ' of Lord Edgware?"

There was no delay or hesitation about her answer. It came swift and pat.

" Why, of course. I want to get married again. What other reason could there be?"

Her great blue eyes opened ingenuously.

" But surely a divorce should be easy to obtain?"

" You don't know my husband, M. Poirot. He's—he's——" she shivered. " I don't know how to explain it. He's a queer man—he's not like other people."

She paused and then went on.

" He should never have married—anyone. I know what I'm talking about. I just can't describe him, but he's—queer. His first wife, you know, ran away from him. Left a baby of three months behind. He never divorced her and she died miserably abroad somewhere. Then he married me. Well—I couldn't stick it. I was frightened. I left him and went to the States. I've no grounds for a divorce, and if I've given him grounds for one, he won't take any notice of them. He's —he's a kind of fanatic."

" In certain American states you could obtain a divorce, Madame."

" That's no good to me—not if I'm going to live in England."

" You want to live in England?"

" Yes."

" Who is the man you want to marry?"

" That's just it. The Duke of Merton."

I drew in my breath sharply. The Duke of Merton had so far been the despair of matchmaking mammas. A young man of monkish tendencies, a violent Anglo-Catholic, he was reported to be completely under the thumb of his mother, the redoubtable dowager duchess. His life was austere in the extreme. He collected Chinese porcelain and was reputed to be of æsthetic tastes. He was supposed to care nothing for women.

" I'm just crazy about him," said Jane sentimentally. " He's unlike anyone I ever met, and Merton Castle is too wonderful. The whole thing is the most romantic business that ever happened. He's so good-looking too—like a dreamy kind of monk."

She paused.

" I'm going to give up the stage when I marry. I just don't seem to care about it any more."

" In the meantime," said Poirot dryly. " Lord Edgware stands in the way of these romantic dreams."

" Yes—and it's driving me to distraction." She leaned back thoughtfully. " Of course if we were only in Chicago I could get him bumped off quite easily, but you don't seem to run to gunmen over here."

" Over here," said Poirot, smiling, " we consider that every human being has the right to live."

" Well, I don't know about that. I guess you'd be better off without some of your politicians, and knowing what I do of Edgware I think he'd be no loss—rather the contrary."

There was a knock at the door, and a waiter entered with supper dishes. Jane Wilkinson continued to discuss her problem with no appreciation of his presence.

" But I don't want you to kill him for me, M. Poirot."

" Merci, Madame."

" I thought perhaps you might argue with him in some clever way. Get him to give in to the idea of divorce. I'm sure you could."

" I think you overrate my persuasive powers, Madame."

" Oh! but you can surely think of *something*, M. Poirot." She leaned forward. Her blue eyes opened wide again. " You'd like me to be happy, wouldn't you?"

Her voice was soft, low and deliciously seductive.

" I should like everybody to be happy," said Poirot cautiously.

" Yes, but I wasn't thinking of everybody. I was thinking of just me."

" I should say you always do that, Madame."

He smiled.

" You think I'm selfish?"

" Oh! I did not say so, Madame."

" I dare say I am. But, you see, I do so hate being unhappy. It affects my acting, even. And I'm going to be ever so unhappy unless he agrees to a divorce—or dies.

" On the whole," she continued thoughtfully, " it would be much better if he died. I mean, I'd feel more finally quit of him."

She looked at Poirot for sympathy.

" You *will* help me, won't you, M. Poirot?" She rose, picking up the white wrap, and stood looking appealingly into his face. I heard the noise of voices outside in the corridor. The door was ajar. " If you don't——" she went on.

" If I don't, Madame?"

She laughed.

" I'll have to call a taxi to go round and bump him off myself."

Laughing, she disappeared through a door to an adjoining room just as Bryan Martin came in with the American girl, Carlotta Adams, and her escort, and the two people who had been supping with him and Jane Wilkinson. They were introduced to me as Mr. and Mrs. Widburn.

" Hello!" said Bryan. " Where's Jane? I want to tell her I've succeeded in the commission she gave me."

Jane appeared in the doorway of the bedroom. She held a lipstick in one hand.

" Have you got her? How marvellous. Miss Adams, I do admire your performance so. I felt I just had to know you. Come in here and talk to me while I fix my face. It's looking too perfectly frightful."

Carlotta Adams accepted the invitation. Bryan Martin flung himself down in a chair.

" Well, M. Poirot," he said. " You were duly captured. Has our Jane persuaded you to fight her battles? You might as well give in sooner as later. She doesn't understand the word ' No.' "

" She has not come across it, perhaps."

" A very interesting character, Jane," said Bryan Martin. He lay back in his chair and puffed cigarette smoke idly towards the ceiling. "Taboos have no meaning for her. No morals whatever. I don't mean she's exactly immoral—she isn't. Amoral is the word, I believe. Just sees one thing only in life—what Jane wants."

He laughed.

" I believe she'd kill somebody quite cheerfully—and feel injured if they caught her and wanted to hang her for it. The trouble is that she *would* be caught. She hasn't any brains. Her idea of a murder would be to drive up in a taxi, sail in under her own name and shoot."

" Now, I wonder what makes you say that?" murmured Poirot.

" Eh?"

" You know her well, Monsieur?"

" I should say I did."

He laughed again, and it struck me that his laugh was unusually bitter.

" You agree, don't you?" he flung out to the others.

" Oh! Jane's an egoist," agreed Mrs Widburn. " An actress has got to be, though. That is, if she wants to express her personality."

Poirot did not speak. His eyes were resting on Bryan Martin's face, dwelling there with a curious speculative expression that I could not quite understand.

At that moment Jane sailed in from the next room, Carlotta Adams behind her. I presume that Jane had now " fixed her face," whatever that term denoted, to her own satisfaction. It looked to me exactly the same as before and quite incapable of improvement.

The supper party that followed was quite a merry one, yet I sometimes had the feeling that there were undercurrents which I was incapable of appreciating.

Jane Wilkinson I acquitted of any subtleties. She was obviously a young woman who saw only one thing at a time. She had desired an interview with Poirot, and had carried her point and obtained her desire without delay. Now she was obviously in high good humour. Her desire to include

Carlotta Adams in the party had been, I decided, a mere whim. She had been highly amused, as a child might be amused, by the clever counterfeit of herself.

No, the undercurrents that I sensed were nothing to do with Jane Wilkinson. In what direction did they lie?

I studied the guests in turn. Bryan Martin? He was certainly not behaving quite naturally. But that, I told myself, might be merely characteristic of a film star. The exaggerated self-consciousness of a vain man too accustomed to playing a part to lay it aside easily.

Carlotta Adams, at anyrate, was behaving naturally enough. She was a quiet girl with a pleasant low voice. I studied her with some attention now that I had a chance to do so at close quarters. She had, I thought, distinct charm, but charm of a somewhat negative order. It consisted in an absence of any jarring or strident note. She was a kind of personified soft agreement. Her very appearance was negative. Soft dark hair, eyes a rather colourless pale blue, pale face and a mobile sensitive mouth. A face that you liked but that you would find it hard to know again if you were to meet her, say, in different clothes.

She seemed pleased at Jane's graciousness and complimentary sayings. Any girl would be, I thought—and then—just at that moment—something occurred that caused me to revise that rather too hasty opinion.

Carlotta Adams looked across the table at her hostess who was at that moment turning her head to talk to Poirot. There was a curious scrutinising quality in the girl's gaze—it seemed a deliberate summing up, and at the same time it struck me that there was a very definite hostility in those pale blue eyes.

Fancy, perhaps. Or possibly professional jealousy. Jane was a successful actress who had definitely arrived. Carlotta was merely climbing the ladder.

I looked at the three other members of the party. Mr. and Mrs. Widburn, what about them? He was a tall cadaverous man, she a plump, fair, gushing soul. They appeared to be wealthy people with a passion for everything connected with the stage. They were, in fact, unwilling to talk on any other subject. Owing to my recent absence from England they found me sadly ill-informed, and finally Mrs. Widburn turned a plump shoulder on me and remembered my existence no more.

The last member of the party was the dark young man with the round cheerful face who was Carlotta Adams' escort. I had had my suspicions from the first that the young man was not quite so sober as he might have been. As he drank more champagne this became even more clearly apparent.

He appeared to be suffering from a profound sense of injury. For the first half of the meal he sat in gloomy silence. Towards the latter half he unbosomed himself to me apparently under the impression that I was one of his oldest friends.

"What I mean to say," he said. "It isn't. No, dear old chap, it isn't——"

I omit the slight slurring together of the words.

"I mean to say," he went on, "I ask you? I mean if you take a girl—well, I mean—butting in. Going round upsetting things. Not as though I'd ever said a word to her I shouldn't have done. She's not the sort. You know— Puritan fathers— the Mayflower—all that. Dash it—the girl's straight. What I mean is—what was I saying?"

"That it was hard lines," I said soothingly.

"Well, dash it all, it is. Dash it, I had to borrow the money for this beano from my tailor. Very obliging chap, my tailor. I've owed him money for years. Makes a sort of bond between us. Nothing like a bond, is there, dear old fellow. You and I. You and I. Who the devil are you, by the way?"

"My name is Hastings."

"You don't say so. Now I could have sworn you were a chap called Spencer Jones. Dear old Spencer Jones. Met him at the Eton and Harrow and borrowed a fiver from him. What I say is one face is very like another face—that's what I say. If we were a lot of Chinks we wouldn't know each other apart."

He shook his head sadly, then cheered up suddenly and drank off some more champagne.

"Anyway," he said. "I'm not a damned nigger."

This reflection seemed to cause him such elation that he presently made several remarks of a hopeful character.

"Look on the bright side, my boy," he adjured me. "What I say is, look on the bright side. One of these days —when I'm seventy-five or so, I'm going to be a rich man. When my uncle dies. Then I can pay my tailor."

He sat smiling happily at the thought.

There was something strangely likeable about the young man. He had a round face and an absurdly small black moustache that gave one the impression of being marooned in the middle of a desert.

Carlotta Adams, I noticed, had an eye on him, and it was after a glance in his direction that she rose and broke up the party.

"It was just sweet of you to come up here," said Jane. "I do so love doing things on the spur of the moment, don't you?"

"No," said Miss Adams. "I'm afraid I always plan a thing out very carefully before I do it. It saves—worry."

There was something faintly disagreeable in her manner.

"Well, at anyrate the results justify you," laughed Jane. "I don't know when I enjoyed anything so much as I did your show to-night."

The American girl's face relaxed.

"Well, that's very sweet of you," she said warmly. "And I guess I appreciate your telling me so. I need encouragement. We all do."

"Carlotta," said the young man with the black moustache. "Shake hands and say thank you for the party to Aunt Jane and come along."

The way he walked straight through the door was a miracle of concentration. Carlotta followed him quickly.

"Well," said Jane, "what was that that blew in and called me Aunt Jane? I hadn't noticed him before."

"My dear," said Mrs. Widburn. "You mustn't take any notice of him. Most brilliant as a boy in the O.U.D.S. You'd hardly think so now, would you? I hate to see early promise come to nothing. But Charles and I positively must toddle."

The Widburns duly toddled and Bryan Martin went with them.

"Well, M. Poirot?"

He smiled at her.

"*Eh bien*, Lady Edgware?"

"For goodness' sake, don't call me that. Let me forget it! If you aren't the hardest-hearted little man in Europe!"

"But no, but no, I am not hard-hearted."

Poirot, I thought, had had quite enough champagne, possibly a glass too much.

"Then you'll go and see my husband? And make him do what I want?"

"I will go and see him," Poirot promised cautiously.

"And if he turns you down—as he will—you'll think of a clever plan. They say you're the cleverest man in England, M. Poirot."

"Madame, when I am hard-hearted, it is Europe you mention. But for cleverness you say only England."

"If you put this through I'll say the universe."

Poirot raised a deprecating hand.

"Madame, I promise nothing. In the interests of the psychology I will endeavour to arrange a meeting with your husband."

"Psycho-analyse him as much as you like. Maybe it would do him good. But you've got to pull it off—for my sake. I've got to have my romance, Mr. Poirot."

She added dreamily: "Just think of the sensation it will make."

CHAPTER III

THE MAN WITH THE GOLD TOOTH

IT WAS a few days later, when we were sitting at breakfast, that Poirot flung across to me a letter that he had just opened.

"Well, *mon ami*," he said. "What do you think of that?"

The note was from Lord Edgware and in stiff formal language it made an appointment for the following day at eleven.

I must say that I was very much surprised. I had taken Poirot's words as uttered lightly in a convivial moment, and I had had no idea that he had actually taken steps to carry out his promise.

Poirot, who was very quick-witted, read my mind and his eyes twinkled a little.

"But yes, *mon ami*, it was not solely the champagne."

"I didn't mean that."

"But yes—but yes—you thought to yourself, the poor old one, he has the spirit of the party, he promises things that he will not perform—that he has no intention of performing. But, my friend, the promises of Hercule Poirot are sacred."

He drew himself up in a stately manner as he said the last words. "Of course. Of course. I know that," I said hastily. "But I thought that perhaps your judgment was slightly— what shall I say—influenced."

"I am not in the habit of letting my judgment be 'influenced' as you call it, Hastings. The best and driest of champagne, the most golden-haired and seductive of women —nothing influences the judgment of Hercule Poirot. No, *mon ami*, I am interested—that is all."

"In Jane Wilkinson's love affair?"

"Not exactly that. Her love affair, as you call it, is a very commonplace business. It is a step in the successful career of a very beautiful woman. If the Duke of Merton had neither a title nor wealth his romantic likeness to a dreamy monk would no longer interest the lady. No, Hastings, what intrigues me is the psychology of the matter. The interplay of character. I welcome the chance of studying Lord Edgware at close quarters."

"You do not expect to be successful in your mission?"

"*Pourquoi pas?* Every man has his weak spot. Do not imagine, Hastings, that because I am studying the case from a psychological standpoint, I shall not try my best to succeed in the commission entrusted to me. I always enjoy exercising my ingenuity."

I had feared an allusion to the little grey cells and was thankful to be spared it.

"So we go to Regent Gate at eleven to-morrow?" I said.

"We?" Poirot raised his eyebrows quizzically.

"Poirot!" I cried. "You are not going to leave me behind. I always go with you."

"If it were a crime, a mysterious poisoning case, an assassination—ah! these are the things your soul delights in. But a mere matter of social adjustment?"

"Not another word," I said determinedly. "I'm coming."

Poirot laughed gently, and at that moment we were told that a gentleman had called.

To our great surprise our visitor proved to be Bryan Martin.

The actor looked older by daylight. He was still handsome,

but it was a kind of ravaged handsomeness. It flashed across my mind that he might conceivably take drugs. There was a kind of nervous tension about him that suggested the possibility.

"Good-morning, M. Poirot," he said in a cheerful manner. "You and Captain Hastings breakfast at a reasonable hour, I am glad to see. By the way, I suppose you are very busy just now?"

Poirot smiled at him amiably.

"No," he said. "At the moment I have practically no business of importance on hand."

"Come now," laughed Bryan. "Not called in by Scotland Yard? No delicate matters to investigate for Royalty? I can hardly believe it."

"You confound fiction with reality, my friend," said Poirot, smiling. "I am, I assure you, at the moment completely out of work, though not yet on the dole. *Dieu merci.*"

"Well, that's luck for me," said Bryan with another laugh. "Perhaps you'll take on something for me."

Poirot considered the young man thoughtfully.

"You have a problem for me—yes?" he said in a minute or two.

"Well—it's like this. I have and I haven't."

This time his laugh was rather nervous. Still considering him thoughtfully, Poirot indicated a chair. The young man took it. He sat facing us, for I had taken a seat by Poirot's side.

"And now," said Poirot, "let us hear all about it."

Bryan Martin still seemed to have a little difficulty in getting under way.

"The trouble is that I can't tell you quite as much as I'd like to." He hesitated. "It's difficult. You see, the whole business started in America."

"In America? Yes?"

"A mere incident first drew my attention to it. As a matter of fact, I was travelling by train and I noticed a certain fellow. Ugly little chap, clean-shaven, glasses, and a gold tooth."

"Ah! a gold tooth."

"Exactly. That's really the crux of the matter."

Poirot nodded his head several times.

"I begin to comprehend. Go on."

" Well, as I say. I just noticed the fellow. I was travelling, by the way, to New York. Six months later I was in Los Angeles, and I noticed the fellow again. Don't know why I should have—but I did. Still, nothing in that."

" Continue."

" A month afterwards I had occasion to go to Seattle, and shortly after I got there who should I see but my friend again, *only this time he wore a beard*."

" Distinctly curious."

" Wasn't it? Of course I didn't fancy it had anything to do with me at that time, but when I saw the man again in Los Angeles, beardless, in Chicago with a moustache and different eyebrows and in a mountain village disguised as a hobo—well, I began to wonder."

" Naturally."

" And at last—well, it seemed odd—but not a doubt about it. I was being what you call shadowed."

" Most remarkable."

" Wasn't it? After that I made sure of it. Wherever I was, there, somewhere near at hand, was my shadow made up in different disguises. Fortunately, owing to the gold tooth, I could always spot him."

" Ah! that gold tooth, it was a very fortunate occurrence."

" It was."

" Pardon me, M. Martin, but did you never speak to the man? Question him as to the reason of his persistent shadowing?"

" No, I didn't." The actor hesitated. " I thought of doing so once or twice, but I always decided against it. It seemed to me that I should merely put the fellow on his guard and learn nothing. Possibly once they had discovered that I had spotted him, they would have put someone else on my track —someone whom I might not recognise."

" *En effet*—someone without that useful gold tooth."

" Exactly. I may have been wrong—but that's how I figured it out."

" Now, M. Martin, you referred to 'they' just now. Whom did you mean by 'they'?"

" It was a mere figure of speech used for convenience. I assumed—I don't know why—a nebulous 'they' in the background."

" Have you any reason for that belief?"

" None."

" You mean you have no conception of who could want you shadowed or for what purpose?"

" Not the slightest. At least——"

" *Continuez*," said Poirot encouragingly.

" I *have* an idea," said Bryan Martin slowly. " It's a mere guess on my part, mind."

" A guess may be very successful sometimes, Monsieur."

" It concerns a certain incident that took place in London about two years ago. It was a slight incident, but an inexplicable and an unforgettable one. I've often wondered and puzzled over it. Just because I could find no explanation of it at the time, I am inclined to wonder if this shadowing business might not be connected in some way with it—but for the life of me I can't see why or how."

" Perhaps I can."

" Yes, but you see——" Bryan Martin's embarrassment returned. " The awkward thing is that I can't tell you about it—not now, that is. In a day or so I might be able to."

Stung into further speech by Poirot's inquiring glance he continued desperately.

" You see—a girl was concerned in it."

" *Ah! parfaitement!* An English girl?"

" Yes. At least—why?"

" Very simple. You cannot tell me now, but you hope to do so in a day or two. That means that you want to obtain the consent of the young lady. Therefore she is in England. Also, she must have been in England during the time you were shadowed, for if she had been in America you would have sought her out then and there. Therefore, since she has been in England for the last eighteen months she is probably, though not certainly, English. It is good reasoning that, eh?"

" Rather. Now tell me, M. Poirot, if I get her permission, will you look into the matter for me?"

There was a pause. Poirot seemed to be debating the matter in his mind. Finally he said:

" Why have you come to me before going to her?"

" Well, I thought——" he hesitated. " I wanted to persuade her to—to clear things up—I mean to let things be cleared up by you. What I mean is, if *you* investigate the affair, nothing need be made public, need it?"

" That depends," said Poirot calmly.

"What do you mean?"

"If there is any question of crime——"

"Oh! there's no crime concerned."

"You do not know. There may be."

"But you would do your best for her—for us?"

"That, naturally."

He was silent for a moment and then said:

"Tell me, this follower of yours—this shadow—of what age was he?"

"Oh! quite youngish. About thirty."

"Ah!" said Poirot. "That is indeed remarkable. Yes, that makes the whole thing very much more interesting."

I stared at him. So did Bryan Martin. This remark of his was, I am sure, equally inexplicable to us both. Bryan questioned me with a lift of his eyebrows. I shook my head.

"Yes," murmured Poirot. "It makes the whole story very interesting."

"He *may* have been older," said Bryan doubtfully, "but I don't think so."

"No, no, I am sure your observation is quite accurate, M. Martin. Very interesting—extraordinarily interesting."

Rather taken aback by Poirot's enigmatical words, Bryan Martin seemed at a loss what to say or do next. He started making desultory conversation.

"An amusing party the other night," he said. "Jane Wilkinson is the most high-handed woman that ever existed."

"She has the single vision," said Poirot, smiling. "One thing at a time."

"She gets away with it, too," said Martin. "How people stand it, I don't know!"

"One will stand a good deal from a beautiful woman, my friend," said Poirot with a twinkle. "If she had the pug nose, the sallow skin, the greasy hair, then—ah! then she would not 'get away with it' as you put it."

"I suppose not," conceded Bryan. "But it makes me mad sometimes. All the same, I'm devoted to Jane, though in some ways, mind you, I don't think she's quite all there."

"On the contrary, I should say she was very much on the spot."

"I don't mean that, exactly. She can look after her interests all right. She's got plenty of business shrewdness. No, I meant morally."

"Ah! morally."

"She's what they call amoral. Right and wrong don't exist for her."

"Ah! I remember you said something of the kind the other evening."

"We were talking of crime just now——"

"Yes, my friend?"

"Well, it would never surprise me if Jane committed a crime."

"And you should know her well," murmured Poirot thoughtfully. "You have acted much with her, have you not?"

"Yes. I suppose I know her through and through, and up and down. I can see her killing anybody quite easily."

"Ah! she has the hot temper, yes?"

"No, no, not at all. Cool as a cucumber. I mean if anyone were in her way she'd just remove them—without a thought. And one couldn't really blame her—morally, I mean. She'd just think that anyone who interfered with Jane Wilkinson had got to go."

There was a bitterness in his last words that had been lacking heretofore. I wondered what memory he was recalling.

"You think she would do—murder?"

Poirot watched him intently.

Bryan drew a deep breath.

"Upon my soul, I do. Perhaps one of these days, you'll remember my words . . . I *know* her, you see. She'd kill as easily as she'd drink her morning tea. *I mean it, M. Poirot.*"

He had risen to his feet.

"Yes," said Poirot quietly. "I can see you mean it."

"I know her," said Bryan Martin again, "through and through."

He stood frowning for a minute, then with a change of tone, he said:

"As to this business we've been talking about, I'll let you know, M. Poirot, in a few days. You will undertake it, won't you?"

Poirot looked at him for a moment or two without replying.

"Yes," he said at last. "I will undertake it. I find it—interesting."

There was something queer in the way he said the last word.

I went downstairs with Bryan Martin. At the door he said to me:

"Did you get the hang of what he meant about that fellow's age? I mean, why was it interesting that he should be about thirty. I didn't get the hang of that at all."

"No more did I," I admitted.

"It doesn't seem to make sense. Perhaps he was just having a game with me."

"No," I said. "Poirot is not like that. Depend upon it, the point has significance since he says so."

"Well, blessed if I can see it. Glad you can't either. I'd hate to feel I was a complete mutt."

He strode away. I rejoined my friend.

"Poirot," I said. "What was the point about the age of the shadower?"

"You do not see? My poor Hastings!" He smiled and shook his head. Then he asked: "What did you think of our interview on the whole?"

"There's so little to go upon. It seems difficult to say. If we knew more——"

"Even without knowing more, do not certain ideas suggest themselves to you, *mon ami*?"

The telephone ringing at that moment saved me from the ignominy of admitting that no ideas whatever suggested themselves to me. I took up the receiver.

A woman's voice spoke, a crisp, clear efficient voice.

"This is Lord Edgware's secretary speaking. Lord Edgware regrets that he must cancel the appointment with M. Poirot for to-morrow morning. He has to go over to Paris to-morrow unexpectedly. He could see M. Poirot for a few minutes at a quarter-past twelve this morning if that would be convenient."

I consulted Poirot.

"Certainly, my friend, we will go there this morning."

I repeated this into the mouthpiece.

"Very good," said the crisp business-like voice. "A quarter-past twelve this morning."

She rang off.

CHAPTER IV

AN INTERVIEW

I ARRIVED with Poirot at Lord Edgware's house in Regent Gate in a very pleasant state of anticipation. Though I had not Poirot's devotion to " the psychology," yet the few words in which Lady Edgware had referred to her husband had aroused my curiosity. I was anxious to see what my own judgment would be.

The house was an imposing one—well-built, handsome and slightly gloomy. There were no window-boxes or such frivolities.

The door was opened to us promptly, and by no aged white-haired butler such as would have been in keeping with the exterior of the house. On the contrary, it was opened by one of the handsomest young men I have ever seen. Tall, fair, he might have posed to a sculptor for Hermes or Apollo. Despite his good looks there was something vaguely effeminate that I disliked about the softness of his voice. Also, in a curious way, he reminded me of someone—someone, too, whom I had met quite lately—but who it was I could not for the life of me remember.

We asked for Lord Edgware.

" This way, sir."

He led us along the hall, past the staircase, to a door at the rear of the hall.

Opening it, he announced us in that same soft voice which I instinctively distrusted.

The room into which we were shown was a kind of library. The walls were lined with books, the furnishings were dark and sombre but handsome, the chairs were formal and not too comfortable.

Lord Edgware, who rose to receive us, was a tall man of about fifty. He had dark hair streaked with grey, a thin face and a sneering mouth. He looked bad-tempered and bitter. His eyes had a queer secretive look about them. There was something, I thought, distinctly odd about those eyes.

His manner was stiff and formal.

30

"M. Hercule Poirot? Captain Hastings? Please be seated."

We sat down. The room felt chilly. There was little light coming in from the one window and the dimness contributed to the cold atmosphere.

Lord Edgware had taken up a letter which I saw to be in my friend's handwriting.

"I am familiar, of course, with your name, M. Poirot. Who is not?" Poirot bowed at the compliment. "But I cannot quite understand your position in this matter. You say that you wish to see me on behalf of"—he paused—"my wife."

He said the last two words in a peculiar way—as though it were an effort to get them out.

"That is so," said my friend.

"I understood that you were an investigator of—crime, M. Poirot?'

"Of problems, Lord Edgware. There are problems of crime, certainly. There are other problems."

"Indeed. And what may this one be?"

The sneer in his words was palpable by now. Poirot took no notice of it.

"I have the honour to approach you on behalf of Lady Edgware," he said. "Lady Edgware, as you may know, desires—a divorce."

"I am quite aware of that," said Lord Edgware coldly.

"Her suggestion was that you and I should discuss the matter."

"There is nothing to discuss."

"You refuse, then?"

"Refuse? Certainly not."

Whatever else Poirot had expected, he had not expected this. It is seldom that I have seen my friend utterly taken aback, but I did on this occasion. His appearance was ludicrous. His mouth fell open, his hands flew out, his eyebrows rose. He looked like a cartoon in a comic paper.

"*Comment?*" he cried. "What is this? You do not refuse?"

"I am at a loss to understand your astonishment, M. Poirot."

"*Ecoutez*, you are willing to divorce your wife?"

"Certainly I am willing. She knows that perfectly well. I wrote and told her so."

"You wrote and told her so?"

"Yes. Six months ago."

"But I do not understand. I do not understand at all."

Lord Edgware said nothing.

"I understood that you were opposed to the principle of divorce."

"I do not see that my principles are your business, M. Poirot. It is true that I did not divorce my first wife. My conscience would not allow me to do so. My second marriage, I will admit frankly, was a mistake. When my wife suggested a divorce, I refused point blank. Six months ago she wrote to me again urging the point. I have an idea she wanted to marry again—some film actor or fellow of that kind. My views had, by this time, undergone modification. I wrote to her at Hollywood telling her so. Why she has sent you to me I cannot imagine. I suppose it is a question of money."

His lips sneered again as he said the last words.

"Extremely curious," muttered Poirot. "Extremely curious. There is something here I do not understand at all."

"As regards money," went on Lord Edgware. "I have no intention of making any financial arrangement. My wife deserted me of her own accord. If she wishes to marry another man, I can set her free to do so, but there is no reason why she should receive a penny from me and she will not do so."

"There is no question of any financial arrangement."

Lord Edgware raised his eyebrows.

"Jane must be marrying a rich man," he murmured cynically.

"There is something here that I do not understand," said Poirot. His face was perplexed and wrinkled with the effort of thought. "I understood from Lady Edgware that she had approached you repeatedly through lawyers?"

"She did," replied Lord Edgware dryly. "English lawyers, American lawyers, every kind of lawyer, down to the lowest kind of scallywag. Finally, as I say, she wrote to me herself."

"You have previously refused?"

"That is so."

"But on receiving her letter, you changed your mind. Why did you change your mind, Lord Edgware?"

"Not on account of anything in that letter," he said sharply. "My views happened to have changed, that is all."

"The change was somewhat sudden."

Lord Edgware did not reply.

"What special circumstance brought about your change of mind, Lord Edgware?"

"That, really, is my own business, M. Poirot. I cannot enter into the subject. Shall we say that gradually I had perceived the advantages of severing what—you will forgive my plain speaking—I considered a degrading association. My second marriage was a mistake."

"Your wife says the same," said Poirot softly.

"Does she?"

There was a queer flicker for a moment in his eyes, but it was gone almost at once.

He rose with an air of finality and as we said good-bye his manner became less unbending.

"You must forgive my altering the appointment. I have to go over to Paris to-morrow."

"Perfectly—perfectly."

"A sale of works of art as a matter of fact. I have my eye on a little statuette—a perfect thing in its way—*a macabre* way, perhaps. But I enjoy the *macabre*. I always have. My taste is peculiar."

Again that queer smile. I had been looking at the books in the shelves near. There were the Memoirs of Casanova, also a volume on the Comte de Sade, another on mediæval tortures.

I remembered Jane Wilkinson's little shudder as she spoke of her husband. That had not been acting. That had been real enough. I wondered exactly what kind of a man George Alfred St. Vincent Marsh, fourth Baron Edgware, was.

Very suavely he bid us farewell, touching the bell as he did so. We went out of the door. The Greek god of a butler was waiting in the hall. As I closed the library door behind me, I glanced back into the room. I almost uttered an exclamation as I did so.

That suave smiling face was transformed. The lips were drawn back from the teeth in a snarl, the eyes were alive with fury and an almost insane rage.

I wondered no longer that two wives had left Lord Edgware. What I did marvel at was the iron self-control of the man. To have gone through that interview with such frozen self-control, such aloof politeness!

Just as we reached the front door, a door on the right opened. A girl stood at the doorway of the room, shrinking back a little as she saw us.

She was a tall slender girl, with dark hair and a white face. Her eyes, dark and startled, looked for a moment into mine. Then, like a shadow, she shrank back into the room again, closing the door.

A moment later we were out in the street. Poirot hailed a taxi. We got in and he told the man to drive to the Savoy.

"Well, Hastings," he said with a twinkle, "that interview did not go at all as I figured to myself it would."

"No, indeed. What an extraordinary man Lord Edgware is."

I related to him how I had looked back before closing the door of the study and what I had seen. He nodded his head slowly and thoughtfully.

"I fancy that he is very near the border line of madness, Hastings. I should imagine he practises many curious vices, and that beneath his frigid exterior he hides a deep-rooted instinct of cruelty."

"It is no wonder both his wives left him."

"As you say."

"Poirot, did you notice a girl as we were coming out? A dark girl with a white face."

"Yes, I noticed her, *mon ami*. A young lady who was frightened and not happy."

His voice was grave.

"Who do you think she was?"

"Probably his daughter. He has one."

"She did look frightened," I said slowly. "That house must be a gloomy place for a young girl."

"Yes, indeed. Ah! here we are, *mon ami*. Now to acquaint her ladyship with the good news."

Jane was in, and after telephoning, the clerk informed us that we were to go up. A page-boy took us to the door.

It was opened by a neat middle-aged woman with glasses and primly arranged grey hair. From the bedroom Jane's voice, with its husky note, called to her.

" Is that M. Poirot, Ellis? Make him sit right down. I'll find a rag to put on and be there in a moment."

Jane Wilkinson's idea of a rag was a gossamer negligée which revealed more than it hid. She came in eagerly, saying: " Well?"

Poirot rose and bowed over her hand.

" Exactly the word, Madame, it *is* well."

" Why—how do you mean?"

" Lord Edgware is perfectly willing to agree to a divorce."

" What?"

Either the stupefaction on her face was genuine, or else she was indeed a most marvellous actress.

" M. Poirot! You've managed it! At once! Like that! Why, you're a genius. How in mercy's name did you set about it?"

" Madame, I cannot take compliments where they are not earned. Six months ago your husband wrote to you withdrawing his opposition."

" What's that you say? *Wrote* to *me*? Where?"

" It was when you were at Hollywood, I understand."

" I never got it. Must have gone astray, I suppose. And to think I've been thinking and planning and fretting and going nearly crazy all these months."

" Lord Edgware seemed to be under the impression that you wished to marry an actor."

" Naturally. That's what I told him." She gave a pleased child's smile. Suddenly it changed to a look of alarm. " Why, M. Poirot, you didn't go and tell him about me and the duke?"

" No, no, reassure yourself. I am discreet. That would not have done, eh?"

" Well, you see, he's got a queer mean nature. Marrying Merton, he'd feel, was perhaps a kind of leg up for me—so then naturally he'd queer the pitch. But a film actor's different. Though, all the same, I'm surprised. Yes, I am. Aren't you surprised, Ellis?"

I had noticed that the maid had come to and fro from the bedroom tidying away various outdoor garments which were lying flung over the backs of chairs. It had been my opinion that she had been listening to the conversation. Now it seemed that she was completely in Jane's confidence.

" Yes, indeed, m'lady. His lordship must have changed a good deal since we knew him," said the maid spitefully.

" Yes, he must."

" You cannot understand his attitude. It puzzles you?" suggested Poirot.

" Oh, it does. But anyway, we needn't worry about that. What does it matter what made him change his mind so long as he has changed it?"

" It may not interest you, but it interests me, Madame." Jane paid no attention to him.

" The thing is that I'm free—at last."

" Not yet, Madame."

She looked at him impatiently.

" Well, going to be free. It's the same thing."

Poirot looked as though he did not think it was.

" The duke is in Paris," said Jane. " I must cable him right away. My—won't his old mother be wild!"

Poirot rose.

" I am glad, Madame, that all is turning out as you wish."

" Good-bye, M. Poirot, and thanks awfully."

" I did nothing."

" You brought me the good news, anyway, M. Poirot, and I'm ever so grateful. I *really* am."

" And that is that," said Poirot to me, as we left the suite. " The single idea—herself! She has no speculation, no curiosity as to why that letter never reached her. You observe, Hastings, she is shrewd beyond belief in the business sense, but she has absolutely no intellect. Well, well, the good God cannot give everything."

" Except to Hercule Poirot," I said slily.

" You mock yourself at me, my friend," he replied serenely. " But come, let me walk along the Embankment. I wish to arrange my ideas with order and method."

I maintained a discreet silence until such time as the oracle should speak.

" That letter," he resumed when we were pacing along by the river. " It intrigues me. There are four solutions of that problem, my friend."

" Four?"

" Yes. First, it was lost in the post. That *does* happen, you know. But not very often. No, not very often. Incorrectly addressed, it would have been returned to Lord

Edgware long before this. No, I am inclined to rule out that solution—though, of course, it may be the true one.

"Solution two, our beautiful lady is lying when she says she never received it. That, of course, is quite possible. That charming lady is capable of telling any lie to her advantage with the most childlike candour. But I cannot see, Hastings, how it could be to her advantage. If she knows that he will divorce her, why send me to ask him to do so? It does not make sense.

"Solution three. Lord Edgware is lying. And if anyone is lying it seems more likely that it is he than his wife. But I do not see much point in such a lie. Why invent a fictitious letter sent six months ago? Why not simply agree to my proposition? No, I am inclined to think that he *did* send that letter—though what the motive was for his sudden change of attitude I cannot guess.

"So we come to the fourth solution—that someone suppressed that letter. And there, Hastings, we enter on a very interesting field of speculation, because that letter could have been suppressed at either end—in America or England.

"Whoever suppressed it was someone who did not want that marriage dissolved. Hastings, I would give a great deal to know what is behind this affair. There is *something*—I swear there is something."

He paused and then added slowly.

"Something of which as yet I have only been able to get a glimpse."

CHAPTER V

MURDER

THE FOLLOWING day was the 30th of June.

It was just half-past nine when we were told that Inspector Japp was below and anxious to see us.

It was some years since we had seen anything of the Scotland Yard inspector.

"*Ah! ce bon Japp,*" said Poirot. "What does he want, I wonder?"

"Help," I snapped. "He's out of his depth over some case and he's come to you."

I had not the indulgence for Japp that Poirot had. It was not so much that I minded his picking Poirot's brains—after all, Poirot enjoyed the process, it was a delicate flattery. What did annoy me was Japp's hypocritical pretence that he was doing nothing of the kind. I liked people to be straight-forward. I said so, and Poirot laughed.

"You are the dog of the bulldog breed, eh, Hastings? But you must remember that the poor Japp he has to save his face. So he makes his little pretence. It is very natural."

I thought it merely foolish and said so. Poirot did not agree.

"The outward form—it is a *bagatelle*—but it matters to people. It enables them to keep the *amour propre*."

Personally I thought a dash of inferiority complex would do Japp no harm, but there was no point in arguing the matter. Besides, I was anxious to learn what Japp had come about.

He greeted us both heartily.

"Just going to have breakfast, I see. Not got the hens to lay square eggs for you yet, M. Poirot?"

This was an allusion to a complaint from Poirot as to the varying sizes of eggs which had offended his sense of sym-metry.

"As yet, no," said Poirot, smiling. "And what brings you to see us so early, my good Japp?"

"It's not early—not for me. I've been up and at work for a good two hours. As to what brings me to see you—well, it's murder."

"Murder?"

Japp nodded.

"Lord Edgware was killed at his house in Regent Gate last night. Stabbed in the neck by his wife."

"By his wife?" I cried.

In a flash I remembered Bryan Martin's words on the previous morning. Had he had a prophetic knowledge of what was going to happen? I remembered, too, Jane's easy reference to "bumping him off." Amoral, Bryan Martin had called her. She was the type, yes. Callous, egotistical and stupid. How right he had been in his judgment.

All this passed through my mind while Japp went on:

"Yes. Actress, you know. Well known. Jane Wilkinson.

Married him three years ago. They didn't get on. She left him."

Poirot was looking puzzled and serious.

"What makes you believe that it was she who killed him?"

"No belief about it. She was recognised. Not much concealment about it, either. She drove up in a taxi——"

"A taxi——" I echoed involuntarily, her words at the Savoy that night coming back to me.

"—rang the bell, asked for Lord Edgware. It was ten o'clock. Butler said he'd see. 'Oh!' she says cool as a cucumber. 'You needn't. I am Lady Edgware. I suppose he's in the library.' And with that she walks along and opens the door and goes in and shuts it behind her.

"Well, the butler thought it was queer, but all right. He went downstairs again. About ten minutes later he heard the front door shut. So, anyway, she hadn't stayed long. He locked up for the night about eleven. He opened the library door, but it was dark, so he thought his master had gone to bed. This morning the body was discovered by a housemaid. Stabbed in the back of the neck just at the roots of the hair."

"Was there no cry? Nothing heard?"

"They say not. That library's got pretty well sound-proof doors, you know. And there's traffic passing, too. Stabbed in that way, death results amazing quick. Straight through the cistern into the medulla, that's what the doctor said—or something very like it. If you hit on exactly the right spot it kills a man instantaneously."

"That implies a knowledge of exactly where to strike. It almost implies medical knowledge."

"Yes—that's true. A point in her favour as far as it goes. But ten to one it was a chance. She just struck lucky. Some people do have amazing luck, you know."

"Not so lucky if it results in her being hanged, *mon ami*," observed Poirot.

"No. Of course she was a fool—sailing in like that and giving her name and all."

"Indeed, very curious."

"Possibly she didn't intend mischief. They quarrelled and she whipped out a penknife and jabbed him one."

"Was it a penknife?"

"Something of that kind, the doctor says. Whatever it was, she took it away with her. It wasn't left in the wound."

Poirot shook his head in a dissatisfied manner.

" No, no, my friend, it was not like that. I know the lady. She would be quite incapable of such a hot-blooded impulsive action. Besides, she would be most unlikely to have a pen-knife with her. Few women have—and assuredly not Jane Wilkinson."

" You know her, you say, M. Poirot?"

" Yes. I know her."

He said no more for the moment. Japp was looking at him inquisitively.

" Got something up your sleeve, M. Poirot?" he ventured at last.

" Ah!" said Poirot. " That reminds me. What has brought you to me? Eh? It is not merely to pass the time of day with an old comrade? Assuredly not. You have here a nice straightforward murder. You have the criminal. You have the motive—what exactly is the motive, by the way?"

" Wanted to marry another man. She was heard to say so not a week ago. Also heard to make threats. Said she meant to call round in a taxi and bump him off."

" Ah!" said Poirot. " You are very well informed—very well informed. Someone has been very obliging."

I thought his eyes looked a question, but if so, Japp did not respond.

" We get to hear things, M. Poirot," he said stolidly.

Poirot nodded. He had reached out for the daily paper. It had been opened by Japp, doubtless while he was waiting, and had been cast impatiently aside on our entry. In a mechanical manner, Poirot folded it back at the middle page, smoothed and arranged it. Though his eyes were on the paper, his mind was deep in some kind of puzzle.

" You have not answered," he said presently. " Since all goes in the swimming fashion, why come to me?"

" Because I heard you were at Regent Gate yesterday morning."

" I see."

" Now, as soon as I heard that, I said to myself, ' Something here.' His lordship sent for M. Poirot. Why? What did he suspect? What did he fear? Before doing anything definite, I'd better go round and have a word with him."

" What do you mean by ' anything definite?' Arresting the lady, I suppose?"

" Exactly."

" You have not seen her yet?"

" Oh! yes, I have. Went round to the Savoy first thing. Wasn't going to risk her giving us the slip."

" Ah!" said Poirot. " So you——"

He stopped. His eyes, which had been fixed thoughtfully and up to now unseeingly on the paper in front of him, now took on a different expression. He lifted his head and spoke in a changed tone of voice.

" And what did she say? Eh! my friend. What did she say?"

" I gave her the usual stuff, of course, about wanting a statement and cautioning her—you can't say the English police aren't fair."

" In my opinion foolishly so. But proceed. What did milady say?"

" Took hysterics—that's what she did. Rolled herself about, threw up her arms and finally flopped down on the ground. Oh! she did it well—I'll say that for her. A pretty bit of acting."

" Ah!" said Poirot blandly. " You formed, then, the impression that the hysterics were not genuine?"

Japp winked vulgarly.

" What do you think? I'm not to be taken in with those tricks. *She* hadn't fainted—not she! Just trying it on, she was. I'll swear she was enjoying it."

"Yes," said Poirot thoughtfully. " I should say that was perfectly possible. What next?"

" Oh! well, she came to—pretended to, I mean. And moaned—*and* groaned and carried on and that sour-faced maid of hers doped her with smelling salts and at last she recovered enough to ask for her solicitor. Wasn't going to say anything without her solicitor. Hysterics one moment, solicitors the next, now I ask you, is that natural behaviour, sir?"

" In this case quite natural, I should say," said Poirot calmly.

" You mean because she's guilty and knows it."

" Not at all, I mean because of her temperament. First she gives you her conception of how the part of a wife suddenly learning of her husband's death should be played. Then, having satisfied her histrionic instinct, her native shrewdness makes her send for a solicitor. That she creates an artificial scene and enjoys it is no proof of her guilt. It merely indicates that she is a born actress."

"Well, she can't be innocent. That's sure."

"You are very positive," said Poirot. "I suppose that it must be so. She made no statement, you say? No statement at all?"

Japp grinned.

"Wouldn't say a word without her solicitor. The maid telephoned for him. I left two of my men there and came along to you. I thought it just as well to get put wise to whatever there was going on before I went on with things."

"And yet you are sure?"

"Of course I'm sure. But I like as many facts as possible. You see, there's going to be a big splash made about this. No hole and corner business. All the papers will be full of it. And you know what papers are."

"Talking of papers," said Poirot. "How do you account for this, my dear friend. You have not read your morning paper very carefully."

He leant across the table, his finger on a paragraph in the society news. Japp read the item aloud.

Sir Montagu Corner gave a very successful dinner-party last night at his house on the river at Chiswick. Among those present were Sir George and Lady du Fisse, Mr. James Blunt, the well-known dramatic critic, Sir Oscar Hammerfeldt of the Overton Film Studios, Miss Jane Wilkinson (Lady Edgware) and others.

For a moment Japp looked taken aback. Then he rallied.

"What's that got to do with it? This thing was sent to the Press beforehand. You'll see. You'll find that our lady wasn't there, or that she came in late—eleven o'clock or so. Bless you, sir, you mustn't believe everything you see in the Press to be gospel. You of all people ought to know better than that."

"Oh! I do, I do. It only struck me as curious, that was all."

"These coincidences do happen. Now, M. Poirot, close as an oyster I know you to be by bitter experience. But you'll come across with things, won't you? You'll tell me why Lord Edgware sent for you?"

Poirot shook his head.

"Lord Edgware did not send for me. It was I who requested him to give me an appointment."

"Really? And for what reason?"

Poirot hesitated a minute.

"I will answer your question," he said slowly. "But I should like to answer it in my own way."

Japp groaned. I felt a sneaking sympathy with him. Poirot can be intensely irritating at times.

"I will request," went on Poirot, "that you permit me to ring up a certain person and ask him to come here."

"What person?"

"Mr. Bryan Martin."

"The film star? What's he got to do with it?"

"I think," said Poirot, "that you may find what he has got to say interesting—and possibly helpful. Hastings, will you be so good?"

I took up the telephone-book. The actor had a flat in a big block of buildings near St. James' Park.

"Victoria 49499."

The somewhat sleepy voice of Bryan Martin spoke after a few minutes.

"Hello—who's speaking?"

"What am I to say?" I whispered, covering the mouth-piece with my hand.

"Tell him," said Poirot, "that Lord Edgware has been murdered, and that I should esteem it a favour if he would come round here and see me immediately."

I repeated this meticulously. There was a startled exclamation at the other end.

"My God," said Martin. "*So she's done it then!* I'll come at once."

"What did he say?" asked Poirot. I told him.

"Ah!" said Poirot. He seemed pleased. "*So she's done it then*. That is what he said? Then it is as I thought, it is as I thought."

Japp looked at him curiously.

"I can't make you out, M. Poirot. First you sound as though you thought the woman might not have done it after all. And now you make out that you knew it all along."

Poirot only smiled.

CHAPTER VI

THE WIDOW

BRYAN MARTIN was as good as his word. In less than ten minutes he had joined us. During the time that we awaited his arrival, Poirot would only talk of extraneous subjects and refused to satisfy Japp's curiosity in the smallest degree.

Evidently our news had upset the young actor terribly. His face was white and drawn.

"Good heavens, M. Poirot," he said as he shook hands. "This is a terrible business. I'm shocked to the core—and yet I can't say I'm surprised. I've always half-suspected that something of this kind might happen. You may remember I was saying so yesterday."

"*Mais oui, mais oui,*" said Poirot. "I remember perfectly what you said to me yesterday. Let me introduce you to Inspector Japp who is in charge of the case."

Bryan Martin shot a glance of reproach at Poirot.

"I had no idea," he murmured. "You should have warned me."

He nodded coldly to the inspector.

He sat down, his lips pressed tightly together.

"I don't see," he objected, "why you asked me to come round. All this has nothing to do with me."

"I think it has," said Poirot gently. "In a case of murder one must put one's private repugnances behind one."

"No, no. I've acted with Jane. I know her well. Dash it all, she's a friend of mine."

"And yet the moment that you hear Lord Edgware is murdered, you jump to the conclusion that it is she who has murdered him," remarked Poirot dryly.

The actor started.

"Do you mean to say——?" His eyes seemed starting out of his head. "Do you mean to say that I'm wrong? That she had nothing to do with it?"

Japp broke in.

"No, no, Mr. Martin. She did it right enough."

The young man sank back again in his chair.

44

"For a moment," he murmured, "I thought I'd made the most ghastly mistake."

"In a matter of this kind friendship must not be allowed to influence you," said Poirot decisively.

"That's all very well, but——"

"My friend, do you seriously wish to range yourself on the side of a woman who has murdered? Murder—the most repugnant of human crimes."

Bryan Martin sighed.

"You don't understand. Jane is not an ordinary murderess. She—she has no sense of right or wrong. Honestly she's not responsible."

"That'll be a question for the jury," said Japp.

"Come, come," said Poirot kindly. "It is not as though you were accusing her. She is already accused. You cannot refuse to tell us what you know. You have a duty to society, young man."

Bryan Martin sighed.

"I suppose you're right," he said. "What do you want me to tell you?"

Poirot looked at Japp.

"Have you ever heard Lady Edgware—or perhaps I'd better call her Miss Wilkinson—utter threats against her husband?" asked Japp.

"Yes, several times."

"What did she say?"

"She said that if he didn't give her her freedom she'd have to 'bump him off'."

"And that was not a joke, eh?"

"No. I think she meant it seriously. Once she said she'd take a taxi and go round and kill him—*you* heard that, M. Poirot?"

He appealed pathetically to my friend.

Poirot nodded.

Japp went on with his questions.

"Now, Mr. Martin, we've been informed that she wanted her freedom in order to marry another man. Do you know who that man was?"

Bryan nodded.

"Who?"

"It was—the Duke of Merton."

"The Duke of Merton! Whew!" The detective whistled.

"Flying at high game, eh? Why, he's said to be one of the richest men in England."

Bryan nodded more dejectedly than ever.

I could not quite understand Poirot's attitude. He was lying back in his chair, his fingers pressed together and the rhythmic motion of his head suggested the complete approval of a man who has put a chosen record on the gramophone and is enjoying the result.

"Wouldn't her husband divorce her?"

"No, he refused absolutely."

"You know that for a fact?"

"Yes."

"And now," said Poirot, suddenly taking part once more in the proceedings. "You see where I come in, my good Japp. I was asked by Lady Edgware to see her husband and try and get him to agree to a divorce. I had an appointment for this morning."

Bryan Martin shook his head.

"It would have been of no use," he declared confidently. "Edgware would never have agreed."

"You think not?" said Poirot, turning an amiable glance on him.

"Sure of it. Jane knew that in her heart of hearts. She'd no real confidence that you'd succeed. She'd given up hope. The man was a monomaniac on the subject of divorce."

Poirot smiled. His eyes grew suddenly very green.

"You are wrong, my dear young man," he said gently. "I saw Lord Edgware yesterday, *and he agreed to a divorce.*"

There was no doubt that Bryan Martin was completely dumbfounded by this piece of news. He stared at Poirot with his eyes almost starting out of his head.

"You—you saw him yesterday?" he spluttered.

"At a quarter-past twelve," said Poirot in his methodical manner.

"And he agreed to a divorce?"

"He agreed to a divorce."

"You should have told Jane at once," cried the young man reproachfully.

"I did, M. Martin."

"You did?" cried Martin and Japp together.

Poirot smiled.

"It impairs the motive a little, does it not?" he murmured. "And now, M. Martin, let me call your attention to this."

He showed him the newspaper paragraph.

Bryan read it, but without much interest.

"You mean this makes an alibi?" he said. "I suppose Edgware was shot some time yesterday evening?"

"He was stabbed, not shot," said Poirot.

Martin laid the paper down slowly.

"I'm afraid this does no good," he said regretfully. "Jane didn't go to that dinner."

"How do you know?"

"I forget. Somebody told me."

"That is a pity," said Poirot thoughtfully.

Japp looked at him curiously.

"I can't make you out, Moosior. Seems now as though you don't want the young woman to be guilty."

"No, no, my good Japp. I am not the partisan you think. But frankly, the case as you present it, revolts the intelligence."

"What do you mean, revolts the intelligence? It doesn't revolt mine."

I could see words trembling on Poirot's lips. He restrained them.

"Here is a young woman who wishes, you say, to get rid of her husband. That point I do not dispute. She told me so frankly. *Eh bien*, how does she set about it? She repeats several times in the loud clear voice before witnesses that she is thinking of killing him. She then goes out one evening, calls at his house, has herself announced, stabs him and goes away. What do you call that, my good friend? Has it even the commonsense?"

"It was a bit foolish, of course."

"Foolish? It is the imbecility!"

"Well," said Japp, rising. "It's all to the advantage of the police when criminals lose their heads. I must go back to the Savoy now."

"You permit that I accompany you?"

Japp made no demur and we set out. Bryan Martin took a reluctant leave of us. He seemed to be in a great state of nervous excitement. He begged earnestly that any further development might be reported to him.

"Nervy sort of chap," was Japp's comment on him.

Poirot agreed.

At the Savoy we found an extremely legal-looking gentleman who had just arrived, and we proceeded all together to Jane's suite. Japp spoke to one of his men.

"Anything?" he inquired laconically.

"She wanted to use the telephone!"

"Who did she telephone to?" inquired Japp eagerly.

"Jay's. For mourning."

Japp swore under his breath. We entered the suite.

The widowed Lady Edgware was trying on hats in front of the glass. She was dressed in a filmy creation of black and white. She greeted us with a dazzling smile.

"Why, M. Poirot, how good of you to come along. Mr. Moxon" (this was to the solicitor) "I'm so glad you've come. Just sit right by me and tell me what questions I ought to answer. This man here seems to think that I went out and killed George this morning."

"Last night, madam," said Japp.

"You said this morning. Ten o'clock."

"I said ten p.m."

"Well. I can never tell which is which—a.m.'s and p.m.'s."

"It's only just about ten o'clock now," added the inspector severely.

Jane's eyes opened very wide.

"Mercy," she murmured. "It's years since I've been awake as early as this. Why, it must have been Early Dawn when you came along."

"One moment, Inspector," said Mr. Moxon in his ponderous legal voice. "When am I to understand that this—er—regrettable—most shocking—occurrence took place?"

"Round about ten o'clock last night, sir."

"Why, that's all right," said Jane sharply. "I was at a party—Oh!" She covered her mouth up suddenly. "Perhaps I oughtn't to have said that."

Her eyes sought the solicitor's in timid appeal.

"If, at ten o'clock last night, you were—er—at a party, Lady Edgware, I—er—I can see no objection to your informing the inspector of the fact—no objection whatever."

"That's right," said Japp. "I only asked you for a statement of your movements yesterday evening."

"You didn't. You said ten something m. And anyway you gave me the most terrible shock. I fainted dead away, Mr. Moxon."

"About this party, Lady Edgware?"

"It was at Sir Montagu Corner's—at Chiswick."

"What time did you go there?"

"The dinner was for eight-thirty."

"You left here—when?"

"I started about eight o'clock. I dropped in at the Piccadilly Palace for a moment to say good-bye to an American friend who was leaving for the States—Mrs. Van Dusen. I got to Chiswick at a quarter to nine."

"What time did you leave?"

"About half-past eleven."

"You came straight back here?"

"Yes."

"In a taxi?"

"No. In my own car. I hire it from the Daimler people."

"And whilst you were at the dinner party you didn't leave it."

"Well—I——"

"So you did leave it?"

It was like a terrier pouncing on a rat.

"I don't know what you mean. I was called to the telephone when we were at dinner."

"Who called you?"

"I guess it was some kind of hoax. A voice said ' Is that Lady Edgware?' And I said ' Yes, that's right,' and then they just laughed and rang off."

"Did you go outside the house to telephone?"

Jane's eyes opened wide in amazement.

"Of course not."

"How long were you away from the dinner table?"

"About a minute and a half."

Japp collapsed after that. I was fully convinced that he did not believe a word she was saying, but having heard her story he could do no more until he had confirmed or disproved it.

Having thanked her coldly, he withdrew.

We also took our leave but she called Poirot back.

"M. Poirot. Will you do something for me?"

"Certainly, Madame."

" Send a cable for me to the Duke in Paris. He's at the Crillon. He ought to know about this. I don't like to send it myself. I guess I've got to look the bereaved widow for a week or two."

" It is quite unnecessary to cable, Madame," said Poirot gently. " It will be in the papers over there."

" Why, what a headpiece you've got! Of course it will. Much better not to cable. I feel it's up to me to keep up my position now everything's gone right. I want to act the way a widow should. Sort of dignified, you know. I thought of sending a wreath of orchids. They're about the most expensive things going. I suppose I shall have to go to the funeral. What do you think?"

" You will have to go to the inquest first, Madame."

" Why, I suppose that's true." She considered for a moment or two. " I don't like that Scotland Yard inspector at all. He just scared me to death. M. Poirot?"

" Yes?"

" Seems it's kind of lucky I changed my mind and went to that party after all."

Poirot had been going towards the door. Suddenly, at these words, he wheeled round.

" What is that you say, Madame? You changed your mind?"

" Yes. I meant to give it a miss. I had a frightful headache yesterday afternoon."

Poirot swallowed once or twice. He seemed to have a difficulty in speaking.

" Did you—say so to anyone?" he asked at last.

" Certainly I did. There was quite a crowd of us having tea and they wanted me to go on to a cocktail party and I said ' No.' I said my head was aching fit to split and that I was going right home and that I was going to cut the dinner too."

" And what made you change your mind, Madame?"

" Ellis went on at me. Said I couldn't afford to turn it down. Old Sir Montagu pulls a lot of strings, you know, and he's a crotchety creature—takes offence easily. Well, I didn't care. Once I marry Merton I'm through with all this. But Ellis is always on the cautious side. She said there's many a slip, etc., and after all I guess she's right. Anyway, off I went."

"You owe Ellis a debt of gratitude, Madame," said Poirot seriously.

"I suppose I do. That inspector had got it all taped out, hadn't he?"

She laughed. Poirot did not. He said in a low voice:

"All the same—this gives one furiously to think. Yes, furiously to think."

"Ellis," called Jane.

The maid came in from the next room.

"M. Poirot says it's very lucky you made me go to that party last night."

Ellis barely cast a glance at Poirot. She was looking grim and disapproving.

"It doesn't do to break engagements, m'lady. You're much too fond of doing it. People don't always forgive it. They turn nasty."

Jane picked up the hat she had been trying on when we came in. She tried it again.

"I hate black," she said disconsolately. "I never wear it. But, I suppose, as a correct widow I've just got to. All those hats are too frightful. Ring up the other hat place, Ellis. I've got to be fit to be seen."

Poirot and I slipped quietly from the room.

CHAPTER VII

THE SECRETARY

WE HAD not seen the last of Japp. He reappeared about an hour later, flung down his hat on the table and said he was eternally blasted.

"You have made the inquiries?" asked Poirot sympathetically.

Japp nodded gloomily.

"And unless fourteen people are lying, she didn't do it," he growled.

He went on:

"I don't mind telling you, M. Poirot, that I expected to find a put-up job. On the face of it, it didn't seem likely that anyone else could have killed Lord Edgware. She's the only person who's got the ghost of a motive."

" I would not say that. *Mais continuez.*"

" Well, as I say, I expected to find a put-up job. You know what these theatrical crowds are—they'd all hang together to screen a pal. But this is rather a different proposition. The people there last night were all big guns, they were none of them close friends of hers and some of them didn't know each other. Their testimony is independent and reliable. I hoped then to find that she'd slipped away for half an hour or so. She could easily have done that—powdering her nose or some excuse. But no, she did leave the dinner table as she told us to answer a telephone call, but the butler was with her—and, by the way, it was just as she told us. He heard what she said. ' Yes, quite right. This is Lady Edgware.' And then the other side rang off. It's curious, that, you know. Not that it's got anything to do with it."

" Perhaps not—but it is interesting. Was it a man or a woman who rang up?"

" A woman, I think she said."

" Curious," said Poirot thoughtfully.

" Never mind that," said Japp impatiently. " Let's get back to the important part. The whole evening went exactly as she said. She got there at a quarter to nine, left at half-past eleven and got back here at a quarter to twelve. I've seen the chauffeur who drove her—he's one of Daimler's regular people. And the people at the Savoy saw her come in and confirm the time."

" *Eh bien*, that seems very conclusive."

" Then what about those two in Regent Gate? It isn't only the butler. Lord Edgware's secretary saw her too. They both swear by all that's holy that it was Lady Edgware who came there at ten o'clock."

" How long has the butler been there?"

" Six months. Handsome chap, by the way."

" Yes, indeed. *Eh bien*, my friend, if he has only been there six months he cannot have recognised Lady Edgware since he had not seen her before."

" Well, he knew her from her pictures in the papers. And anyway the secretary knew her. She's been with Lord Edgware five or six years, and she's the only one who's absolutely positive."

" Ah!" said Poirot. " I should like to see the secretary."

" Well, why not come along with me now?"

"Thank you, *mon ami*, I should be delighted to do so. You include Hastings in your invitation, I hope?"

Japp grinned.

"What do you think? Where the master goes, there the dog follows," he added in what I could not think was the best of taste.

"Reminds me of the Elizabeth Canning Case," said Japp. "You remember? How at least a score of witnesses on either side swore they had seen the gipsy, Mary Squires, in two different parts of England. Good reputable witnesses, too. And she with such a hideous face there couldn't be two like it. That mystery was never cleared up. It's very much the same here. Here's a separate lot of people prepared to swear a woman was in two different places at the same time. Which of 'em is speaking the truth?"

"That ought not to be difficult to find out?"

"So you say—but this woman—Miss Carroll, really *knew* Lady Edgware. I mean she'd lived in the house with her day after day. She wouldn't be likely to make a mistake."

"We shall soon see."

"Who comes into the title?" I asked.

"A nephew, Captain Ronald Marsh. Bit of a waster, I understand."

"What does the doctor say as to the time of death?" asked Poirot.

"We'll have to wait for the autopsy to be exact, you know. See where the dinner had got to." Japp's way of putting things was, I am sorry to say, far from refined. "But ten o'clock fits in well enough. He was last seen alive at a few minutes past nine when he left the dinner table and the butler took whisky and soda into the library. At eleven o'clock when the butler went up to bed the light was out—so he must have been dead then. He wouldn't have been sitting in the dark."

Poirot nodded thoughtfully. A moment or two later we drew up to the house, the blinds of which were now down.

The door was opened to us by the handsome butler.

Japp took the lead and went in first. Poirot and I followed. The door opened to the left, so that the butler stood against the wall on that side. Poirot was on my right and, being smaller than I was, it was only just as we stepped into the hall that the butler saw him. Being close to him, I heard the

sudden intake of his breath and looked sharply at the man
to find him staring at Poirot with a kind of startled fear
visible on his face. I put the fact away in my mind for what
it might be worth.

Japp marched into the dining-room, which lay on our right,
and called the butler in after him.

" Now then, Alton, I want to go into this again very carefully. It was ten o'clock when this lady came?"

" Her ladyship? Yes, sir."

" How did you recognise her?" asked Poirot.

" She told her name, sir, and besides I've seen her portrait
in the papers. I've seen her act, too."

Poirot nodded.

"How was she dressed?"

" In black, sir. Black walking dress, and a small black
hat. A string of pearls and grey gloves."

Poirot looked a question at Japp.

" White taffeta evening dress and ermine wrap," said the
latter succinctly.

The butler proceeded. His tale tallied exactly with that
which Japp had already passed on to us.

" Did anybody else come to see your master that evening?"
asked Poirot.

" No, sir."

" How was the front door fastened?"

" It has a Yale lock, sir. I usually draw the bolts when
I go to bed, sir. At eleven, that is. But last night Miss
Geraldine was at the Opera so it was left unbolted."

" How was it fastened this morning?"

" It was bolted, sir. Miss Geraldine had bolted it when
she came in."

" When did she come in? Do you know?"

" I think it was about a quarter to twelve, sir."

" Then during the evening until a quarter to twelve, the
door could not be opened from outside without a key? From
the inside it could be opened by simply drawing back the
handle."

" Yes, sir."

" How many latchkeys were there?"

" His lordship had his, sir, and there was another key in
the hall drawer which Miss Geraldine took last night. I don't
know if there were any others."

" Does nobody else in the house have a key?"

" No, sir. Miss Carroll always rings."

Poirot intimated that that was all he wished to ask and we went in search of the secretary.

We found her busily writing at a large desk.

Miss Carroll was a pleasant efficient-looking woman of about forty-five. Her fair hair was turning grey and she wore pince-nez through which a pair of shrewd blue eyes gleamed out on us. When she spoke I recognised the clear business-like voice that had spoken to me through the telephone.

" Ah! M. Poirot," she said as she acknowledged Japp's introduction. " Yes. It was with you I made that appointment for yesterday morning."

" Precisely, Mademoiselle."

I thought that Poirot was favourably impressed by her. Certainly she was neatness and precision personified.

" Well, Inspector Japp?" said Miss Caroll. " What more can I do for you?"

" Just this. Are you absolutely certain that it was Lady Edgware who came here last night?"

" That's the third time you've asked me. Of course I'm sure. I saw her."

" Where did you see her, Mademoiselle?"

" In the hall. She spoke to the butler for a minute then she went along the hall and in at the library door."

" And where were you?"

" On the first floor—looking down."

" And you were positive you were not mistaken?"

" Absolutely. I saw her face distinctly."

" You could not have been misled by a resemblance?"

" Certainly not. Jane Wilkinson's features are quite unique. It was her."

Japp threw a glance at Poirot as much as to say: " You see."

" Had Lord Edgware any enemies?" asked Poirot suddenly.

" Nonsense," said Miss Carroll.

" How do you mean—nonsense, Mademoiselle?"

" Enemies! People in these days don't have *enemies*. Not English people!"

" Yet Lord Edgware was murdered."

" That was his wife," said Miss Carroll.

" A wife is not an enemy—no?"

" I'm sure it was a most extraordinary thing to happen. I've never heard of such a thing happening—I mean to anyone in our class of life."

It was clearly Miss Carroll's idea that murders were only committed by drunken members of the lower classes.

" How many keys are there to the front door?"

" Two," replied Miss Carroll promptly. " Lord Edgware always carried one. The other was kept in the drawer in the hall, so that anybody who was going to be late in could take it. There was a third one, but Captain Marsh lost it. Very careless."

" Did Captain Marsh come much to the house?"

" He used to live here until three years ago."

" Why did he leave?" asked Japp.

" I don't know. He couldn't get on with his uncle, I suppose."

" I think you know a little more than that, Mademoiselle," said Poirot gently.

She darted a quick glance at him.

" I am not one to gossip, M. Poirot."

" But you can tell us the truth concerning the rumours of a serious disagreement between Lord Edgware and his nephew."

" It wasn't so serious as all that. Lord Edgware was a difficult man to get on with."

" Even you found that?"

" I'm not speaking of myself. I never had any disagreements with Lord Edgware. He always found me perfectly reliable."

" But as regards Captain Marsh——"

Poirot stuck to it, gently continuing to goad her into further revelations.

Miss Carroll shrugged her shoulders.

" He was extravagant. Got into debt. There was some other trouble—I don't know exactly what. They quarrelled. Lord Edgware forbade him the house. That's all."

Her mouth closed firmly. Evidently she intended to say no more.

The room we had interviewed her in was on the first floor. As we left it, Poirot took me by the arm.

" A little minute. Remain here if you will, Hastings. I

am going down with Japp. Watch till we have gone into the library, then join us there."

I have long ago given up asking Poirot questions beginning "Why?" Like the Light Brigade "Mine not to reason why, mine but to do or die," though fortunately it has not yet come to dying! I thought that possibly he suspected the butler of spying on him and wanted to know if such were really the case.

I took up my stand looking over the banisters. Poirot and Japp went first to the front door—out of my sight. Then they reappeared walking slowly along the hall. I followed their backs with my eye until they had gone into the library. I waited a minute or two in case the butler appeared, but there was no sign of anyone, so I ran down the stairs and joined them.

The body had, of course, been removed. The curtains were drawn and the electric light was on. Poirot and Japp were standing in the middle of the room looking round them.

"Nothing here," Japp was saying.

And Poirot replied with a smile:

"Alas! not the cigarette ash—nor the footprint—nor a lady's glove—nor even a lingering perfume! Nothing that the detective of fiction so conveniently finds."

"The police are always made out to be as blind as bats in detective stories," said Japp with a grin.

"I found a clue once," said Poirot dreamily. "But since it was four feet long instead of four centimetres no one would believe in it."

I remembered the circumstance and laughed. Then I remembered my mission.

"It's all right, Poirot," I said. "I watched, but no one was spying upon you as far as I could see."

"The eyes of my friend Hastings," said Poirot in a kind of gentle mockery. "Tell me, my friend, did you notice the rose between my lips?"

"The rose between your lips?" I asked in astonishment. Japp turned aside spluttering with laughter.

"You'll be the death of me, M. Poirot," he said. "The death of me. A rose. What next?"

"I had the fancy to pretend I was Carmen," said Poirot quite undisturbed.

I wondered if they were going mad or if I was.

"You did not observe it, Hastings?" There was reproach in Poirot's voice.

"No," I said, staring. "But then I couldn't see your face."

"No matter." He shook his head gently.

Were they making fun of me?

"Well," said Japp. "No more to do here, I fancy. I'd like to see the daughter again if I could. She was too upset before for me to get anything out of her."

He rang the bell for the butler.

"Ask Miss Marsh if I can see her for a few moments?"

The man departed. It was not he, however, but Miss Carroll who entered the room a few minutes later.

"Geraldine is asleep," she said. "She's had a terrible shock, poor child. After you left I gave her something to make her sleep and she's fast asleep now. In an hour or two, perhaps."

Japp agreed.

"In any case there's nothing she can tell you that I can't," said Miss Carroll firmly.

"What is your opinion of the butler?" asked Poirot.

"I don't like him much and that's a fact," replied Miss Carroll. "But I can't tell you why."

We had reached the front door.

"It was up there that you stood, was it not, last night, Mademoiselle?" said Poirot suddenly, pointing with his hand up the stairs.

"Yes. Why?"

"And you saw Lady Edgware go along the hall into the study?"

"Yes."

"And you saw her face distinctly?"

"Certainly."

"*But you could not have seen her face, Mademoiselle.* You can only have seen the back of her head from where you were standing."

Miss Carroll flushed angrily. She seemed taken aback.

"Back of her head, her voice, her walk! It's all the same thing. Absolutely unmistakable! I tell you I *know* it was Jane Wilkinson—a thoroughly bad woman if there ever was one."

And turning away she flounced upstairs.

CHAPTER VIII

POSSIBILITIES

JAPP HAD to leave us. Poirot and I turned into Regent's Park and found a quiet seat.

"I see the point of your rose between the lips now," I said, laughing. "At the moment I thought you had gone mad."

He nodded without smiling.

"You observe, Hastings, that the secretary is a dangerous witness. Dangerous because inaccurate. You notice that she stated positively that she saw the visitor's *face*? At the time I thought that impossible. Coming *from* the study—yes, but not going *to* the study. So I made my little experiment which resulted as *I* thought, and then sprung my trap upon her. She immediately changed her ground."

"Her belief was quite unaltered, though," I argued. "And after all, a voice and a walk are just as unmistakable."

"No, no."

"Why, Poirot, I think a voice and the general gait are about the most characteristic things about a person."

"I agree. And therefore they are the most easily counterfeited."

"You think——"

"Cast your mind back a few days. Do you remember one evening as we sat in the stalls of a theatre——"

"Carlotta Adams? Ah! but then she is a genius."

"A well-known person is not so difficult to mimic. But I agree she has unusual gifts. I believe she could carry a thing through without the aid of footlights and distance——"

A sudden thought flashed into my mind.

"Poirot," I cried. "You don't think that possibly—no, that would be too much of a coincidence."

"It depends how you look at it, Hastings. Regarded from one angle it would be no coincidence at all."

"But why should Carlotta Adams wish to kill Lord Edgware? She did not even know him."

"How do you know she did not know him? Do not

assume things, Hastings. There may have been some link between them of which we know nothing. Not that that is precisely my theory."

" Then you have a theory?"

" Yes. The possibility of Carlotta Adams being involved struck me from the beginning."

" But, Poirot——"

" Wait, Hastings. Let me put together a few facts for you. Lady Edgware, with a complete lack of reticence, discusses the relations between her and her husband, and even goes so far as to talk of killing him. Not only you and I hear this. A waiter hears it, her maid probably has heard it many times, Bryan Martin hears it, and I imagine Carlotta Adams herself hears it. And there are the people to whom these people repeat it. Then, on that same evening, the excellence of Carlotta Adams', imitation of Jane is commented upon. Who had a motive for killing Lord Edgware? His wife.

" Now supposing that someone else wishes to do away with Lord Edgware. Here is a scapegoat ready to his hand. On the day when Jane Wilkinson announces that she has a headache and is going to have a quiet evening—*the plan is put into operation.*

" Lady Edgware must be seen to enter the house in Regent Gate. Well, she is seen. She even goes so far as to announce her identity. *Ah! c'est un peu trop, ça!* It would awaken suspicion in an oyster.

" And another point—a small point, I admit. The woman who came to the house last night wore black. *Jane Wilkinson never wears black.* We heard her say so. Let us assume then, that the woman who came to the house last night was *not* Jane Wilkinson—that it was a woman impersonating Jane Wilkinson. Did that woman kill Lord Edgware?

" Did a third person enter that house and kill Lord Edgware? If so, did the person enter before or after the supposed visit of Lady Edgware? If after, what did the woman say to Lord Edgware? How did she explain her presence? She might deceive the butler who did not know her, and the secretary who did not see her at close quarters but she could not hope to deceive a husband. Or was there only a dead body in the room? Was Lord Edgware killed *before* she entered the house—sometime between nine and ten?"

"Stop, Poirot!" I cried. "You are making my head spin."

"No, no, my friend. We are only considering possibilities. It is like trying on the clothes. Does this fit? No, it wrinkles on the shoulder? This one? Yes, that is better—but not quite large enough. This other one is too small. So on and so on—until we reach the perfect fit—the truth."

"Who do you suspect of such a fiendish plot?" I asked.

"Ah! that is too early to say. One must go into the question of who has a motive for wishing Lord Edgware dead. There is, of course, the nephew who inherits. A little obvious that, perhaps. And then, in spite of Miss Carroll's dogmatic pronouncement, there is the question of enemies. Lord Edgware struck me as a man who very easily might make enemies."

"Yes," I agreed. "That is so."

"Whoever it was must have fancied himself pretty safe. Remember, Hastings, but for her change of mind at the last minute, Jane Wilkinson would have had no alibi. She might have been in her room at the Savoy, and it would have been difficult to prove it. She would have been arrested, tried—probably hanged."

I shivered.

"But there is one thing puzzles me," went on Poirot. "The desire to incriminate her is clear—but what then of the telephone call? Why did someone ring her up at Chiswick and, once satisfied of her presence there, immediately ring off. It looks, does it not, as if someone wanted to be sure of her presence there before proceeding to—what? That was at nine-thirty, almost certainly before the murder. The intention then seems—there is no other word for it—*beneficent*. It *cannot* be the murderer who rings up—the murderer has laid all his plans to incriminate Jane. Who, then, was it? It looks as though we have here two entirely different sets of circumstances."

I shook my head, utterly fogged.

"It might be just a coincidence," I suggested.

"No, no, everything cannot be a coincidence. Six months ago, a letter was suppressed. Why? There are too many things here unexplained. There must be some reason linking them together."

He sighed. Presently he went on:

"That story that Bryan Martin came to tell us——"

"Surely, Poirot, that has got no connection with this business."

"You are blind, Hastings, blind and wilfully obtuse. Do you not see that the whole thing makes a pattern? A pattern confused at present but which will gradually become clear. . . ."

I felt Poirot was being over-optimistic. I did not feel that anything would ever become clear. My brain was frankly reeling.

"It's no good," I said suddenly. "I can't believe it of Carlotta Adams. She seemed such a—well, such a thoroughly nice girl."

Yet, even as I spoke, I remembered Poirot's words about love of money. Love of money—was that at the root of the seemingly incomprehensible? I felt that Poirot had been inspired that night. He had seen Jane in danger—the result of her strange egotistical temperament. He had seen Carlotta led astray by avarice.

"I do not think she committed the murder, Hastings. She is too cool and level-headed for that. Possibly she was not even told that murder would be done. She may have been used innocently. But then——"

He broke off, frowning.

"Even so, she's an acccessory after the fact now. I mean, she will see the news to-day. She will realise——"

A hoarse sound broke from Poirot.

"Quick, Hastings, Quick! I have been blind—imbecile. A taxi. At once."

I stared at him.

He waved his arms.

"A taxi—at once."

One was passing. He hailed it and we jumped in.

"Do you know her address?"

"Carlotta Adams, do you mean?"

"*Mais oui, mais oui*. Quickly, Hastings, quickly. Every minute is of value. Do you not see?"

"No," I said. "I don't."

Poirot swore under his breath.

"The telephone book? No, she would not be in it. The theatre."

At the theatre they were not disposed to give Carlotta's

address, but Poirot managed it. It was a flat in a block of mansions near Sloane Square. We drove there, Poirot in a fever of impatience.

"If I am not too late, Hastings. If I am not too late."

"What is all this haste? I don't understand. What does it mean?"

"It means that I have been slow. Terribly slow to realise the obvious. Ah! *mon Dieu*, if only we may be in time."

CHAPTER IX

THE SECOND DEATH

Though I did not understand the reason for Poirot's agitation, I knew him well enough to be sure that he had a reason for it.

We arrived at Rosedew Mansions. Poirot sprang out, paid the driver and hurried into the building. Miss Adams' flat was on the first floor, as a visiting-card stuck on a board informed us.

Poriot hurried up the stairs, not waiting to summon the lift which was at one of the upper floors.

He knocked and rang. There was a short delay, then the door was opened by a neat middle-aged woman with hair drawn tightly back from her face. Her eyelids were reddened as though with weeping.

"Miss Adams?" demanded Poirot eagerly.

The woman looked at him.

"Haven't you heard?"

"Heard? Heard what?"

His face had gone deadly pale, and I realised that this, whatever it was, was what he had feared.

The woman continued slowly to shake her head.

"She's dead. Passed away in her sleep. It's terrible."

Poirot leaned against the doorpost.

"Too late," he murmured.

His agitation was so apparent that the woman looked at him with more attention.

"Excuse me, sir, but are you a friend of hers? I do not remember seeing you come here before?"

Poirot did not reply to this directly. Instead he said:

" You have had a doctor? What did he say?"

"Took an overdose of a sleeping draught. Oh! the pity of it! Such a nice young lady. Nasty dangerous things—these drugs. Veronal, he said it was."

Poirot suddenly stood upright. His manner took on a new authority.

" I must come in," he said.

The woman was clearly doubtful and suspicious.

" I don't think——" she began.

But Poirot meant to have his way. He took probably the only course that would have obtained the desired result.

"You must let me in," he said. "I am a detective and I have got to inquire into the circumstances of your mistress's death."

The woman gasped. She stood aside and we passed into the flat.

From there on Poirot took command of the situation.

"What I have told you," he said authoritatively, "is strictly confidential. It must not be repeated. Everyone must continue to think that Miss Adams' death was accidental. Please give me the name and address of the doctor you summoned."

" Dr. Heath, 17 Carlisle Street."

" And your own name?"

" Bennett—Alice Bennett."

"You were attached to Miss Adams, I can see, Miss Bennett."

"Oh! yes, sir. She were a nice young lady. I worked for her last year when she were over here. It wasn't as though she were one of those actresses. She were a real young lady. Dainty ways she had and liked everything just so."

Poirot listened with attention and sympathy. He had now no signs of impatience. I realised that to proceed gently was the best way of extracting the information he wanted.

"It must have been a great shock to you," he observed gently.

"Oh! it was, sir. I took her in her tea—at half-past nine as usual and there she was lying—asleep I thought. And I put the tray down. And I pulled the curtains—one of the rings caught, sir, and I had to jerk it hard. Such a noise it made. I was surprised when I looked round to see she hadn't woken. And then all of a sudden something seemed to take hold of me. Something not quite natural about the way she lay. And I went to the side of the bed, and I touched her hand. Icy cold it was, sir, and I cried out."

She stopped, tears coming into her eyes.

"Yes, yes," said Poirot sympathetically. "It must have been terrible for you. Did Miss Adams often take stuff to make her sleep?"

"She'd take something for a headache now and again, sir. Some little tablets in a bottle, but it was some other stuff she took last night, or so the doctor said."

"Did anyone come to see her last night? A visitor?"

"No, sir. She was out yesterday evening, sir."

"Did she tell you where she was going?"

"No, sir. She went out about seven o'clock."

"Ah! How was she dressed?"

"She had on a black dress, sir. A black dress and a black hat."

Poirot looked at me.

"Did she wear any jewellery?"

"Just the string of pearls she always wore, sir."

"And gloves—grey gloves?"

"Yes, sir. Her gloves were grey."

"Ah! Now describe to me, if you will, what her manner was. Was she gay? Excited? Sad? Nervous?"

"It seemed to me she was pleased about something, sir. She kept smiling to herself, as though there were some kind of joke on."

"What time did she return?"

"A little after twelve o'clock, sir."

"And what was her manner then? The same?"

"She was terribly tired, sir."

"But not upset? Or distressed?"

"Oh! no, sir. I think she was pleased about something, but just done up, if you know what I mean. She started to ring someone up on the telephone, and then she said she couldn't bother. She'd do it to-morrow morning."

"Ah!" Poirot's eyes gleamed with excitement. He leaned forward and spoke in a would-be indifferent voice.

"Did you hear the name of the person she rang up?"

"No, sir. She just asked for the number and waited and then the Exchange must have said: 'I'm trying to get them' as they do, sir, and she said 'All right,' and then suddenly she yawned and said: 'Oh! I can't bother. I'm too tired,' and she put the receiver back and started undressing."

"And the number she called? Do you recollect that? Think. It may be important."

"I'm sorry I can't say, sir. It was a Victoria number and that's all I can remember. I wasn't paying special heed, you see."

"Did she have anything to eat or drink before she went to bed?"

"A glass of hot milk, sir, like she always did."

"Who prepared it?"

"I did, sir."

"And nobody came to the flat that evening?"

"Nobody, sir."

"And earlier in the day?"

"Nobody came that I can remember, sir. Miss Adams was out to lunch and tea. She came in at six o'clock."

"When did the milk come? The milk she drank last night?"

"It was the new milk she had, sir. The afternoon delivery. The boy leaves it outside the door at four o'clock. But, oh! sir, I'm sure there wasn't nothing wrong with the milk. I had it myself for tea this morning. And the doctor he said positive as she'd taken the nasty stuff herself."

"It is possible that I am wrong," said Poirot. "Yes, it is possible that I am entirely wrong. I will see the doctor. But, you see, Miss Adams had enemies. Things are very different in America——"

He hesitated, but the good Alice leapt at the bait.

"Oh! I know, sir. I've read about Chicago and them gunmen and all that. It must be a wicked country and what the police can be about, I can't think. Not like our policemen."

Poirot left it thankfully at that, realising that Alice Bennet"s insular proclivities would save him the trouble of explanations.

His eye fell on a small suitcase—more of an attaché case, that was lying on a chair.

"Did Miss Adams take that with her when she went out last night?"

"In the morning she took it, sir. She didn't have it when she came back at tea-time, but she brought it back last thing."

" Ah! You permit that I open it?"

Alice Bennett would have permitted anything. Like most canny and suspicious women, once she had overcome her distrust she was child's play to manipulate. She would have assented to anything Poirot suggested.

The case was not locked. Poirot opened it. I came forward and looked over his shoulder.

"You see, Hastings, you see?" he murmured excitedly.

The contents were certainly suggestive.

There was a box of make-up materials, two objects which I recognised as elevators to place in shoes and raise the height an inch or so, there was a pair of grey gloves and, folded in tissue paper, an exquitely-made wig of golden hair, the exact shade of gold of Jane Wilkinson's and dressed like hers with a centre parting and curls in the back of the neck.

" Do you doubt now, Hastings?" asked Poirot.

I believe I had up to that moment. But now I doubted no longer.

Poirot closed the case again and turned to the maid.

"You do not know with whom Miss Adams dined yesterday evening?"

" No, sir."

" Do you know with whom she had lunch or tea?"

" I know nothing about tea, sir. I believed she lunched with Miss Driver."

" Miss Driver?"

"Yes, her great friend. She has a hat-shop in Moffat Street, just off Bond Street. Genevieve it's called."

Poirot noted the address in his notebook just below that of the doctor.

"One thing more, Madame. Can you remember anything —anything at all—that Mademoiselle Adams said or did after she came in at six o'clock that strikes you as at all unusual or significant?"

The maid thought for a moment or two.

" I really can't say that I do, sir," she said at last. " I asked her if she would have tea and she said she'd had some."

" Oh! she said she had had it," interrupted Poirot.

" Pardon. Continue."

" And after that she was writing letters till just on the time she went out."

"Letters, eh? You do not know to whom?"

"Yes, sir. It was just one letter—to her sister in Washington. She wrote her sister twice a week regular. She took the letter out with her to post because of catching the mail. But she forgot it."

"Then it is here still?"

"No, sir. I posted it. She remembered last night just as she was getting into bed. And I said I'd run out with it. By putting an extra stamp on it and putting it in the late fee box it would be all right."

"Ah!—and is that far?"

"No, sir, the post office is just round the corner."

"Did you shut the door of the flat behind you?"

Bennett stared.

"No, sir. I just left it to—as I always do when I go out to post."

Poirot seemed about to speak—then checked himself.

"Would you like to look at her, sir?" asked the maid tearfully. "Looks beautiful she does."

We followed her into the bedroom.

Carlotta Adams looked strangely peaceful and much younger than she had appeared that night at the Savoy. She looked like a tired child asleep.

There was a strange expression on Poirot's face as he stood looking down on her. I saw him make the sign of the Cross.

"*J'ai fait un serment*, Hastings," he said as we went down the stairs.

I did not ask him what his vow was. I could guess.

A minute or two later he said:

"There is one thing off my mind at least. I could not have saved her. By the time I heard of Lord Edgware's death she was already dead. That comforts me. Yes, that comforts me very much."

CHAPTER X

JENNY DRIVER

OUR NEXT proceeding was to call upon the doctor whose address the maid had given us.

He turned out to be a fussy elderly man somewhat vague

in manner. He knew Poirot by repute and expressed a lively pleasure at meeting him in the flesh.

"And what can I do for you, M. Poirot?" he asked after this opening preamble.

"You were called this morning, M. le docteur, to the bedside of a Miss Carlotta Adams."

"Ah! yes, poor girl. Clever actress too. I've been twice to her show. A thousand pities it's ended this way. Why these girls must have drugs I can't think."

"You think she was addicted to drugs, then?"

"Well, professionally, I should hardly have said so. At all events she didn't take them hypodermically. No marks of the needle. Evidently always took it by the mouth. Maid said she slept well naturally, but then maids never know. I don't suppose she took veronal every night, but she'd evidently taken it for some time."

"What makes you think so?"

"This. Dash it—where did I put the thing?"

He was peering into a small case.

"Ah! here it is."

He drew out a small black morocco handbag.

"There's got to be an inquest, of course. I brought this away so that the maid shouldn't meddle with it."

Opening the pochette he took out a small gold box. On it were the initials C.A. in rubies. It was a valuable and expensive trinket. The doctor opened it. It was nearly full of a white powder.

"Veronal," he explained briefly. "Now look what's written inside."

On the inside of the lid of the box was engraved:

C.A. from D. Paris, Nov. 10th.
Sweet Dreams.

"November 10th," said Poirot thoughtfully.

"Exactly, and we're now in June. That seems to show that she's been in the habit of taking the stuff for at least six months, and as the year isn't given, it might be eighteen months or two years and a half—or any time."

"Paris. D," said Poirot, frowning.

"Yes. Convey anything to you? By the way, I haven't asked you what your interest is in the case. I'm assuming you've got good grounds. I suppose you want to know if it's suicide? Well, I can't tell you. Nobody can. According to the maid's account she was perfectly cheerful yesterday. That looks like accident, and in my opinion accident it is. Veronal's very uncertain stuff. You can take a devil of a lot and it won't kill you, and you can take very little and off you go. It's a dangerous drug for that reason.

"I've no doubt they'll bring it in Accidental Death at the inquest. I'm afraid I can't be of any more help to you."

"May I examine the little bag of Mademoiselle?"

"Certainly. Certainly."

Poirot turned out the contents of the pochette. There was a fine handkerchief with C.M.A. in the corner, a powder puff, a lipstick, a pound note and a little change, and a pair of pince-nez.

These last Poirot examined with interest. They were gold-rimmed and rather severe and academic in type.

"Curious," said Poirot. "I did not know that Miss Adams wore glasses. But perhaps they are for reading?"

The doctor picked them up.

"No, these are outdoor glasses," he affirmed. "Pretty powerful too. The person who wore these must have been very short-sighted."

"You do not know if Miss Adams——"

"I never attended her before. I was called in once to see a poisoned finger of the maid's. Otherwise I have never been in the flat. Miss Adams whom I saw for a moment on that occasion was certainly not wearing glasses then."

Poirot thanked the doctor and we took our leave.

Poirot wore a puzzled expression.

"It can be that I am mistaken," he admitted.

"About the impersonation?"

"No, no. That seems to me proved. No, I mean as to her death. Obviously she had veronal in her possession. It is possible that she was tired and strung up last night and determined to ensure herself a good night's rest."

Then he suddenly stopped dead—to the great surprise of the passers-by—and beat one hand emphatically on the other.

"No, no, no, no!" he declared emphatically. "Why should that accident happen so conveniently? It was no accident. It was not suicide. No, she played her part and in doing so she signed her death warrant. Veronal may have been chosen simply because it was known that she occasionally took it and that she had that box in her posession. But, if so, the murderer must have been someone who knew her well. Who is D? Hastings. I would give a good deal to know who D. was."

"Poirot," I said, as he remained wrapt in thought. "Hadn't we better go on. Everyone is staring at us."

"Eh? Well, perhaps you are right. Though it does not incommode me that people should stare. It does not interfere in the least with my train of thought."

"People were beginning to laugh," I murmured.

"That has no importance."

I did not quite agree. I have a horror of doing anything conspicuous. The only thing that affects Poirot is the possibility of the damp or the heat affecting the set of his famous moustache.

"We will take a taxi," said Poirot, waving his stick.

One drew up by us, and Poirot directed it to go to Genevieve in Moffat Street.

Genevieve turned out to be one of those establishments where one nondescript hat and a scarf display themselves in a glass box downstairs and where the real centre of operations is one floor up a flight of musty-smelling stairs.

Having climbed the stairs we came to a door with "Genevieve. Please Walk In" on it, and having obeyed this command we found ourselves in a small room full of hats while an imposing blonde creature came forward with a suspicious glance at Poirot.

"Miss Driver?" asked Poirot.

"I do not know if Modom can see you. What is your business, please?"

"Please tell Miss Driver that a friend of Miss Adams would like to see her."

The blonde beauty had no need to go on this errand. A black velvet curtain was violently agitated and a small vivacious creature with flaming red hair emerged.

"What's that?" she demanded.

"Are you Miss Driver?"

"Yes. What's that about Carlotta?"

"You have heard the sad news?"

"What sad news?"

"Miss Adams died in her sleep last night. An overdose of veronal."

The girl's eyes opened wide.

"How awful!" she exclaimed. "Poor Carlotta. I can hardly believe it. Why, she was full of life yeterday."

"Nevertheless it is true, Mademoiselle," said Poirot. "Now see—it is just on one o'clock. I want you to do me the honour of coming out to lunch with me and my friend. I want to ask you several questions."

The girl looked him up and down. She was a pugilistic little creature. She reminded me in some ways of a fox terrier.

"Who are you?" she demanded bluntly.

"My name is Hercule Poirot. This is my friend Captain Hastings."

I bowed.

Her glance travelled from one to the other of us.

"I've heard of you," she said abruptly. "I'll come." She called to the blonde:

"Dorothy?"

"Yes, Jenny."

"Mrs. Lester's coming in about that Rose Descrates model we're making for her. Try the different feathers. Bye-bye, shan't be long, I expect."

She picked up a small black hat, affixed it to one ear, powdered her nose furiously, and then looked at Poirot.

"Ready," she said abruptly.

Five minutes afterwards we were sitting in a small restaurant in Dover Street. Poirot had given an order to the waiter and cocktails were in front of us.

"Now," said Jenny Driver, "I want to know the meaning of all this. What has Carlotta been getting herself mixed up in?"

"She had been getting herself mixed up in something, then, Mademoiselle?"

"Now then, who is going to ask the questions, you or me?"

"My idea was that I should," said Poirot, smiling. "I have been given to understand that you and Miss Adams were great friends."

"Right."

"Eh bien, then I ask you, Mademoiselle, to accept my solemn assurance that what I do, I am doing in the interests of your dead friend. I assure you that that is so."

There was a moment's silence while Jenny Driver considered this question. Finally she gave a quick assenting nod of the head.

"I believe you. Carry on. What do you want to know?"

"I understand, Mademoiselle, that your friend lunched with you yesterday."

"She did."

"Did she tell you what her plans were for last night?"

"She didn't exactly mention last night."

"But she said something?"

"Well, she mentioned something that maybe is what you're driving at. Mind you, she spoke in confidence."

"That is understood."

"Well, let me see now. I think I'd better explain things in my own words."

"If you please, Mademoiselle."

"Well, then, Carlotta was excited. She isn't often excited. She's not that kind. She wouldn't tell me anything definite, said she'd promised not to, but she'd got something on. Something, I gathered, in the nature of a gigantic hoax."

"A hoax?"

"That's what she said. She didn't say how or when or where. Only—" She paused, frowning. "Well—you see —Carlotta's not the kind of person who enjoys practical jokes or hoaxes or things of that kind. She's one of those serious, nice-minded, hard-working girls. What I mean is, somebody had obviously put her up to this stunt. And I think— she didn't say so, mind——"

"No, no, I quite understand. What was it that you thought?"

"I thought—I was sure—that in some way money was concerned. Nothing really ever excited Carlotta except money. She was made that way. She'd got one of the best heads for business I've ever met. She wouldn't have been so excited and so pleased unless money—quite a lot of money —had been concerned. My impression was that she'd taken on something for a bet—and that she was pretty sure of winning. And yet that isn't quite true. I mean, Carlotta didn't bet. I've never known her make a bet. But anyway, somehow or other, I'm sure money was concerned."

"She did not actually say so?"

"N-no-o. Just said that she'd be able to do this, that and the other in the near future. She was going to get her sister over from America to meet her in Paris. She was crazy about her little sister. Very delicate, I believe, and musical. Well, that's all I know. Is that what you want?"

Poirot nodded his head.

"Yes. It confirms my theory. I had hoped, I admit, for more. I had anticipated that Miss Adams would have been bound to secrecy. But I hoped that, being a woman, she would not have counted revealing the secret to her best friend."

"I tried to make her tell me," admitted Jenny. "But she only laughed and said she'd tell me all about it some day."

Poirot was silent for a moment. Then he said:

"You know the name of Lord Edgware?"

"What? The man who was murdered? On a poster half an hour ago."

"Yes. Do you know if Miss Adams was acquainted with him?"

"I don't think so. I'm sure she wasn't. Oh! wait a minute."

"Yes, Mademoiselle?" said Poirot eagerly.

"What was it now?" she frowned, knitting her brow as she tried to remember. "Yes, I've got it now. She mentioned him once. Very bitterly."

"Bitterly?"

"Yes. She said—what was it?—that men like that shouldn't be allowed to ruin other people's lives by their cruelty and lack of understanding. She said—why, so she did—that he was the kind of man whose death would probably be a good thing for everybody."

"When was it she said this, Mademoiselle?"

"Oh! about a month ago, I think it was."

"How did the subject come up?"

Jenny Driver racked her brains for some minutes and finally shook her head.

"I can't remember," she confessed. "His name cropped up or something. It might have been in the newspaper. Anyway, I remember thinking it odd that Carlotta should be so vehement all of a sudden when she didn't even know the man."

"Certainly it is odd," agreed Poirot thoughtfully. Then he asked:

" Do you know if Miss Adams was in the habit of taking veronal?"

" Not that I knew. I never saw her take it or mention taking it."

" Did you ever see in her bag a small gold box with the initials C.A. on it in rubies?"

" A small gold box—no, I am sure I didn't."

" Do you happen to know where Miss Adams was last November?"

" Let me see. She went back to the States in November, I think—towards the end of the month. Before that she was in Paris."

" Alone?"

" Alone, of course! Sorry—perhaps you didn't mean that! I don't know why any mention of Paris always suggests the worst. And it's such a nice respectable place really. But Carlotta wasn't the week-ending sort, if that's what you're driving at."

" Now, Mademoiselle, I am going to ask you a very important question. Was there any man Miss Adams was specially interested in?"

" The answer to that is 'No,'" said Jenny slowly. " Carlotta, since I've known her, has been wrapped up in her work and in her delicate sister. She's had the 'head of the family all depends on me' attitude very strongly. So the answer's NO—strictly speaking."

" Ah! and not speaking so strictly?"

" I shouldn't wonder if—lately—Carlotta hadn't been getting interested in some man."

" Ah!"

" Mind you, that's entirely guesswork on my part. I've gone simply by her manner. She's been—different—not exactly dreamy, but abstracted. And she's looked different, somehow. Oh! I can't explain. It's the sort of thing that another woman just feels—and, of course, may be quite wrong about."

Poirot nodded.

" Thank you, Mademoiselle. One thing more. Is there any friend of Miss Adams whose initial is D?"

" D," said Jenny Driver thoughtfully. " D? No, I'm sorry. I can't think of anyone."

CHAPTER XI

THE EGOIST

I DO NOT think Poirot had expected any other answer to his question. All the same he shook his head sadly. He remained lost in thought. Jenny Driver leant forward, her elbows on the table.

" And now," she said, " am I going to be told anything?"

" Mademoiselle," said Poirot. " First of all let me compliment you. Your answers to my questions have been singularly intelligent. Clearly you have brains, Mademoiselle. You ask whether I am going to tell you anything. I answer—not very much. I will tell you just a few bare facts, Mademoiselle."

He paused, and then said quietly:

" Last night Lord Edgware was murdered in his library. At ten o'clock yesterday evening a lady whom I believed to have been your friend Miss Adams came to the house, asked to see Lord Edgware, and announced herself as Lady Edgware. She wore a golden wig and was made up to resemble the real Lady Edgware who, as you probably know, is Miss Jane Wilkinson, the actress. Miss Adams (if it were she) only remained a few moments. She left the house at five minutes past ten but she did not return home till after midnight. She went to bed, having taken an overdose of veronal. Now, Mademoiselle, you see the point, perhaps, of some of the questions I have been asking you."

Jenny drew a deep breath.

" Yes," she said. " I see now. I believe you're right, M. Poirot. Right about its having been Carlotta, I mean. For one thing, she bought a new hat off me yesterday."

" A new hat?"

" Yes. She said she wanted one to shade the left side of her face."

Here I must insert a few words of explanation as I do not know when these words will be read. I have seen many fashions of hats in my time—the cloche that shaded the face so completely that one gave up in despair the task of recognising one's friends. The tilted forward hat, the hat attached

76

airily to the back of the head, the beret, and many other styles. In this particular June the hat of the moment was shaped like an inverted soup plate and was worn attached (as if by suction) over one ear, leaving the other side of the face and hair open to inspection.

"These hats are usually worn on the right side of the head?" asked Poirot.

The little modiste nodded.

"But we keep a few to be worn on the opposite side," she explained. "Because there are people who much prefer their right profile to the left or who have a habit of parting the hair on one side only. Now, would there be any special reason for Carlotta's wanting that side of her face to be in shadow?"

I remembered that the door of the house in Regent Gate opened to the left, so that anyone entering would be in full view of the butler that side. I remembered also that Jane Wilkinson (so I had noticed the other night) had a tiny mole at the corner of the left eye.

I said as much excitedly. Poirot agreed, nodding his head vigorously.

"It is so. It is so. *Vous avez parfaitement raison*, Hastings. Yes, that explains the purchase of the hat."

"M. Poirot?" Jenny sat suddenly bolt upright. "You don't think—you don't for one moment think—that Carlotta did it? Killed him, I mean. You can't think that? Not just because she spoke so bitterly about him."

"I do not think so. But it is curious, all the same—that she should have spoken so, I mean. I would like to know the reason for it. What had he done—what did she know of him to make her speak in such a fashion?"

"I don't know—but she didn't kill him. She's—oh! she was—well—too refined."

Poirot nodded approvingly.

"Yes, yes. You put that very well. It is a point psychological. I agree. This was a scientific crime—but not a refined one."

"Scientific?"

"The murderer knew exactly where to strike so as to reach the vital nerve centres at the base of the skull where it joins the cord."

"Looks like a doctor," said Jenny thoughtfully.

" Did Miss Adams know any doctors? I mean, was any particular doctor a friend of hers?"

Jenny shook her head.

" Never heard of one. Not over here, anyway."

" Another question. Did Miss Adams wear pince-nez?"

" Glasses? Never."

" Ah!" Poirot frowned.

A vision rose in my mind. A doctor, smelling of carbolic, with short-sighted eyes magnified by powerful lenses. Absurd!

" By the way, did Miss Adams know Bryan Martin, the film actor?"

" Why, yes. She used to know him as a child, she told me. I don't think she saw much of him, though. Just once in a while. She told me she thought he'd got very swollen-headed."

She looked at her watch and uttered an exclamation.

" Goodness, I must fly. Have I helped you at all, M. Poirot?"

"You have. I shall ask you for further help by and by."

" It's yours. Someone staged this devilry. We've got to find out who it is."

She gave us a quick shake of the hand, flashed her white teeth in a sudden smile and left us with characteristic abruptness.

" An interesting personality," said Poirot as he paid the bill.

" I like her," I said.

" It is always a pleasure to meet a quick mind."

" A little hard, perhaps," I reflected. " The shock of her friend's death did not upset her as much as I should have thought it would have done."

" She is not the sort that weeps, certainly," agreed Poirot dryly.

" Did you get what you hoped from the interview?"

He shook his head.

" No—I hoped—very much I hoped—to get a clue to the personality of D, the person who gave her the little gold box. There I have failed. Unfortunately Carlotta Adams was a reserved girl. She was not one to gossip about her friends or her possible love affairs. On the other hand, the person who suggested the hoax may not have been a friend at all. It may have been a mere acquaintance who proposed it—doubtless for some 'sporting' reason—on a money basis. This person may have seen the gold box she carried about with her and made some opportunity to discover what it contained."

"But how on earth did they get her to take it? And when?"

"Well, there was the time during which the flat door was open—when the maid was out posting a letter. Not that that satisfies me. It leaves too much to chance. But now—to work. We have still two possible clues."

"Which are?"

"The first is the telephone call to a Victoria number. It seems to me quite a probability that Carlotta Adams would ring up on her return to announce her success. On the other hand, where was she between five minutes past ten and midnight. She may have had an appointment with the instigator of the hoax. In that case the telephone call may have been merely one to a friend."

"What is the second clue?"

"Ah! that I do have hopes of. The letter, Hastings. The letter to the sister. It is possible—I only say possible—that in that she may have described the whole business. She would not regard it as a breach of faith, since the letter would not be read till a week later and in another country at that."

"Amazing, if that is so!"

"We must not build too much upon it, Hastings. It is a chance, that is all. No, we must work now from the other end."

"What do you call the other end?"

"A careful study of those who profit in any degree by Lord Edgware's death."

I shrugged my shoulders.

"Apart from his nephew and his wife——"

"And the man the wife wanted to marry," added Poirot.

"The Duke? He is in Paris."

"Quite so. But you cannot deny that he is an interested party. Then there are the people in the house—the butler—the servants. Who knows what grudges they may have had? But I think myself our first point of attack should be a further interview with Mademoiselle Jane Wilkinson. She is shrewd. She may be able to suggest something."

Once more we made our way to the Savoy. We found the lady surrounded by boxes and tissue paper, whilst exquisite black draperies were strewn over the back of every chair. Jane had a rapt and serious expression and was just trying on yet another small black hat before the glass.

"Why, M. Poirot. Sit down. That is, if there's anything to sit on. Ellis, clear something, will you?"

"Madame, you look charming."

Jane looked serious.

"I don't want exactly to play the hypocrite, M. Poirot. But one must observe appearances, don't you think? I mean, I think I ought to be careful. Oh! by the way, I've had the sweetest telegram from the Duke."

"From Paris?"

"Yes, from Paris. Guarded, of course, and supposed to be condolences, but put so that I can read between the lines."

"My felicitations, Madame."

"M. Poirot." She clasped her hands, her husky voice dropped. She looked like an angel about to give vent to thoughts of exquisite holiness. "I've been thinking. It all seems so *miraculous*, if you know what I mean. Here I am—all my troubles over. No tiresome business of divorce. No bothers. Just my path cleared and all plain sailing. It makes me feel almost religious—if you know what I mean."

I held my breath. Poirot looked at her, his head a little on one side. She was quite serious.

"That is how it strikes you, Madame, eh?"

"Things happen right for me," said Jane in a sort of awed whisper. "I've thought and I've thought lately—if Edgware was to die. And there—he's dead! It's—it's almost like an answer to prayer."

Poirot cleared his throat.

"I cannot say I look at it quite like that, Madame. Somebody killed your husband."

She nodded.

"Why, of course."

"Has it not occurred to you to wonder who that someone was?"

She stared at him. "Does it matter? I mean—what's that to do with it? The Duke and I can be married in about four or five months. . . ."

With difficulty Poirot controlled himself.

"Yes, Madame, I know that. But apart from that has it not occurred to you to ask yourself *who killed your husband?*"

"No." She seemed quite surprised by the idea. We could see her thinking about it.

"Does it not interest you to know?" asked Poirot.

"Not very much, I'm afraid," she admitted. "I suppose the police will find out. They're very clever, aren't they?"

"So it is said. I, too, am going to make it my business to find out."

"Are you? How funny."

"Why funny?"

"Well, I don't know." Her eyes strayed back to the clothes. She slipped on a satin coat and studied herself in the glass.

"You do not object, eh?" said Poirot, his eyes twinkling.

"Why, of course not, M. Poirot. I should just love you to be clever about it all. I wish you every success."

"Madame—I want your more than wishes. I want your opinion."

"Opinion?" said Jane absently, as she twisted her head over her shoulder. "What on?"

"Who do you think likely to have killed Lord Edgware?"

Jane shook her head. "I haven't any idea!"

She wriggled her shoulders experimentally and took up the hand-glass.

"Madame!" said Poirot in a loud, emphatic voice. "Who DO *you* THINK KILLED YOUR HUSBAND?"

This time it got through. Jane threw him a startled glance.

"Geraldine, I expect," she said.

"Who is Geraldine?"

But Jane's attention was gone again.

"Ellis, take this up a little on the right shoulder. So. What, M. Poirot? Geraldine's his daughter. No Ellis, the *right* shoulder. That's better. Oh! must you go, M. Poirot? I'm terribly grateful for everything. I mean, for the divorce, even though it isn't necessary after all. I shall always think you were wonderful."

I only saw Jane Wilkinson twice again. Once on the stage, once when I sat opposite her at a luncheon party. I always think of her as I saw her then, absorbed heart and soul in clothes, her lips carelessly throwing out the words that were to influence Poirot's further actions, her mind concentrated firmly and beatifically on herself.

"*Epatant*," said Poirot with reverence as we emerged into the Strand.

CHAPTER XII

THE DAUGHTER

THERE WAS a letter sent by hand lying on the table when we got back to our rooms. Poirot picked it up, slit it open with his usual neatness, and then laughed.

"What is it you say—'Talk of the devil'? See here, Hastings."

I took the note from him.

The paper was stamped 17 Regent Gate and was written in very upright characteristic handwriting which looked easy to read and, curiously enough, was not.

" Dear Sir (it ran),
            I hear you were at the house this morning with the inspector. I am sorry not to have had the opportunity of speaking to you. If convenient to yourself I should be much obliged if you could spare me a few minutes any time this afternoon.
                              Yours truly,
                                  GERALDINE MARSH."

"Curious," I said. "I wonder why she wants to see you?"

"Is it curious that she should want to see me? You are not polite, my friend."

Poirot has the most irritating habit of joking at the wrong moment.

"We will go round at once, my friend," he said, and lovingly brushing an imagined speck of dust from his hat he put it on his head.

Jane Wilkinson's careless suggestion that Geraldine might have killed her father seemed to me particularly absurd. Only a particularly brainless person could have suggested it. I said as much to Poirot.

" Brains. Brains. What do we really mean by the term? In your idiom you would say that Jane Wilkinson has the brains of a rabbit. That is a term of disparagement. But consider the rabbit for a moment. He exists and multiplies, does he not? That, in Nature, is a sign of mental superiority. The lovely Lady Edgware she does not know history, or geography, nor the classics *sans doute*. The name of Lao Tse would suggest to her a prize Pekingese dog, the name of Molière a *maison de couture*. But when it comes to choosing clothes, to making rich and advantageous marriages, and to getting her own way—her success is phenomenal. The opinion of a philosopher as to who murdered Lord Edgware would be no good to me—the motive for murder from a philosopher's point of view would be the greatest good of the greatest number, and as that is difficult to decide, few philosophers are murderers. But a careless opinion from Lady Edgware *might* be useful to me because her point of view would be material-istic and based on a knowledge of the worst side of human nature."

" Perhaps there's something in that," I conceded.

" *Nous voici*," said Poirot. " I am curious to know why the young lady wishes so urgently to see me."

" It is a natural desire," I said, getting my own back. " You said so a quarter of an hour ago. The natural desire to see something unique at close quarters."

" Perhaps it is you, my friend, who make an impression on her heart the other day," replied Poirot as he rang the bell.

I recalled the startled face of the girl who had stood in the doorway. I could still see those burning dark eyes in the white face. That momentary glimpse had made a great impression on me.

We were shown upstairs to a big drawing-room and in a minute or two Geraldine Marsh came to us there.

The impression of intensity which I had noticed before was heightened on this occasion. This tall, thin, white-faced girl with her big haunting black eyes was a striking figure.

She was extremely composed—in view of her youth, remarkably so.

" It is very good of you to come so promptly, M. Poirot," she said. " I am sorry to have missed you this morning."

" You were lying down?"

" Yes, Miss Carroll—my father's secretary, you know—insisted. She has been very kind."

There was a queer grudging note in the girl's voice that puzzled me.

" In what way can I be of service to you, Mademoiselle?" asked Poirot.

She hesitated a minute and then said:

" On the day before my father was killed you came to see him?"

" Yes, Mademoiselle."

" Why? Did he—send for you?"

Poirot did not reply for a moment. He seemed to be deliberating. I believe, now, that it was a cleverly calculated move on his part. He wanted to goad her into further speech. She was, he realised, of the impatient type. She wanted things in a hurry.

" Was he afraid of something? Tell me. Tell me. I must know. Who was he afraid of? Why? What did he say to you? Oh! why can't you speak?"

I had thought that that forced composure was not natural. It had soon broken down. She was leaning forward now, her hands twisting themselves nervously on her lap.

" What passed between Lord Edgware and myself was in confidence," said Poirot slowly.

His eyes never left her face.

" Then it was about—I mean, it must have been something to do with—the family. Oh! you sit there and torture me. Why won't you tell me? It's necessary for me to know. It's necessary. I tell you."

Again, very slowly, Poirot shook his head, apparently a prey to deep perplexity.

" M. Poirot." She drew herself up. " I'm his daughter. It is my right to know—what my father dreaded on the last day but one of his life. It isn't fair to leave me in the dark. It isn't fair to him—not to tell me."

" Were you so devoted to your father, then, Mademoiselle?" asked Poirot gently.

She drew back as though stung.

" Fond of him?" she whispered. " Fond of him. I—I——"

And suddenly her self-control snapped. Peals of laughter

broke from her. She lay back in her chair and laughed and laughed.

"It's so funny," she gasped. "It's so funny—to be asked that."

That hysterical laughter had not passed unheard. The door opened and Miss Carroll came in. She was firm and efficient.

"Now, now, Geraldine, my dear, that won't do. No, no. Hush, now. I insist. No. Stop it. I mean it. Stop it at once."

Her determined manner had its effect. Geraldine's laughter grew fainter. She wiped her eyes and sat up.

"I'm sorry," she said in a low voice. "I've never done that before."

Miss Carroll was still looking at her anxiously.

"I'm all right now, Miss Carroll. It was idiotic."

She smiled suddenly. A queer bitter smile that twisted her lips. She sat up very straight in her chair and looked at no one.

"He asked me," she said in a cold clear voice, "if I had been very fond of my father."

Miss Caroll made a sort of indeterminate cluck. It denoted irresolution on her part. Geraldine went on, her voice high and scornful.

"I wonder if it is better to tell lies or the truth? The truth, I think. I wasn't fond of my father. I hated him!"

"Geraldine dear."

"Why pretend? You didn't hate him because he couldn't touch you! You were one of the few people in the world that he couldn't get at. You saw him as the employer who paid you so much a year. His rages and his queernesses didn't interest you—you ignored them. I know what you'd say, 'Everyone has got to put up with something.' You were cheerful and uninterested. You're a very strong woman. You're not really human. But then you could have walked out of the house any minute. I couldn't. I belonged."

"Really, Geraldine, I don't think it's necessary going into all this. Fathers and daughters often don't get on. But the less said in life the better, I've found."

Geraldine turned her back on her. She addressed herself to Poirot.

"M. Poirot, I _hated_ my father! I am glad he is dead! It means freedom for me—freedom and independence. I am

not in the least anxious to find his murderer. For all we
know the person who killed him may have had reasons—
ample reasons—justifying that action."

Poirot looked at her thoughtfully.

"That is a dangerous principle to adopt, Mademoiselle."

"Will hanging someone else bring father back to life?"

"No," said Poirot dryly. "But it may save other
innocent people from being murdered."

"I don't understand."

"A person who has once killed, Mademoiselle, nearly
always kills again—sometimes again and again."

"I don't believe it. Not—not a real person."

"You mean—not a homicidal maniac? But yes, it is true.
One life is removed—perhaps after a terrific struggle with
the murderer's conscience. Then—danger threatens—the
second murder is morally easier. At the slightest threatening
of suspicion a third follows. And little by little an artistic
pride arises—it is a *métier*—to kill. It is done at last almost
for pleasure."

The girl had hidden her face in her hands.

"Horrible. Horrible. It isn't true."

"And supposing I told you that it *had already happened*?
That already—to save himself—*the murderer has killed a
second time*?"

"What's that, M. Poirot?" cried Miss Carroll. "Another
murder? Where? Who?"

Poirot gently shook his head.

"It was an illustration only. I ask pardon."

"Oh! I see. For a moment I really thought—— Now,
Geraldine, if you've finished talking arrant nonsense."

"You are on my side, I see," said Poirot with a little bow.

"I don't believe in capital punishment," said Miss Carroll
briskly. "Otherwise I am certainly on your side. Society
must be protected."

Geraldine got up. She smoothed back her hair.

"I am sorry," she said. "I am afraid I have been making
rather a fool of myself. You still refuse to tell me why my
father called you in?"

"Called him?" said Miss Carroll in lively astonishment.

"You misunderstand, Miss Marsh. I have not refused to
tell you."

Poirot was forced to come out into the open.

"I was only considering how far that interview might have been said to be confidential. Your father did not call me in. *I* sought an interview with *him* on behalf of a client. That client was Lady Edgware."

"Oh! I see."

An extraordinary expression came over the girl's face. I thought at first it was disappointment. Then I saw it was relief.

"I have been very foolish," she said slowly. "I thought my father had perhaps thought himself menaced by some danger. It was stupid."

"You know, M. Poirot, you gave me quite a turn just now," said Miss Carroll, "when you suggested that woman had done a second murder."

Poirot did not answer her. He spoke to the girl.

"Do you believe Lady Edgware committed the murder, Mademoiselle?"

She shook her head.

"No, I don't. I can't see her doing a thing like that. She's much too—well, artificial."

"I don't see who else can have done it," said Miss Carroll. "And I don't think women of that kind have got any moral sense."

"It needn't have been her," argued Geraldine. "She may have come here and just had an interview with him and gone away, and the real murderer may have been some lunatic who got in afterwards."

"All murderers are mentally deficient—of that I am assured," said Miss Carroll. "Internal gland secretion."

At that moment the door opened and a man came in—then stopped awkwardly.

"Sorry," he said. "I didn't know anyone was in here."

Geraldine made a mechanical introduction.

"My cousin, Lord Edgware. M. Poirot. It's all right, Ronald. You're not interrupting."

"Sure, Dina? How do you do, M. Poirot? Are your grey cells functioning over our particular family mystery?"

I cast my mind back trying to remember. That round, pleasant, vacuous face, the eyes with slight pouches underneath them, the little moustache marooned like an island in the middle of the expanse of face.

Of course! It was Carlotta Adams' escort on the night of the supper party in Jane Wilkinson's suite.

Captain Ronald Marsh. Now Lord Edgware,

CHAPTER XIII

THE NEPHEW

THE NEW Lord Edgware's eye was a quick one. He noticed the slight start I gave.

"Ah! you've got it," he said amiably. "Aunt Jane's little supper party. Just a shade bottled, wasn't I? But I fancied it passed quite unperceived."

Poirot was saying good-bye to Geraldine Marsh and Miss Carroll.

"I'll come down with you," said Ronald genially.

He led the way down the stairs, talking as he went.

"Rum thing—life. Kicked out one day, lord of the manor the next. My late unlamented uncle kicked me out, you know, three years ago. But I expect you know all about that, M. Poirot?"

"I had heard the fact mentioned—yes," replied Poirot composedly.

"Naturally. A thing of that kind is sure to be dug up. The earnest sleuth can't afford to miss it."

He grinned.

Then he threw open the dining-room door.

"Have a spot before you go."

Poirot refused. So did I. But the young man mixed himself a drink and continued to talk.

"Here's to murder," he said cheerfully. "In the space of one short night I am converted from the creditor's despair to the tradesman's hope. Yesterday ruin stared me in the face, to-day all is affluence. God bless Aunt Jane."

He drained his glass. Then, with a slight change of manner, he spoke to Poirot.

"Seriously, though, M. Poirot, what *are* you doing here? Four days ago Aunt Jane was dramatically declaiming, 'Who will rid me of this insolent tyrant?' and lo and behold she is ridded! Not by your agency, I hope? The perfect crime, by Hercule Poirot, ex-sleuth hound."

Poirot smiled.

" I am here this afternoon in answer to a note from Miss Geraldine Marsh."

" A discreet answer, eh? No, M. Poirot, what are you really doing here? For some reason or other you are interesting yourself in my uncle's death."

" I am always interested in murder, Lord Edgware."

" But you don't commit it. Very cautious. You should teach Aunt Jane caution. Caution and a shade more camouflage. You'll excuse me calling her Aunt Jane. It amuses me. Did you see her blank face when I did it the other night? Hadn't the foggiest notion who I was."

" *En verité?*"

" No. I was kicked out of here three months before she came along."

The fatuous expression of good nature on his face failed for a moment. Then he went on lightly:

" Beautiful woman. But no subtlety. Methods are rather crude, eh?"

Poirot shrugged his shoulders.

" It is possible."

Ronald looked at him curiously.

" I believe you think she didn't do it. So she's got round you too, has she?"

" I have a great admiration for beauty," said Poirot evenly. " But also for—evidence."

He brought the last word out very quietly.

" Evidence?" said the other sharply.

" Perhaps you do not know, Lord Edgware, that Lady Edgware was at a party at Chiswick last night at the time she was supposed to have been seen here."

Ronald swore.

" So she went after all! How like a woman! At six o'clock she was throwing her weight about, declaring that nothing on earth would make her go, and I suppose about ten minutes after she'd changed her mind! When planning a murder never depend upon a woman doing what she says she'll do. That's how the best laid-plans of murder gang agley. No, M. Poirot, I'm not incriminating myself. Oh, yes, don't think I can't read what's passing through your mind. Who is the Natural Suspect? The well-known Wicked Ne'er-do-Weel Nephew."

He leaned back in his chair chuckling.

"I'm saving your little grey cells for you, M. Poirot. No need for you to hunt round for someone who saw me in the offing when Aunt Jane was declaring she never, never, never would go out that night, etc. I was there. So you ask yourself did the wicked nephew in very truth come here last night disguised in a fair wig and a Paris hat?"

Seemingly enjoying the situation, he surveyed us both. Poirot, his head a little on one side, was regarding him with close attention. I felt rather uncomfortable.

"I had a motive—oh! yes, motive admitted. And I'm going to give you a present of a very valuable and significant piece of information. I called to see my uncle yesterday morning. Why? To ask for money. Yes, lick your lips over that. To ASK FOR MONEY. And I went away without getting any. And that same evening—that very same evening —Lord Edgware dies. Good title that, by the way. Lord Edgware Dies. Look well on a bookstall."

He paused. Still Poirot said nothing.

"I'm really flattered by your attention, M. Poirot. Captain Hastings looks as though he had seen a ghost—or were going to see one any minute. Don't get so strung up, my dear fellow. Wait for the anti-climax. Well, where were we? Oh! yes, case against the Wicked Nephew. Guilt is to be thrown on the hated Aunt by Marriage. Nephew, celebrated at one time for acting female parts, does his supreme histrionic effort. In a girlish voice he announces himself as Lady Edgware and sidles past the butler with mincing steps. No suspicions are aroused. 'Jane,' cries my fond uncle. 'George,' I squeak. I fling my arms about his neck and neatly insert the penknife. The next details are purely medical and can be omitted. Exit the spurious lady. And so to bed at the end of a good day's work."

He laughed, and rising, poured himself out another whisky and soda. He returned slowly to his chair.

"Works out well, doesn't it? But you see, here comes the crux of the matter. The disappointment! The annoying sensation of having been led up the garden. For now, M. Poirot, we come to the alibi!"

He finished off his glass.

"I always find alibis very enjoyable," he remarked. "Whenever I happen to be reading a detective story I sit up and take notice when the alibi comes along. This is a remark-ably good alibi. Three strong, and Jewish at that. In plainer language, Mr., Mrs. and Miss Dortheimer. Extremely rich and extremely musical. They have a box at Covent Garden. Into that box they invite young men with prospects. I, M. Poirot, am a young man with prospects—as good a one, shall we say, as they can hope to get. Do I like the opera? Frankly, no. But I enjoy the excellent dinner in Grosvenor Square first, and I also enjoy an excellent supper somewhere else afterwards, even if I do have to dance with Rachel Dortheimer and have a stiff arm for two days afterwards. So you see, M. Poirot, there you are. When uncle's lifeblood is flowing, I am whispering cheerful nothings into the diamond encrusted ears of the fair (I beg her pardon, dark) Rachel in a box at Covent Garden. Her long Jewish nose is quivering with emotion. And so you see, M. Poirot, why I can afford to be so frank."

He leaned back in his chair.

"I hope I have not bored you. Any question to ask?"

"I can assure you that I have not been bored," said Poirot. "Since you are so kind, there is one little question that I would like to ask."

"Delighted."

"How long, Lord Edgware, have you known Miss Carlotta Adams?"

Whatever the young man had expected, it certainly had not been this. He sat up sharply with an entirely new expres-sion on his face.

"Why on earth do you want to know that? What's that got to do with what we've been talking about?"

"I was curious, that was all. For the other, you have explained so fully everything there is to explain that there is no need for me to ask questions."

Ronald shot a quick glance at him. It was almost as though he did not care for Poirot's amiable acquiescence. He would, I thought, have preferred him to be more suspicious.

"Carlotta Adams? Let me see. About a year. A little more. I got to know her last year when she gave her first show."

"You knew her well?"

"Pretty well. She's not the sort of girl you ever got to know frightfully well. Reserved and all that."

" But you liked her?"

Ronald stared at him.

" I wish I knew why you were so interested in the lady. Was it because I was with her the other night? Yes, I like her very much. She's sympathetic—listens to a chap and makes him feel he's something of a fellow after all."

Poirot nodded.

" I comprehend. Then you will be sorry."

" Sorry? What about?"

" That she is dead!"

" What?" Ronald sprang up in astonishment. " Carlotta dead?"

He looked absolutely dumbfounded by the news.

" You're pulling my leg, M. Poirot. Carlotta was perfectly well the last time I saw her."

" When was that?" asked Poirot quickly.

" Day before yesterday, I think. I can't remember."

" *Tout de même*, she is dead."

" It must have been frightfully sudden. What was it? A street accident?"

Poirot looked at the ceiling.

"No. She took an overdose of veronal."

"Oh! I say. Poor kid. How frightfully sad."

" *N'est ce pas?*"

"I *am* sorry. And she was getting on so well. She was going to get her kid sister over and had all sorts of plans. Dash it, I'm more sorry than I can say."

" Yes," said Poirot. " It is sad to die when you are young—when you do not want to die—when all life is open before you and you have everything to live for."

Ronald looked at him curiously.

" I don't think I quite get you, M. Poirot."

" No?"

Poirot rose and held out his hand.

" I express my thoughts—a little strongly, perhaps. For I do not like to see youth deprived of its right to live, Lord Edgware. I feel—very strongly about it. I wish you good-day."

" Oh—er—good-bye."

He looked rather taken aback.

As I opened the door I almost collided with Miss Carroll.

" Ah! M. Poirot, they told me you hadn't gone yet. I'd

like a word with you if I may. Perhaps you wouldn't mind coming up to my room.

" It's about that child, Geraldine," she said when we had entered her sanctum and she had closed the door.

" Yes, Mademoiselle?"

" She talked a lot of nonsense this afternoon. Now don't protest. Nonsense! That's what I call it and that's what it was. She broods."

" I could see that she was suffering from over-strain," said Poirot gently.

" Well—to tell the truth—she hasn't had a very happy life. No, one can't pretend she has. Frankly, M. Poirot, Lord Edgware was a peculiar man—not the sort of man who ought to have had anything to do with the upbringing of children. Quite frankly, he terrorised Geraldine."

Poirot nodded.

"Yes, I should imagine something of the kind."

" He was a peculiar man. He—I don't quite know how to put it—but he enjoyed seeing anyone afraid of him. It seemed to give him a morbid kind of pleasure."

" Quite so."

" He was an extremely well-read man, and a man of considerable intellect. But in some ways—well, I didn't come across that side of him myself, but it was there. I'm not really surprised his wife left him. This wife, I mean. I didn't approve of her, mind. I've no opinion of that young woman at all. But in marrying Lord Edgware she got all and more than she deserved. Well, she left him—and no bones broken, as they say. But Geraldine couldn't leave him. For a long time he'd forget all about her, and then, suddenly, he'd remember. I sometimes think—though perhaps I shouldn't say it——"

" Yes, yes. Mademoiselle, say it."

" Well, I sometimes thought he revenged himself on the mother—his first wife—that way. She was a gentle creature, I believe, with a very sweet disposition. I've always been sorry for her. I shouldn't have mentioned all this, M. Poirot, if it hadn't been for that very foolish outburst of Geraldine's just now. Things she said—about hating her father—they might sound peculiar to anyone who didn't know."

" Thank you very much, Mademoiselle. Lord Edgware, I

fancy, was a man who would have done much better not to marry."

" Much better."

" He never thought of marrying for a third time? "

" How could he? His wife was alive."

" By giving her her freedom he would have been free himself."

" I should think he had had enough trouble with two wives as it was," said Miss Carroll grimly.

" So you think there would have been no question of a third marriage. There was no one? Think, Mademoiselle. No one? "

Miss Carroll's colour rose.

" I cannot understand the way you keep harping on the point. Of course there was no one."

CHAPTER XIV

FIVE QUESTIONS

" WHY DID you ask Miss Carroll about the possibility of Lord Edgware's wanting to marry again? " I asked with some curiosity as we were driving home.

" It just occurred to me that there was the possibility of such a thing, *mon ami.*"

" Why? "

" I have been searching in my mind for something to explain Lord Edgware's sudden *volte face* regarding the matter of divorce. There is something curious there, my friend."

" Yes," I said thoughtfully. " It is rather odd."

"You see, Hastings, Lord Edgware confirmed what Madame had told us. She had employed the lawyers of all kinds, but he refused to budge the inch. No, he would not agree to the divorce. And then, all of a sudden, he yields! "

" Or so he says," I reminded him.

" Very true, Hastings. It is very just, the observation you make there. *So he says.* We have no proof, whatever, that that letter was written. *Eh bien*, on one part, *ce* Monsieur is lying. For some reason he tells us the fabrication, the embroidery. Is it not so? Why, we do not know. But, on the hypothesis that he *did* write that letter, there must have been a *reason* for so doing. Now the reason that presents itself most naturally to the imagination is that he has suddenly met someone whom he desires to marry. That explains perfectly his sudden change of face. And so, naturally, I make the inquiries."

"Miss Carroll turned the idea down very decisively," I said.

"Yes. Miss Carroll . . ." said Poirot in a meditative voice.

"Now what are you driving at?" I asked in exasperation. Poirot is an adept at suggesting doubts by the tone of his voice.

"What reason should she have for lying about it?" I asked.

"*Aucune—aucune.*"

"But, you see, Hastings, it is difficult to trust her evidence."

"You think she's lying? But why? She looks a most upright person."

"That is just it. Between the deliberate falsehood and the disinterested inaccuracy it is very hard to distinguish sometimes."

"What *do* you mean?"

"To deceive deliberately—that is one thing. But to be so sure of your facts, of your ideas and of their essential truth that the details do not matter—that, my friend, is a special characteristic of particularly honest persons. Already, mark you, she has told us one lie. She said she saw Jane Wilkinson's face when she could not possibly have done so. Now how did that come about? Look at it this way. She looks down and sees Jane Wilkinson in the hall. No doubt enters her head that it *is* Jane Wilkinson. She knows it is. She says she saw her face distinctly because—being so sure of her facts—exact details do not matter! It is pointed out to her that she could not have seen her face. Is that so? Well, what does it matter if she saw her face or not—it *was* Jane Wilkinson. And so with any other question. She *knows*. And so she answers questions in the light of her knowledge, not by reason of remembered facts. The positive witness should always be treated with suspicion, my friend. The uncertain witness who doesn't remember, isn't sure, will think a minute—ah! yes, that's how it was—is infinitely more to be depended upon!"

"Dear me, Poirot," I said. "You upset all my preconceived ideas about witnesses."

"In reply to my question as to Lord Edgware's marrying again she ridicules the idea—simply because it has never occurred to her. She will not take the trouble to remember whether any infinitesimal signs may have pointed that way. Therefore we are exactly where we were before."

"She certainly did not seem at all taken aback when you pointed out she could not have seen Jane Wilkinson's face," I remarked thoughtfully.

"No. That is why I decided that she was one of those honestly inaccurate persons, rather than a deliberate liar. I can see no motive for deliberate lying unless—true, that is an idea!"

"What is?" I asked eagerly.

But Poirot shook his head.

"An idea suggested itself to me. But it is too impossible—yes, much too impossible."

And he refused to say more.

"She seems very fond of the girl," I said.

"Yes. She certainly was determined to assist at our interview. What was your impression of the Honourable Geraldine Marsh, Hastings?"

"I was sorry for her—deeply sorry for her."

"You have always the tender heart, Hastings. Beauty in distress upsets you every time."

"Didn't you feel the same?"

He nodded gravely.

"Yes—she has not had a happy life. That is written very clearly on her face."

"At any rate," I said warmly, "you realise how preposterous Jane Wilkinson's suggestion was—that she should have had anything to do with the crime, I mean."

"Doubtless her alibi is satisfactory, but Japp has not communicated it to me as yet."

"My dear Poirot—do you mean to say that even after seeing her and talking to her, you are still not satisfied and want an alibi?"

"*Eh bien*, my friend, what is the result of seeing and talking to her? We perceive that she has passed through great unhappiness, she admits that she hated her father and is glad that he is dead, and she is deeply uneasy about what he may have said to us yesterday morning. And after that you say—no alibi is necessary!"

"Her mere frankness proves her innocence," I said warmly.

"Frankness is a characteristic of the family. The new Lord Edgware—with what a gesture he laid his cards on the table."

"He did indeed," I said, smiling at the remembrance. "Rather an original method."

Poirot nodded.

"He—what do you say?—cuts the ground before our feet."

"From under," I corrected. "Yes—it made us look rather foolish."

"What a curious idea. You may have looked foolish. I did not feel foolish in the least and I do not think I looked it. On the contrary, my friend, I put him out of countenance."

"Did you?" I said doubtfully, not remembering having seen signs of anything of the kind.

"*Si, si.* I listen—and listen. And at last I ask a question about something quite different, and that, you may have noticed, disconcerts our brave Monsieur very much. You do not observe, Hastings."

"I thought his horror and astonishment at hearing of Carlotta Adams' death was genuine," I said. "I suppose you will say it was a piece of clever acting."

"Impossible to tell. I agree it *seemed* genuine."

"Why do you think he flung all those facts at our head in that cynical way? Just for amusement?"

"That is always possible. You English, you have the most extraordinary notions of humour. But it may have been policy. Facts that are concealed acquire a suspicious importance. Facts that are frankly revealed tend to be regarded as less important than they really are."

"The quarrel with his uncle that morning, for instance?"

"Exactly. He knows that the fact is bound to leak out. *Eh bien*, he will parade it."

"He is not so foolish as he looks."

"Oh! he is not foolish at all. He has plenty of brains when he cares to use them. He sees exactly where he stands and, as I said, he lays his cards on the table. You play the bridge, Hastings. Tell me, when does one do that?"

"You play bridge yourself," I said, laughing. "You know well enough—when all the rest of the tricks are yours and you want to save time and get on to a new hand."

"Yes, *mon ami*, that is all very true. But occasionally there is another reason. I have remarked it once or twice when playing with *les dames*. There is perhaps a little doubt. *Eh bien, la dame*, she throws down the cards, says 'and all the rest are mine,' and gathers up the cards and cuts the new pack. And possibly the other players agree—especially if they are a little inexperienced. The thing is not obvious, mark you. It requires to be followed out. Half-way through dealing the next hand, one of the players thinks: 'Yes, but she would have to have taken over that fourth diamond in dummy whether she wanted to or not, and then she would have had to lead a little club and my nine would have made.'"

"So you think?"

"I think, Hastings, that too much bravado is a very interesting thing. And I also think that it is time we dined. *Une petite omelette, n'est ce pas?* And after that, about nine o'clock, I have one more visit I wish to make."

"Where is that?"

"We will dine first, Hastings. And until we drink our coffee, we will not discuss the case further. When engaged in eating, the brain should be the servant of the stomach."

Poirot was as good as his word. We went to a little restaurant in Soho where he was well known, and there we had a delicious omelette, a sole, a chicken and a Baba au Rhum of which Poirot was inordinately fond.

Then, as we sipped our coffee, Poirot smiled affectionately across the table at me.

"My good friend," he said. "I depend upon you more than you know."

I was confused and delighted by these unexpected words. He had never said anything of the kind to me before. Sometimes, secretly, I had felt slightly hurt. He seemed almost to go out of his way to disparage my mental powers.

Although I did not think his own powers were flagging, I did realise suddenly that perhaps he had come to depend on my aid more than he knew.

"Yes," he said dreamily. "You may not always comprehend just how it is so—but you do often and often point the way."

I could hardly believe my ears.

"Really, Poirot," I stammered. "I'm awfully glad. I suppose I've learnt a good deal from you one way or another——"

He shook his head.

"*Mais non, ce n'est pas ça.* You have learnt nothing."

"Oh!" I said, rather taken aback.

"That is as it should be. No human being should learn from another. Each individual should develop his own powers to the uttermost, not try to imitate those of someone else. I do not wish you to be a second and inferior Poirot. I wish you to be the supreme Hastings. And you are the supreme Hastings. In you, Hastings, I find the normal mind almost perfectly illustrated."

"I'm not abnormal, I hope," I said.

"No, no. You are beautifully and perfectly balanced. In you sanity is personified. Do you realise what that means to me? When the criminal sets out to do a crime his first effort is to deceive. Who does he seek to deceive? The image in his mind is that of the normal man. There is probably no such thing actually—it is a mathematical abstraction. But you come as near to realising it as is possible. There are moments when you have flashes of brilliance when you rise above the average, moments (I hope you will pardon me) when you descend to curious depths of obtuseness, but take it all for all, you are amazingly normal. *Eh bien*, how does this profit me? Simply in this way. As in a mirror I see reflected in your mind exactly what the criminal wishes me to believe. That is terrifically helpful and suggestive."

I did not quite understand. It seemed to me that what Poirot was saying was hardly complimentary. However, he quickly disabused me of that impression.

"I have expressed myself badly," he said quickly. "You have an insight into the criminal mind, which I myself lack. You show me what the criminal wishes me to believe. It is a great gift."

"Insight," I said thoughtfully. "Yes, perhaps I have got insight,"

I looked across the table at him. He was smoking his tiny cigarettes and regarding me with great kindliness.

"*Ce cher* Hastings," he murmured. "I have indeed much affection for you."

I was pleased but embarrassed and hastened to change the subject.

"Come," I said in a business-like manner. "Let us discuss the case."

"*Eh bien*." Poirot threw his head back, his eyes narrowed. He slowly puffed out smoke.

"*Je me pose des questions*," he said,

"Yes?" I said eagerly.

"You, too, doubtless?"

"Certainly," I said. And also leaning back and narrowing my own eyes I threw out:

"Who killed Lord Edgware?"

Poirot immediately sat up and shook his head vigorously.

"No, no. Not at all. Is it a question, that? You are like someone who reads the detective story and who starts guessing each of the characters in turn without rhyme or reason. Once, I agree, I had to do that myself. It was a very exceptional case. I will tell you about it one of these days. It was a feather in my cap. But of what were we speaking?"

"Of the questions you were 'posing' to yourself," I replied dryly. It was on the tip of my tongue to suggest that my real use to Poirot was to provide him with a companion to whom he could boast, but I controlled myself. If he wished to instruct then let him.

"Come on," I said. "Let's hear them."

That was all that the vanity of the man wanted. He leaned back again and resumed his former attitude.

"The first question we have already discussed. *Why did Lord Edgware change his mind on the subject of divorce?* One or two ideas suggest themselves to me on that subject. One of them you know.

"The second question I ask myself is *What happened to that letter?* To whose interest was it that Lord Edgware and his wife should continue to be tied together?

"Three, *What was the meaning of the expression on his face that you saw when you looked back yesterday morning on leaving the library?* Have you any answer to that, Hastings?"

I shook my head.

" I can't understand it."

" You are sure that you didn't imagine it? Sometimes, Hastings, you have the imagination *un peu vif*."

" No, no." I shook my head vigorously. " I'm quite sure I wasn't mistaken."

" *Bien*. Then it is a fact to be explained. My fourth question concerns those pince-nez. Neither Jane Wilkinson nor Carlotta Adams wore glasses. What, then, are the glasses doing in Carlotta Adams' bag?

" And for my fifth question. *Why did someone telephone to find out if Jane Wilkinson were at Chiswick and who was it?*

" Those, my friend, are the questions with which I am tormenting myself. If I could answer those, I should feel happier in my mind. If I could even evolve a theory that explained them satisfactorily my *amour propre* would not suffer so much."

" There are several other questions," I said.

" Such as?"

" Who incited Carlotta Adams to this hoax? Where was she that evening before and after ten o'clock? Who is D who gave her the golden box?"

" Those questions are self-evident," said Poirot. " There is no subtlety about them. They are simply things we do not know. They are questions of *fact*. We may get to know them any minute. My questions, *mon ami*, are psychological. The little grey cells of the brain——"

" Poirot," I said desperately. I felt that I must stop him at all costs. I could not bear to hear it all over again. " You spoke of making a visit to-night?"

Poirot looked at his watch.

" True," he said. " I will telephone and find out if it is convenient."

He went away and returned a few minutes later.

" Come," he said. " All is well."

" Where are we going?" I asked.

" To the house of Sir Montagu Corner at Chiswick. I would like to know a little more about that telephone call."

CHAPTER XV

SIR MONTAGU CORNER

IT WAS about ten o'clock when we reached Sir Montagu Corner's house on the river at Chiswick. It was a big house standing back in its own grounds. We were admitted into a beautifully-panelled hall. On our right, through an open door, we saw the dining-room with its long polished table lit with candles.

" Will you come this way, please?"

The butler led the way up a broad staircase and into a long room on the first floor overlooking the river.

" M. Hercule Poirot," announced the butler.

It was a beautifully-proportioned room, and had an old world air with its carefully-shaded dim lamps. In one corner of the room was a bridge table, set near the open window, and round it sat four people. As we entered the room one of the four rose and came towards us.

" It is a great pleasure to make your acquaintance, M. Poirot."

I looked with some interest at Sir Montagu Corner. He had a distinctly Jewish cast of countenance, very small intelligent black eyes and a carefully-arranged toupée. He was a short man—five foot eight at most, I should say. His manner was affected to the last degree.

" Let me introduce you. Mr. and Mrs. Widburn."

" We've met before," said Mrs. Widburn brightly.

" And Mr. Ross."

Ross was a young fellow of about twenty-two with a pleasant face and fair hair.

" I disturb your game. A million apologies," said Poirot.

" Not at all. We have not started. We were commencing to deal the cards only. Some coffee, M. Poirot?"

Poirot declined but accepted an offer of old brandy. It was brought us in immense goblets.

As we sipped it, Sir Montagu discoursed.

He spoke of Japanese prints, of Chinese lacquer, of Persian carpets, of the French impressionists, of modern music and of the theories of Einstein.

Then he sat back and smiled at us beneficently. He had evidently thoroughly enjoyed his performance. In the dim light he looked like some genie of the mediæval age. All around the room were exquisite examples of art and culture.

"And now, Sir Montagu," said Poirot. "I will trespass on your kindness no longer but will come to the object of my visit."

Sir Montagua waved a curious claw-like hand.

"There is no hurry. Time is infinite."

"One always feels that in this house," sighed Mrs. Widburn. "So wonderful."

"I would not live in London for a million pounds," said Sir Montagu. "Here one is in the old-world atmosphere of peace that—alas!—we have put behind us in these jarring days."

A sudden impish fancy flashed over me that if someone were really to offer Sir Montagu a million pounds, old-world peace might go to the wall, but I trod down such heretical sentiments.

"What is money, after all?" murmured Mrs. Widburn.

"Ah!" said Mr. Widburn thoughtfully, and rattled some coins absent-mindedly in his trousers pocket.

"Archie," said Mrs. Widburn reproachfully.

"Sorry," said Mr. Widburn and stopped.

"To speak of crime in such an atmosphere is, I feel, unpardonable," began Poirot apologetically.

"Not at all." Sir Montagu waved a gracious hand. "A crime can be a work of art. A detective can be an artist. I do not refer, of course, to the police. An inspector has been here to-day. A curious person. He had never heard of Benvenuto Cellini, for instance."

"He came about Jane Wilkinson, I suppose," said Mrs. Widburn with instant curiosity.

"It was fortunate for the lady that she was at your house last night," said Poirot.

"So it seems," said Sir Montagu. "I asked her here knowing that she was beautiful and talented and hoping that I might be able to be of use to her. She was thinking of going into management. But it seems that I was fated to be of use to her in a very different way."

"Jane's got luck," said Mrs. Widburn. "She's been dying to get rid of Edgware and here's somebody gone and saved her the trouble. She'll marry the young Duke of Merton now. Everyone says so. His mother's wild about it."

" I was favourably impressed by her," said Sir Montagu graciously. " She made several most intelligent remarks about Greek art."

I smiled to myself picturing Jane saying " Yes " and " No," " Really how wonderful," in her magical husky voice. Sir Montagu was the type of man to whom intelligence consisted of the faculty of listening to his own remarks with suitable attention.

" Edgware was a queer fish, by all accounts," said Widburn. " I daresay he's got a good few enemies."

" Is it true, M. Poirot," asked Mrs. Widburn, " that somebody ran a penknife into the back of his brain?"

" Perfectly true, Madame. It was very neatly and efficiently done—scientific, in fact."

" I note your artistic pleasure, M. Poirot," said Sir Montagu.

" And now," said Poirot, " let me come to the object of my visit. Lady Edgware was called to the telephone when she was here at dinner. It is about that telephone call that I seek information. Perhaps you will allow me to question your domestics on the subject?"

" Certainly. Certainly. Just press that bell, will you, Ross."

The butler answered the bell. He was a tall middle-aged man of ecclesiastical appearance.

Sir Montagu explained what was wanted. The butler turned to Poirot with polite attention.

" Who answered the telephone when it rang?" began Poirot.

" I answered it myself, sir. The telephone is in a recess leading out of the hall."

" Did the person calling ask to speak to Lady Edgware or to Miss Jane Wilkinson?"

" To Lady Edgware, sir."

" What did they say exactly?"

The butler reflected for a moment.

" As far as I remember, sir, I said ' Hello.' A voice then asked if I was Chiswick 43434. I replied that that was so. It then asked me to hold the line. Another voice then asked if that was Chiswick 43434 and on my replying ' yes ' it said

'Is Lady Edgware dining there?' I said her ladyship *was* dining here. The voice said, 'I would like to speak to her, please.' I went and informed her ladyship who was at the dinner table. Her ladyship rose, and I showed her where the 'phone was."

"And then?"

"Her ladyship picked up the receiver and said: 'Hello—who's speaking?' Then she said: 'Yes—that's all right. Lady Edgware speaking.' I was just about to leave her ladyship when she called to me and said they had cut her off. She said someone had laughed and evidently hung up the receiver. She asked me if the person ringing up had given any name. They had not done so. That was all that occurred, sir."

Poirot frowned to himself.

"Do you really think the telephone call has something to do with the murder, M. Poirot?" asked Mrs. Widburn.

"Imposible to say, Madame. It is just a curious circumstance."

"People do ring up for a joke sometimes. It's been done to me."

"*C'est toujours possible, Madame.*"

He spoke to the butler again.

"Was it a man's voice or a woman's who rang up?"

"A lady's, I think, sir."

"What kind of a voice, high or low?"

"Low, sir. Careful and rather distinct." He paused. "It may be my fancy, sir, but it sounded like a *foreign* voice. The R's were very noticeable."

"As far as that goes it might have been a Scotch voice, Donald," said Mrs. Widburn, smiling at Ross.

Ross laughed.

"Not guilty," he said. "I was at the dinner table."

Poirot spoke once again to the butler.

"Do you think," he asked, "that you would recognise that voice if you were to hear it any time?"

The butler hesitated.

"I couldn't quite say, sir. I might do so. I think it is possible that I should do so."

"I thank you, my friend."

"Thank you, sir."

The butler inclined his head and withdrew, pontifical to the last.

Sir Montagu Corner continued to be very friendly and to play his rôle of old-world charm. He persuaded us to remain and play bridge. I excused myself—the stakes were bigger than I cared about. Young Ross seemed relieved also at the prospect of someone taking his hand. He and I sat looking on while the other four played. The evening ended in a heavy financial gain to Poirot and Sir Montagu.

Then we thanked our host and took our departure. Ross came with us.

"A strange little man," said Poirot as we stepped out into the night.

The night was fine and we had decided to walk until we picked up a taxi instead of having one telephoned for.

"Yes, a strange little man," said Poirot again.

"A very rich little man," said Ross with feeling.

"I suppose so."

"He seems to have taken a fancy to me," said Ross. "Hope it will last. A man like that behind you means a lot."

"You are an actor, Mr. Ross?"

Ross said that he was. He seemed sad that his name had not brought instant recognition. Apparently he had recently won marvellous notices in some gloomy play translated from the Russian.

When Poirot and I between us had soothed him down again, Poirot asked casually:

"You knew Carlotta Adams, did you not?"

"No. I saw her death announced in the paper to-night. Overdose of some drug or other. Idiotic the way all these girls dope."

"It is sad, yes. She was clever, too."

"I suppose so."

He displayed a characteristic lack of interest in anyone else's performance but his own.

"Did you see her show at all?" I asked.

"No. That sort of thing's not much in my line. Kind of craze for it at present, but I don't think it will last."

"Ah!" said Poirot. "Here is a taxi."

He waved a stick.

"Think I'll walk," said Ross. "I get a tube straight home from Hammersmith."

Suddenly he gave a nervous laugh.

"Odd thing," he said. "That dinner last night."

" Yes?"

" We were thirteen. Some fellow failed at the last minute. We never noticed it till just the end of dinner."

" And who got up first?" I asked.

He gave a queer little nervous cackle of laughter.

" I did," he said.

CHAPTER XVI

MAINLY DISCUSSION

WHEN WE got home we found Japp waiting for us.

" Thought I'd just call round and have a chat with you before turning in, M. Poirot," he said cheerfully.

" *Eh bien*, my good friend, how goes it?"

" Well, it doesn't go any too well. And that's a fact."

He looked depressed.

" Got any help for me, M. Poirot?"

" I have one or two little ideas that I should like to present to you," said Poirot.

" You and your ideas! In some ways, you know, you're a caution. Not that I don't want to hear them. I do. There's some good stuff in that funny-shaped head of yours."

Poirot acknowledged the compliment somewhat coldly.

" Have you any ideas about the double lady problem— that's what I want to know? Eh, M. Poirot? What about it? Who was she?"

" That is exactly what I wish to talk to you about."

He asked Japp if he had ever heard of Carlotta Adams.

"I've heard the name. For the moment I can't just place it."

Poirot explained.

" Her! Does imitations does she? Now what made you fix on her? What have you got to go on?"

Poirot related the steps we had taken and the conclusion we had drawn.

" By the Lord, it looks as though you were right. Clothes, hat, gloves, etc., and the fair wig. Yes, it must be. I will say —you're the goods, M. Poirot. Smart work, that! Not that I think there's anything to show she was put out of the way. That seems a bit far fetched. I don't quite see eye to eye with you there. Your theory is a bit fantastical for me. I've more experience than you have. I don't believe in this villain-behind-the-scenes motif. Carlotta Adams was the woman all right, but I should put it one of two ways. She went there for purposes of her own—blackmail, maybe, since she hinted she was going to get money. They had a bit of a dispute. He turned nasty, she turned nasty, and she finished him off. And I should say that when she got home she went all to pieces. She hadn't meant murder. It's my belief she took an overdose on purpose as the easiest way out."

" You think that covers all the facts?"

" Well, naturally there are a lot of things we don't know yet. It's a good working hypothesis to go on with. The other explanation is that the hoax and the murder had nothing to do with each other. It's just a damned queer coincidence."

Poirot did not agree, I knew. But he merely said non-committally:

" *Mais oui, c'est possible.*"

" Or, look here, how's this? The hoax is innocent enough. Someone gets to hear of it and thinks it will suit their purpose jolly well. That's not a bad idea?" He paused and went on: " But personally I prefer idea No. 1. What the link was between his lordship and the girl we'll find out somehow or other."

Poirot told him of the letter to America posted by the maid, and Japp agreed that that might possibly be of great assistance.

" I'll get on to that at once," he said, making a note of it in his little book.

" I'm the more in favour of the lady being the killer because I can't find anyone else," he said, as he put the book away. " Captain Marsh, now, his lordship as now is. He's got a motive sticking out a yard. A bad record too. Hard up and none too scrupulous over money. What's more he had a row with his uncle yesterday morning. He told me that himself as a matter of fact—which rather takes the taste out of it. Yes, he'd be a likely customer. But he's got an alibi for yesterday evening. He was at the opera with the Dortheimers. Rich Jews. Grosvenor Square. I've looked into that and it's all right. He dined with them, went to the opera and they went on to supper at Sobranis. So that's that."

" And Mademoiselle?"

" The daughter, you mean? She was out of the house too.
Dined with some people called Carthew West. They took her
to the opera and saw her home afterwards. Quarter to twelve
he got in. That disposes of *her*. The secretary woman seems
all right—very efficient decent woman. Then there's the butler.
I can't say I take to him much. It isn't natural for a man to
have good looks like that. There's something fishy about him
—and something odd about the way he came to enter Lord
Edgware's service. Yes, I'm checking up on him all right.
I can't see any motive for murder, though."

" No fresh facts have come to light?"

" Yes, one or two. It's hard to say whether they mean anything or not. For one thing, Lord Edgware's key's missing."

" The key to the front door?"

" Yes."

" That is interesting, certainly."

" As I say, it may mean a good deal or nothing at all.
Depends. What *is* a bit more significant to my mind is this.
Lord Edgware cashed a cheque yesterday—not a particularly
large one—a hundred pounds as a matter of fact. He took
the money in French notes—that's why he cashed the cheque
because of his journey to Paris to-day. Well, that money has
disappeared."

" Who told you of this?"

" Miss Carroll. She cashed the cheque and obtained the
money. She mentioned it to me, and then I found that it had
gone."

" Where was it yesterday evening?"

" Miss Carroll doesn't know. She gave it to Lord Edgware
about half-past three. It was in a Bank envelope. He was in
the library at the time. He took it and laid it down beside
him on a table."

" That certainly gives one to think. It is a complication."

" Or a simplification. By the way—the wound."

" Yes?"

" The doctor says it wasn't made by an ordinary penknife.
Something of that kind but a different shaped blade. And it
was amazingly sharp."

" Not a razor?"

" No, no. Much smaller."

Poirot frowned thoughtfully.

" The new Lord Edgware seems to be fond of his joke,"

remarked Japp. "He seems to think it amusing to be suspected of murder. He made sure we *did* suspect him o
murder, too. Looks a bit queer, that."

"It might be merely intelligence."

"More likely guilty conscience. His uncle's death cam
very pat for him. He's moved into the house, by the way."

"Where was he living before?"

"Martin Street, St. George's Road. Not a very swel
neighbourhood."

"You might make a note of that, Hastings."

I did so, though I wondered a little. If Ronald had move
to Regent Gate, his former address was hardly likely to be
needed.

"*I* think the Adams girl did it," said Japp, rising. "A fin
bit of work on your part, M. Poirot, to tumble to that. Bu
there, of course, you go about to theatres and amusing your
self. Things strike you that don't get the chance of striking
me. Pity there's no apparent motive, but a little spade wor
will soon bring it to light, I expect."

"There is one person with a motive to whom you hav
given no attention," remarked Poirot.

"Who's that, sir?"

"The gentleman who is reputed to have wanted to marry
Lord Edgware's wife. I mean the Duke of Merton."

"Yes, I suppose there is a *motive*." Japp laughed. "Bu
a gentleman in his position isn't likely to do murder. An
anyway, he's over in Paris."

"You do not regard him as a serious suspect, then?"

"Well, M. Poirot, do you?"

And laughing at the absurdity of the idea, Japp left us.

CHAPTER XVII

THE BUTLER

THE FOLLOWING day was one of inactivity for us, and activity
for Japp. He came round to see us about teatime.

He was red and wrathful.

"I've made a bloomer."

"Impossible, my friend," said Poirot soothingly.

"Yes, I have. I've let that (here he gave way to profanity) —of a butler slip through my fingers."

"He has disappeared?"

"Yes. Hooked it. What makes me kick myself for a double-dyed idiot is that I didn't particularly suspect him."

"Calm yourself—but calm yourself then."

"All very well to talk. *You* wouldn't be calm if you'd been hauled over the coals at headquarters. Oh! he's a slippery customer. It isn't the first time he's given anyone the slip. He's an old hand."

Japp wiped his forehead and looked the picture of misery. Poirot made sympathetic noises—somewhat suggestive of a hen laying an egg. With more insight into the English character, I poured out a stiff whisky and soda and placed it in front of the gloomy inspector. He brightened a little.

"Well," he said. "I don't mind if I do."

Presently he began to talk more cheerfully.

"I'm not so sure even now that he's the murderer! Of course it looks bad his bolting this way, but there might be other reasons for that. I'd begun to get on to him, you see. Seems he's mixed up with a couple of rather disreputable night clubs. Not the usual thing. Something a great deal more recherché and nasty. In fact, he's a real bad hat."

"*Tout de même*, that does not necessarily mean that he is a murderer."

"Exactly! He may have been up to some funny business or other, but not necessarily murder. No, I'm more than ever convinced it was the Adams girl. I've got nothing to prove it as yet, though. I've had men going all through her flat to-day, but we've found nothing that's helpful. She was a canny one. Kept no letters except a few business ones about financial contracts. They're all neatly docketed and labelled. Couple of letters from her sister in Washington. Quite straight and aboveboard. One or two pieces of good old-fashioned jewellery—nothing new or expensive. She didn't keep a diary. Her passbook and cheque-book don't show anything helpful. Dash it all, the girl doesn't seem to have had any private life at all!"

"She was of a reserved character," said Poirot thoughtfully. "From our point of view that is a pity."

"I've talked to the woman who did for her. Nothing there. I've been and seen that girl who keeps a hat shop and who, it seems, was a friend of hers."

" Ah! and what do you think of Miss Driver?"

" She seems a smart wide-awake bit of goods. She couldn't help me, though. Not that that surprises me. The amount of missing girls I've had to trace and their family and their friends always say the same things. ' She was of a bright and affectionate disposition and had no men friends.' That's never true. It's unnatural. Girls ought to have men friends. If not there's something wrong about them. It's the muddle-headed loyalty of friends and relations that makes a detective's life so difficult."

He paused for want of breath, and I replenished his glass.

" Thank you, Captain Hastings, I don't mind if I do. Well, there you are. You've got to hunt and hunt about. There's about a dozen young men she went out to supper and danced with, but nothing to show that one of them meant more than another. There's the present Lord Edgware, there's Mr. Bryan Martin, the film star, there's half a dozen others—but nothing special and particular. Your man behind idea is all wrong. I think you'll find that she played a lone hand, M. Poirot. I'm looking now for the connection between her and the murdered man. That must exist. I think I'll have to go over to Paris. There was Paris written in that little gold box, and the late Lord Edgware ran over to Paris several times last Autumn, so Miss Carroll tells me, attending sales and buying curios. Yes, I think I must go over to Paris. Inquest's to-morrow. It'll be adjourned, of course. After that I'll take the afternoon boat."

" You have a furious energy, Japp. It amazes me."

" Yes, you're getting lazy. You just sit here and *think!* What you call employing the little grey cells. No good, you've got to go out to things. They won't come to you."

The little maidservant opened the door.

" Mr. Bryan Martin, sir. Are you busy or will you see him?"

" I'm off, M. Poirot." Japp hoisted himself up. " All the stars of the theatrical world seem to consult you."

Poirot shrugged a modest shoulder, and Japp laughed.

" You must be a millionaire by now, M. Poirot. What do you do with the money? Save it?"

" Assuredly I practise the thrift. And talking of the disposal of money, how did Lord Edgware dispose of his?"

" Such property as wasn't entailed he left to his daughter.

Five hundred to Miss Carroll. No other bequests. Very simple will."

"And it was made—when?"

"After his wife left him—just over two years ago. He expressly excludes her from participation, by the way."

"A vindictive man," murmured Poirot to himself.

With a cheerful "So long," Japp departed.

Bryan Martin entered. He was faultlessly attired and looked extremely handsome. Yet I thought that he looked haggard and not too happy.

"I am afraid I have been a long time coming, M. Poirot," he said apologetically. "And, after all, I have been guilty of taking up your time for nothing."

"*En verité?*"

"Yes. I have seen the lady in question. I've argued with her, pleaded with her, but all to no purpose. She won't hear of my interesting you in the matter. So I'm afraid we'll have to let the thing drop. I'm very sorry—very sorry to have bothered you——"

"*Du tout—du tout,*" said Poirot genially. "I expected this."

"Eh?" The young man seemed taken aback.

"You expected this?" he asked in a puzzled way.

"*Mais oui.* When you spoke of consulting your friend—I could have predicted that all would have arrived as it has done."

"You have a theory, then?"

"A detective, M. Martin, always has a theory. It is expected of him. I do not call it a theory myself. I say that I have a little idea. That is the first stage."

"And the second stage?"

"If the little idea turns out to be right—then I *know!* It is quite simple, you see."

"I wish you'd tell me what your theory—or your little idea —is?"

Poirot shook his head gently.

"That is another rule. The detective never tells."

"Can't you suggest it even?"

"No. I will only say that I formed my theory as soon as you mentioned a gold tooth."

Bryan Martin stared at him.

"I'm absolutely bewildered," he declared: "I can't make

out what you are driving at. If you'd just give me a hint."

Poirot smiled and shook his head.

" Let us change the subject."

" Yes, but first—your fee—you must let me."

Poirot waved an imperious hand.

" *Pas un sou!* I have done nothing to aid you."

" I took up your time——"

" When a case interests me, I do not touch money. Your case interested me very much."

" I'm glad," said the actor uneasily.

He looked supremely unhappy.

" Come," said Poirot kindly. " Let us talk of something else."

" Wasn't that the Scotland Yard man whom I met on the stairs?"

" Yes, Inspector Japp."

" The light was so dim, I wasn't sure. By the way, he came round and asked me some questions about that poor girl, Carlotta Adams, who died of an overdose of veronal."

" You knew her well—Miss Adams?"

" Not very well. I knew her as a child in America. I came across her here once or twice but I never saw very much of her. I was very sorry to hear of her death."

" You liked her?"

" Yes. She was extraordinarily easy to talk to."

" A personality very sympathetic—yes, I found the same."

" I suppose they think it might be suicide? I knew nothing that could help the inspector. Carlotta was always very reserved about herself."

" I do not think it was suicide," said Poirot.

" Far more likely to be an accident, I agree."

There was a pause.

Then Poirot said with a smile:

" The affair of Lord Edgware's death becomes intriguing, does it not?"

" Absolutely amazing. Do you know—have they any idea —who did it—now that Jane is definitely out of it?"

" *Mais oui*—they have a very strong suspicion."

Bryan Martin looked excited.

" Really? Who?"

" The butler has disappeared. You comprehend—flight is as good as a confession."

" The butler! Really, you surprise me."

" A singularly good-looking man. *Il vous ressemble un peu*," he bowed in a complimentary fashion.

Of course! I realised now why the butler's face had struck me as being faintly familiar when I first saw it.

" You flatter me," said Bryan Martin with a laugh.

" No, no, no. Do not all the young girls, the servant girls, the flappers, the typists, the girls of society, do they not all adore M. Bryan Martin? Is there one who can resist you?"

" A lot, I should think," said Martin. He got up abruptly.

" Well, thank you very much, M. Poirot. Let me apologise again for having troubled you."

He shook hands with us both. Suddenly, I noticed, he looked much older. The haggard look was more apparent.

I was devoured with curiosity, and as soon as the door closed behind him, I burst out with what I wanted to know.

" Poirot, did you really expect him to come back and relinquish all idea of investigating those queer things that happened to him in America?"

" You heard me say so, Hastings."

" But then——" I followed the thing out logically.

" Then you must know who this mysterious girl is that he had to consult?"

He smiled.

" I have a little idea, my friend. As I told you, it started from the mention of the gold tooth, and if my little idea is correct, I know who the girl is, I know why she will not let M. Martin consult me. I know the truth of the whole affair. And so could you know it if you would only use the brains the good God has given you. Sometimes I really am tempted to believe that by inadvertence He passed you by."

CHAPTER XVIII

THE OTHER MAN

I DO NOT propose to describe either the inquest on Lord Edgware or that on Carlotta Adams. In Carlotta's case the verdict was Death by Misadventure. In the case of Lord Edgware the inquest was adjourned, after evidence of identification and the medical evidence had been given. As a result of the analysis of the stomach, the time of death was fixed as having occurred not less than an hour after the completion of dinner, with possible extension to an hour after that. This put it as between ten and eleven o'clock, with the probability in favour of the earlier time.

None of the facts concerning Carlotta's impersonation of Jane Wilkinson were allowed to leak out. A description of the wanted butler was published in the Press, and the general impression seemed to be that the butler was the man wanted. His story of Jane Wilkinson's visit was looked upon as an impudent fabrication. Nothing was said of the secretary's corroborating testimony. There were columns concerning the murder in all the papers, but little real information.

Meanwhile Japp was actively at work, I knew. It vexed me a little that Poirot adopted such an inert attitude. The suspicion that approaching old age had something to do with it flashed across me—not for the first time. He made excuses to me which did not ring very convincingly.

"At my time of life one saves oneself the trouble," he explained.

"But, Poirot, my dear fellow, you mustn't think of yourself as old," I protested.

I felt that he needed bracing. Treatment by suggestion—that, I know, is the modern idea.

"You are as full of vigour as ever you were," I said earnestly. "You're in the prime of life, Poirot. At the height of your powers. You could go out and solve this case magnificently if you only would."

Poirot replied that he preferred to solve it sitting at home.

"But you can't do that, Poirot."

"Not entirely, it is true."

"What I mean is, we are doing nothing! Japp is doing everything."

"Which suits me admirably."

"It doesn't suit me at all. I want you to be doing things."

"So I am."

"What are you doing?"

"Waiting."

"Waiting for what?"

"*Pour que mon chien de chasse me rapporte le gibier,*" replied Poirot with a twinkle.

"What *do* you mean?"

"I mean the good Japp. Why keep a dog and bark yourself? Japp brings us here the result of the physical energy you admire so much. He has various means at his disposal which I have not. He will have news for us very soon, I do not doubt."

By dint of persistent inquiry, it was true that Japp was slowly getting together material. He had drawn a blank in Paris, but a couple of days later he came in looking pleased with himself.

"It's slow work," he said. "But we're getting somewhere at last."

"I congratulate you, my friend. What has happened?"

"I've discovered that a fair-haired lady deposited an attaché-case in the cloak-room at Euston at nine o'clock that night. They've been shown Miss Adams' case and identify it positively. It's of American make and so just a little different."

"Ah! Euston. Yes, the nearest of the big stations to Regent Gate. She went there doubtless, made herself up in the lavatory, and then left the case. When was it taken out again?"

"At half-past ten. The clerk says by the same lady."

Poirot nodded.

"And I've come on something else too. I've reason to believe that Carlotta Adams was in Lyons Corner House in the Strand at eleven o'clock."

"Ah! c'est très bien ça! How did you come across that?"

"Well, really more or less by chance. You see, there's been a mention in the papers of the little gold box with the ruby initials. Some reporter wrote it up—he was doing an article on the prevalence of dope-taking among young actresses. Sunday paper romantic stuff. The fatal little gold box with its deadly contents—pathetic figure of a young girl with all the world before her! And just a wonder expressed as to where she passed her last evening and how she felt and so on and so on.

"Well, it seems a waitress at the Corner House read this and she remembered that a lady she had served that evening had had such a box in her hand. She remembered the C.A. on it. And she got excited and began talking to all her friends —perhaps a paper would give her something?

"A young newspaper man soon got on to it and there's going to be a good sobstuff article in to-night's *Evening Shriek*.

The last hours of the talented actress. Waiting—for the man who never came—and a good bit about the waitress's sympathetic intuition that something was not well with her sister woman. You know the kind of bilge, M. Poirot?"

"And how has it come to your ears so quickly?"

"Oh! well, we're on very good terms with the *Evening Shriek*. It got passed on to me while their particular bright young man tried to get some news out of me about something else. So I rushed along to the Corner House straight away—"

Yes, that was the way things ought to be done. I felt a pang of pity for Poirot. Here was Japp getting all this news at first hand—quite possibly missing valuable details, and here was Poirot placidly content with stale news.

"I saw the girl—and I don't think there's much doubt about it. She couldn't pick out Carlotta Adams' photograph, but then she said she didn't notice the lady's face particularly. She was young and dark and slim, and very well dressed, the girl said. Had got on one of the new hats. I wish women looked at faces a bit more and hats a bit less."

"The face of Miss Adams is not an easy one to observe," said Poirot. "It had the mobility, the sensitiveness—the fluid quality."

"I daresay you're right. I don't go in for analysing these things. Dressed in black the lady was, so the girl said, and she had an attaché-case with her. The girl noticed that particularly, because it struck her as odd that a lady so well dressed should be carrying a case about. She ordered some scrambled eggs and some coffee, but the girl thinks she was putting in time and waiting for someone. She'd got a wrist-watch on and she kept looking at it. It was when the girl came to give her the bill that she noticed the box. The lady took it out of her handbag and had it on the table looking at it. She opened the lid and shut it down again. She was smiling in a pleased dreamy sort of way. The girl noticed the box particular because it was such a lovely thing. 'I'd like to have a gold box with my initials in rubies on it!' she said.

"Apparently Miss Adams sat there some time after paying her bill. Then, finally, she looked at her watch once more, seemed to give it up and went out."

Poirot was frowning.

"It was a *rendez-vous*," he murmured. "A *rendez-vous*

with someone who did not turn up. Did Carlotta Adams meet that person afterwards? Or did she fail to meet him and go home and try to ring him up? I wish I knew—oh! how I wish I knew."

"That's *your* theory, M. Poirot. Mysterious Man-in-the-Background. That Man-in-the-Background's a myth. I don't say she mayn't have been waiting for someone—that's possible. She may have made an appointment to meet some-one there after her business with his lordship was settled satis-factorily. Well, we know what happened. She lost her head and stabbed him. But she's not one to lose her head for long. She changes her appearance at the station, gets out her case, goes to the rendezvous, and then what they call the ' reaction ' gets her. Horror of what she's done. And when her friend doesn't turn up, that finishes her. He may be someone who knew she was going to Regent Gate that evening. She feels the game's up. So she takes out her little box of dope. An overdose of that and it'll be all over. At anyrate she won't be hanged. Why, it's as plain as the nose on your face."

Poirot's hand strayed doubtfully to his nose, then his fingers dropped to his moustaches. He caressed them tenderly with a proud expression.

"There was no evidence at all of a mysterious Man-in-the-Background," said Japp, pursuing his advantage doggedly. "I haven't got evidence yet of a connection between her and his lordship, but I shall do—it's only a question of time. I must say I'm disappointed about Paris, but nine months ago is a long time. I've still got someone making inquiries over there. Something may come to light yet. I know you don't think so. You're a pig-headed old boy, you know."

"You insult first my nose and then my head!"

"Figure of speech, that's all," said Japp soothingly. " No offence meant."

"The answer to that," I said, " is ' nor taken.' "

Poirot looked from one to the other of us completely puzzled.

"Any orders?" inquired Japp facetiously from the door₂

Poirot smiled forgivingly at him.

"An order, no. A suggestion—yes."

"Well, what is it? Out with it."

"A suggestion that you circularise the taxi-cabs. Find one that took a fare—or more probably two fares—yes, two fares —from the neighbourhood of Covent Garden to Regent Gate on the night of the murder. As to time it would probably be about twenty minutes to eleven."

Japp cocked an eye alertly. He had the look of a smart terrier dog.

"So, that's the idea, is it?" he said. "Well, I'll do it. Can't do any harm—and you sometimes know what you're talking about."

No sooner had he left than Poirot arose and with great energy began to brush his hat.

"Ask me no questions, my friend. Instead bring me the benzine. A morsel of omelette this morning descended on my waistcoat."

I brought it to him.

"For once," I said. "I do not think I need to ask questions. It seems fairly obvious. But do you think it really is so?"

"*Mon ami*, at the moment I concern myself solely with the toilet. If you will pardon me saying so, your tie does not please me."

"It's a jolly good tie," I said.

"Possibly—once. It feels the old age as you have been kind enough to say I do. Change it, I beseech you, and also brush the right sleeve."

"Are we proposing to call on King George?" I inquired sarcastically.

"No. But I saw in the newspaper this morning that the Duke of Merton had returned to Merton House. I understand he is a premier member of the English aristocracy. I wish to do him all honour."

There is nothing of the Socialist about Poirot.

"Why are we going to call on the Duke of Merton?"

"I wish to see him."

That was all I could get out of him. When my attire was at last handsome enough to please Poirot's critical eye, we started out.

At Merton House, Poirot was asked by a footman if he had an appointment. Poirot replied in the negative. The footman bore away the card and returned shortly to say that His Grace was very sorry but he was extremely busy this morning. Poirot immediately sat down in a chair.

"*Très bien*," he said. "I wait. I will wait several hours if need be."

This, however, was not necessary. Probably as the shortest way of getting rid of the importunate caller, Poirot was bidden to the presence of the gentleman he desired to see.

The Duke was about twenty-seven years of age. He was hardly prepossessing in appearance, being thin and weakly. He had nondescript thin hair going bald at the temples, a small bitter mouth and vague dreamy eyes. There were several crucifixes in the room and various religious works of art. A wide shelf of books seemed to contain nothing but theological works. He looked far more like a weedy young haberdasher than like a duke. He had, I knew, been educated at home, having been a terribly delicate child. This was the man who had fallen an immediate prey to Jane Wilkinson! It was really ludicrous in the extreme. His manner was priggish and his reception of us just short of courteous.

"You may, perhaps, know my name," began Poirot.

"I have no acquaintance with it."

"I study the psychology of crime."

The Duke was silent. He was sitting at a writing-table, an unfinished letter before him. He tapped impatiently on the desk with his pen.

"For what reason do you wish to see me?" he inquired coldly.

Poirot was sitting opposite him. His back was to the window. The Duke was facing it.

"I am at present engaged on investigating the circumstances connected with Lord Edgware's death."

Not a muscle of the weak but obstinate face moved.

"Indeed? I was not acquainted with him."

"But you are, I think, acquainted with his wife—with Miss Jane Wilkinson?"

"That is so."

"You are aware that she is supposed to have had a strong motive for desiring the death of her husband?"

"I am really not aware of anything of the kind."

"I should like to ask you outright, your Grace. Are you shortly going to marry Miss Jane Wilkinson?"

"When I am engaged to marry anyone the fact will be announced in the newspapers. I consider your question an impertinence." He stood up. "Good-morning."

Poirot stood up also. He looked awkward. He hung his head. He stammered.

" I did not mean . . . I . . . *Je vous demande pardone* . . ."

" Good-morning," repeated the Duke, a little louder.

This time Poirot gave it up. He made a characteristic gesture of hopelessness, and we left. It was an ignominious dismissal.

I felt rather sorry for Poirot. His usual bombast had not gone well. To the Duke of Merton a great detective was evidently lower than a blackbeetle.

" That didn't go too well," I said sympathetically. " What a stiff-necked tartar the man is. What did you really want to see him for?"

" I wanted to know whether he and Jane Wilkinson are really going to marry."

" She said so."

" Ah! she said so. But, you realise, she is one of those who say anything that suits their purpose. She might have decided to marry him and he—poor man—might not yet be aware of the fact."

" Well, he certainly sent you away with a flea in the ear."

" He gave me the reply he would give to a reporter—yes." Poirot chuckled. " But I know! I know exactly how the case stands."

" How do you know? By his manner?"

" Not at all. You saw he was writing a letter?"

" Yes."

" *Eh bien*, in my early days in the police force in Belgium I learned that it was very useful to read handwriting upside down. Shall I tell you what he was saying in that letter? ' *My dearest, I can hardly bear to wait through the long months. Jane, my adored, my beautiful angel, how can I tell you what you are to me? You who have suffered so much! Your beautiful nature——*' "

" Poirot! " I cried, scandalised, stopping him.

" That was as far as he had got. '*Your beautiful nature—only I know it.*' "

I felt very upset. He was so naïvely pleased with his performance.

" Poirot," I cried. " You can't do a thing like that. Overlook a private letter."

" You say the imbecilities, Hastings. Absurd to say I ' cannot do ' a thing which I have just done! "

" It's not—not playing the game."

"I do not play games. You know that. Murder is not a game. It is serious. And anyway, Hastings, you should not use that phrase—playing the game. It is not said any more. I have discovered that. It is dead. Young people laugh when they hear it. *Mais oui*, young beautiful girls will laugh at you if you say ' playing the game ' and ' not cricket.' "

I was silent. I could not bear this thing that Poirot had done so light-heartedly.

"It was so unnecessary," I said. "If you had only told him that you had gone to Lord Edgware at Jane Wilkinson's request, then he would have treated you very differently."

"Ah! but I could not do that. Jane Wilkinson was my client. I cannot speak of my client's affairs to another. I undertake a mission in confidence. To speak of it would not be honourable."

"Honourable!"

"Precisely."

"But she's going to marry him?"

"That does not mean that she has no secrets from him. Your ideas about marriage are very old-fashioned. No, what you suggest, I couldn't possibly have done. I have my honour as a detective to think of. The honour, it is a very serious thing."

"Well, I suppose it takes all kinds of honour to make a world."

CHAPTER XIX

A GREAT LADY

THE VISIT that we received on the following morning was to my mind one of the most surprising things about the whole affair.

I was in my room when Poirot slipped in with his eyes shining.

"*Mon ami*, we have a visitor."

"Who is it?"

"The Dowager Duchess of Merton."

"How extraordinary! What does she want?"

"If you accompany me downstairs, *mon ami*, you will know."

I hastened to comply. We entered the room together.

The Duchess was a small woman with a high-bridged nose and autocratic eyes. Although she was short one would not have dared to call her dumpy. Dressed though she was in unfashionable black, she was yet every inch a *grande dame*. She also impressed me as having an almost ruthless personality. Where her son was negative, she was positive. Her will-power was terrific. I could almost feel waves of force emanating from her. No wonder this woman had always dominated all those with whom she came in contact!

She put up a lorgnette and studied first me and then my companion. Then she spoke to him. Her voice was clear and compelling, a voice accustomed to command and to be obeyed.

" You are M. Hercule Poirot?"

My friend bowed.

" At your service, Madame la Duchesse."

She looked at me.

" This is my friend, Captain Hastings. He assists me in my cases."

Her eyes looked momentarily doubtful. Then she bent her head in acquiescence.

She took the chair that Poirot offered.

" I have come to consult you on a very delicate matter, M. Poirot, and I must ask that what I tell you shall be understood to be entirely confidential."

" That without saying, Madame."

" It was Lady Yardly who told me about you. From the way in which she spoke of you and the gratitude she expressed, I felt that you were the only person likely to help me."

" Rest assured, I will do my best, Madame."

Still she hesitated. Then, at last, with an effort, she came to the point, came to it with a simplicity that reminded me in an odd way of Jane Wilkinson on that memorable night at the Savoy.

" M. Poirot, I want to ensure that my son does not marry the actress, Jane Wilkinson."

If Poirot felt astonishment, he refrained from showing it. He regarded her thoughtfully and took his time about replying.

" Can you be a little more definite, Madame, as to what you want me to do?"

" That is not easy. I feel that such a marriage would be a great disaster. It would ruin my son's life."

"Do you think so, Madame?"

"I am sure of it. My son has very high ideals. He knows really very little of the world. He has never cared for the young girls of his own class. They have struck him as empty-headed and frivolous. But as regards this woman—well, she is very beautiful, I admit that. And she has the power of enslaving men. She has bewitched my son. I have hoped that the infatuation would run its course. Mercifully she was not free. But now that her husband is dead——"

She broke off.

"They intend to be married in a few months' time. The whole happiness of my son's life is at stake." She spoke more peremptorily. "It must be stopped, M. Poirot."

Poirot shrugged his shoulders.

"I do not say that you are not right, Madame. I agree that the marriage is not a suitable one. But what can one do?"

"It is for you to do something."

Poirot slowly shook his head.

"Yes, yes, you must help me."

"I doubt if anything would avail, Madame. Your son, I should say, would refuse to listen to anything against the lady! And also, I do not think there is very much against her to say! I doubt if there are any discreditable incidents to be raked up in her past. She has been—shall we say—careful?"

"I know," said the Duchess grimly.

"Ah! So you have already made the inquiries in that direction."

She flushed a little under his keen glance.

"There is nothing I would not do, M. Poirot, to save my son from this marriage." She reiterated that word emphatically. "*Nothing!*"

She paused, then went on:

"Money is nothing in this matter. Name any fee you like. But the marriage must be stopped. You are the man to do it."

Poirot slowly shook his head.

"It is not a question of money. I can do nothing—for a reason which I will explain to you presently. But also, I may say, I do not see there is anything to be done. I cannot give you help, Madame la Duchesse. Will you think me impertinent if I give you advice?"

"What advice?"

"*Do not antagonise your son!* He is of an age to choose for himself. Because his choice is not your choice, do not assume that you must be right. If it is a misfortune—then accept misfortune. Be at hand to aid him when he needs aid. But do not turn him against you."

"You hardly understand."

She rose to her feet. Her lips were trembling.

"But yes, Madame la Duchesse, I understand very well. I comprehend the mother's heart. No one comprehends it better than I, Hercule Poirot. And I say to you with authority —be patient. Be patient and calm, and disguise your feelings. There is yet a chance that the matter may break itself. Opposition will merely increase your son's obstinacy."

"Good-bye, M. Poirot," she said coldly. "I am disappointed."

"I regret infinitely, Madame, that I cannot be of service to you. I am in a difficult position. Lady Edgware, you see, has already done me the honour to consult me herself."

"Oh! I see." Her voice cut like a knife. "You are in the opposite camp. That explains, no doubt, why Lady Edgware has not yet been arrested for her husband's murder."

"*Comment*, Madame la Duchesse?"

"I think you heard what I said. Why is she not arrested? She was there that evening. She was seen to enter the house— to enter his study. No one else went near him and he was found dead? And yet she is not arrested! Our police force must be corrupt through and through."

With shaking hands she arranged the scarf round her neck, then with the slightest of bows, she swept out of the room.

"Whew!" I said. "What a tartar! I admire her, though, don't you?"

"Because she wishes to arrange the universe to her manner of thinking?"

"Well, she's only got her son's welfare at heart."

Poirot nodded his head.

"That is true enough, and yet, Hastings, will it really be such a bad thing for M. le Duc to marry Jane Wilkinson?"

"Why, you don't think she is really in love with him?"

"Probably not. Almost certainly not. But she is very much in love with his position. She will play her part carefully. She is an extremely beautiful woman and very ambitious. It is not such a catastrophe. The Duke might very easily have married a young girl of his own class who would have accepted him from the same reasons—but no one would have made the song and the dance about that."

"That is quite true, but——"

"And suppose he marries a girl who loves him passionately, is there such a great advantage in that? Often I have observed that it is a great misfortune for a man to have a wife who loves him. She creates the scenes of jealousy, she makes him look ridiculous, she insists on having all his time and attention. Ah! *non*, it is not the bed of roses."

"Poirot," I said. "You're an incurable old cynic."

"*Mais non, mais non*, I only make the reflections. See you, really, I am on the side of the good mamma."

I could not refrain from laughing at hearing the haughty Duchess described in this way.

Poirot remained quite serious.

"You should not laugh. It is of great importance—all this. I must reflect. I must reflect a great deal."

"I don't see what you can do in the matter," I said.

Poirot paid no attention.

"You observed, Hastings, how well-informed the Duchess was? And how vindictive. She knew all the evidence there was against Jane Wilkinson."

"The case for the prosecution, but not the case for the defence," I said, smiling.

"How did she come to know of it?"

"Jane told the Duke. The Duke told her," I suggested.

"Yes, that is possible. Yet I have——"

The telephone rang sharply. I answered it.

My part consisted of saying Yes at varying intervals. Finally I put down the receiver and turned excitedly to Poirot.

"That was Japp. Firstly, you're 'the goods' as usual. Secondly, he's had a cable from America. Thirdly, he's got the taxi-driver. Fourthly, would you like to come round and hear what the taxi-driver says. Fifthly you're 'the goods' again, and all along he's been convinced that you'd hit the nail on the head when you suggested that there was some man behind all this! I omitted to tell him that we'd just had a visitor here who says the police force is corrupt."

"So Japp is convinced at last," murmured Poirot. "Curious that the Man-in-the-Background theory should be proved just at the moment when I was inclining to another possible theory."

"What theory?"

"The theory that the motive for the murder might have nothing to do with Lord Edgware himself. Imagine someone who hated Jane Wilkinson, hated her so much that they would have even had her hanged for murder. *C'est une idée, ça!*"

He sighed—then rousing himself:

"Come, Hastings, let us hear what Japp has to say."

CHAPTER XX

THE TAXI-DRIVER

WE FOUND Japp interrogating an old man with a ragged moustache and spectacles. He had a hoarse self-pitying voice.

"Ah! there you are," said Japp. "Well, things are all plain sailing, I think. This man—his name's Jobson—picked up two people in Long Acre on the night of June 29th."

"That's right," assented Jobson hoarsely. "Lovely night it were. Moon and all. The young lady and gentleman were by the tube station and hailed me."

"They were in evening dress?"

"Yes, gent in white waistcoat and the young lady all in white with birds embroidered on it. Come out of the Royal Opera, I guess."

"What time was this?"

"Some time afore eleven."

"Well, what next?"

"Told me to go to Regent Gate—they'd tell me which house when they got there. And told me to be quick, too. People always says that. As though you wanted to loiter. Sooner you get there and get another fare the better for you. They never think of that. And, mind you, if there's an accident you'll get the blame for dangerous driving!"

"Cut it out," said Japp impatiently. "There wasn't an accident this time, was there?"

"N-no," agreed the man as though unwilling to abandon his claim to such an occurrence. "No, as a matter of fact, there weren't. Well, I got to Regent Gate—not above seven minutes it didn't take me, and there the gentleman rapped on the glass, and I stopped. About at number 8 that were. Well, the gentleman and lady got out. The gentleman stopped where he was and told me to do the same. The lady crossed the road, and began walking back along the houses the other side. The gentleman stayed by the cab—standing on the sidewalk with his back to me, looking after her. Had his hands in his pockets. It was about five minutes when I heard him say something—kind of exclamation under his breath and then off he goes too. I looks after him because I wasn't going to be bilked. It'd been done afore to me, so I kept my eye on him. He went up the steps of one of the houses on the other side and went in."

" Did he push the door open?"

" No, he had a latchkey."

" What number was the house?"

" It would be 17 or 19, I fancy. Well, it seemed odd to me my being told to stay where I was. So I kept watching. About five minutes later him and the young lady came out together. They got back into the cab and told me to drive back to Covent Garden Opera House. They stopped me just before I got there and paid me. Paid me handsome, I will say. Though I expect I've got into trouble over it—seems there's nothing but trouble."

" You're all right," said Japp. " Just run your eye over these, will you, and tell me if the young lady is among them."

There were half a dozen photographs all fairly alike as to type. I looked with some interest over his shoulder.

" That were her," said Jobson. He pointed a decisive finger at one of Geraldine Marsh in evening dress.

" Sure?"

" Quite sure. Pale she was and dark."

" Now the man."

Another sheaf of photographs was handed to him.

He looked at them attentively and then shook his head.

" Well, I couldn't say—not for sure. Either of these two might be him."

The photographs included one of Ronald Marsh, but Jobson had not selected it. Instead he indicated two other men not unlike Marsh in type.

Jobson then departed and Japp flung the photographs on the table.

" Good enough. Wish I could have got a clearer identification of his lordship. Of course it's an old photograph, taken seven or eight years ago. The only one I could get hold of.

Yes, I'd like a clearer identification, although the case is clear enough. Bang go a couple of alibis. Clever of you to think of it, M. Poirot."

Poirot looked modest.

"When I found that she and her cousin were both at the opera it seemed to me possible that they might have been together during one of the intervals. Naturally the parties they were with would assume that they had not left the Opera House. But a half-hour interval gives plenty of time to get to Regent Gate and back. The moment the new Lord Edgware laid such stress upon his alibi, I was sure something was wrong with it."

"You're a nice suspicious sort of fellow, aren't you?" said Japp affectionately. "Well, you're about right. Can't be too suspicious in a world like this. His lordship is our man all right. Look at this."

He produced a paper.

"Cable from New York. They got into touch with Miss Lucie Adams. The letter was in the mail delivered to her this morning. She was not willing to give up the original unless absolutely necessary, but she willingly allowed the officer to take a copy of it and cable it to us. Here it is, and it's as damning as you could hope for."

Poirot took the cable with great interest. I read it over his shoulder.

Following is text letter to Lucie Adams, dated June 29th, 8 Rosedew Mansions, London, S.W.3. Begins, Dearest little Sister, I'm sorry I wrote such a scrappy bit last week but things were rather busy and there was a lot to see to. Well, darling, it's been ever such a success! Notices splendid, box office good, and everybody most kind. I've got some real good friends over here and next year I'm thinking of taking a theatre for two months. The Russian dancer sketch went very well and the American woman in Paris too, but the Scenes at a Foreign Hotel are still the favourites, I think. I'm so excited that I hardly know what I'm writing, and you'll see why in a minute, but first I must tell you what people have said. Mr. Hergsheimer was ever so kind and he's going to ask me to lunch to meet Sir Montagu Corner, who might do great things for me. The other night I met Jane Wilkinson and she was ever so sweet about my show and my take off of her, which brings me round to what I am going to tell you. I don't really like her very much because I've been hearing a lot about her lately from someone I know and she's behaved cruelly, I think, and in a very underhand way—but I won't go into that now. You know that she really is Lady Edgware? I've heard a lot about him too lately, and he's no beauty, I can tell you. He treated his nephew, the Captain Marsh I have mentioned to you, in the most shameful way—literally turned him out of the house and discontinued his allowance. He told me all about it and I felt awfully sorry for him. He enjoyed my show very much, he said ' I believe it would take in Lord Edgware himself. Look here, will you take something on for a bet?' I laughed and said ' How much?' Lucie darling, the answer fairly took my breath away. Ten thousand dollars. Ten thousand dollars, think of it—just to help someone win a silly bet. ' Why,' I said, ' I'd play a joke on the King in Buckingham Palace and risk lèse majesté for that.' Well, then, we laid our heads together and got down to details.

" I'll tell you all about it next week—whether I'm spotted or not. But anyway, Lucie darling, whether I succeed or fail, I'm to have the ten thousand dollars. Oh! Lucie, little sister, what that's going to mean to us. No time for more—just going off to do my 'hoax.' Lots and lots and lots of love, little sister mine.

" *Yours,*

" *Carlotta."*

Poirot laid down the letter. It had touched him, I could see. Japp, however, reacted in quite a different way.

" We've got him," said Japp exultantly.

" Yes," said Poirot.

His voice sounded strangely flat.

Japp looked at him curiously.

" What is it, M. Poirot?"

" Nothing," said Poirot. " It is not, somehow, just as I thought. That is all."

He looked acutely unhappy.

" But still it must be so," he said as though to himself. " Yes, it must be so."

" Of course it is so. Why, you've said so all along!"

" No, no. You misunderstand me."

" Didn't you say there was someone back of all this who got the girl into doing it innocently?"

" Yes, yes."

" Well, what more do you want?"

Poirot sighed and said nothing.

" You are an odd sort of cove. Nothing ever satisfies you. I say, it was a piece of luck the girl wrote this letter."

Poirot agreed with more vigour than he had yet shown.

" *Mais oui*, that is what the murderer did not expect. When Miss Adams accepted that ten thousand dollars she signed her death warrant. The murderer thought he had taken all precautions—and yet in sheer innocence she outwitted him. The dead speak. Yes, sometimes the dead speak."

" I never thought she'd done it off her own bat," said Japp unblushingly.

" No, no," said Poirot absently.

" Well, I must get on with things."

" You are going to arrest Captain Marsh—Lord Edgware, I mean?"

" Why not? The case against him seems proved up to the hilt."

" True."

" You seem very despondent about it, M. Poirot. The truth is, you like things to be difficult. Here's your own theory proved and even that does not satisfy you. Can you see any flaw in the evidence we've got?"

Poirot shook his head.

" Whether Miss Marsh was accessory or not, I don't know," said Japp. " Seems as though she must have known about it, going there with him from the opera. If she wasn't, why did he take her? Well, we'll hear what they've both got to say."

" May I be present?"

Poirot spoke almost humbly.

" Certainly you can. I owe the idea to you!"

He picked up the telegram on the table.

I drew Poirot aside.

" What is the matter, Poirot?"

" I am very unhappy, Hastings. This seems the plain sailing and the above board. But *there is something wrong*. Somewhere or other, Hastings, there is a fact that escapes us. It all fits together, it is as I imagined it, and yet, my friend, there is something wrong."

He looked at me piteously.
I was at a loss what to say,

CHAPTER XXI

RONALD'S STORY

I FOUND it hard to understand Poirot's attitude. Surely this was what he had predicted all along?

All the way to Regent Gate, he sat perplexed and frowning, paying no attention to Japp's self-congratulations.

He came out of his reverie at last with a sigh.

" At all events," he murmured. " We can see what he has to say."

" Next to nothing if he's wise," said Japp. " There's any amount of men that have hanged themselves by being too eager to make a statement. Well, no one can say as we don't warn them! It's all fair and above board. And the more guilty they are, the more anxious they are to pipe up and tell you the lies they've thought out to meet the case. They don't know that you should always submit your lies to a solicitor first."

He sighed and said:

" Solicitors and coroners are the worst enemies of the police. Again and again I've had a perfectly clear case messed up by the Coroner fooling about and letting the guilty party get away with it. Lawyers you can't object to so much, I suppose. They're paid for their artfulness and twisting things this way and that."

On arrival at Regent Gate we found that our quarry was at home. The family were still at the luncheon table. Japp proffered a request to speak to Lord Edgware privately. We were shown into the library.

In a minute or two the young man came to us. There was an easy smile on his face which changed a little as he cast a quick glance over us. His lips tightened.

" Hello, Inspector," he said. " What's all this about?"

Japp said his little piece in the classic fashion.

" So that's it, is it?" said Ronald.

He drew a chair towards him and sat down. He pulled out a cigarette case.

" I think, Inspector, I'd like to make a statement."

" That's as you please, my lord."

" Meaning that it's damned foolish on my part. All the same, I think I will. 'Having no reason to fear the truth,' as the heroes in books always say."

Japp said nothing. His face remained expressionless.

" There's a nice handy table and chair," went on the young man. " Your minion can sit down and take it all down in shorthand."

I don't think that Japp was used to having his arrangements made for him so thoughtfully. Lord Edgware's suggestion was adopted.

" To begin with," said the young man. " Having some grains of intelligence, I strongly suspect that my beautiful alibi has bust. Gone up in smoke. Exit the useful Dortheimers. Taxi-driver, I suppose?"

" We know all about your movements on that night," said Japp woodenly.

" I have the greatest admiration for Scotland Yard. All the same, you know, if I had really been planning a deed of violence I shouldn't have hired a taxi and driven straight to the place and kept the fellow waiting. Have you thought of that? Ah! I see M. Poirot has."

" It had occurred to me, yes," said Poirot.

" Such is not the manner of premeditated crime," said Ronald. " Put on a red moustache and horn-rimmed glasses and drive to the next street and pay the man off. Take the tube—well—well, I won't go into it all. My Counsel, at a fee of several thousand guineas, will do it better than I can. Of course, I see the answer. Crime was a sudden impulse. There was I, waiting in the cab, etc., etc. It occurs to me, ' Now, my boy, up and doing.'

" Well, I'm going to tell you the truth. I was in a hole for money. That's been pretty clear, I think. It was rather a desperate business. I had to get it by the next day or drop out of things. I tried my uncle. He'd no love for me, but I thought he might care for the honour of his name. Middle-aged men sometimes do. My uncle proved to be lamentably modern in his cynical indifference.

" Well—it looked like just having to grin and bear it. I was going to try and have a shot at borrowing from Dortheimer, but I knew there wasn't a hope. And marry his daughter I couldn't. She's much too sensible a girl to take me, anyway. Then, by chance, I met my cousin at the opera. I don't often come across her, but she was always a decent kid when I lived in the house. I found myself telling her all about it. She'd heard something from her father anyway. Then she showed her mettle. She suggested I should take her pearls. They'd belonged to her mother."

He paused. There was something like real emotion, I think, in his voice. Or else he suggested it better than I could have believed possible.

"Well—I accepted the blessed child's offer. I could raise the money I wanted on them, and I swore I'd turn to and redeem them even if it meant working to manage it. But the pearls were at home in Regent Gate. We decided that the best thing to do would be to go and fetch them at once. We jumped in a taxi and off we went.

"We made the fellow stop on the opposite side of the street in case anyone should hear the taxi draw up at the door. Geraldine got out and went across the road. She had her latchkey with her. She would go in quietly, get the pearls and bring them out to me. She didn't expect to meet anyone except, possibly, a servant. Miss Carroll, my uncle's secretary, usually went to bed at half-past nine. He, himself, would probably be in the library.

"So off Dina went. I stood on the pavement smoking a cigarette. Every now and then I looked over towards the house to see if she was coming. And now I come to the part of the story that you may believe or not as you like. A man passed me on the sidewalk. I turned to look after him. To my surprise he went up the steps and let himself in to No. 17. At least I thought it was No. 17, but, of course, I was some distance away. That surprised me very much for two reasons. One was that the man had let himself in with a key, and the second was that I thought I recognised in him a certain well-known actor.

"I was so surprised that I determined to look into matters. I happened to have my own key of No. 17 in my pocket. I'd lost it or thought I'd lost it three years ago, had come across it unexpectedly a day or two ago and had been meaning to give it back to my uncle this morning. However, in the heat of our discussion, it had slipped my memory. I had transferred it with the other contents of my pockets when I changed.

" Telling the taxi man to wait. I strode hurriedly along the pavement, crossed the road, went up the steps of No. 17, and opened the door with my key. The hall was empty. There was no sign of any visitor having just entered. I stood for a minute looking about me. Then I went towards the library door. Perhaps the man was in with my uncle. If so, I should hear the murmur of voices. I stood outside the library door, but I heard nothing.

" I suddenly felt I had made the most abject fool of myself. Of course the man must have gone into some other house—the house beyond, probably. Regent Gate is rather dimly lighted at night. I felt an absolute idiot. What on earth had possessed me to follow the fellow, I could not think. It had landed me here, and a pretty fool I should look if my uncle were to come suddenly out of the library and find me. I should get Geraldine into trouble and altogether the fat would be in the fire. All because something in the man's manner had made me imagine that he was doing something that he didn't want known. Luckily no one had caught me. I must get out of it as soon as I could.

" I tiptoed back towards the front door and at the same moment Geraldine came down the stairs with the pearls in her hand.

" She was very startled at seeing me, of course. I got her out of the house, and then explained."

He paused.

" We hurried back to the opera. Got there just as the curtain was going up. No one suspected that we'd left it. It was a hot night and several people went outside to get a breath of air."

He paused.

" I know what you'll say: Why didn't I tell you this right away? And now I put it to you: Would you, with a motive for murder sticking out a yard, admit light-heartedly that you'd actually been at the place the murder was committed on the night in question?

" Frankly, I funked it! Even if we were believed, it was going to be a lot of worry for me and for Geraldine. We'd nothing to do with the murder, we'd seen nothing, we'd heard nothing. Obviously, I thought, Aunt Jane had done it. Well, why bring myself in? I told you about the quarrel and my lack of money because I knew you'd ferret it out, and if I'd tried to conceal all that you'd be much more suspicious and you'd probably examine that alibi much more closely. As it was, I thought that if I bucked enough about it it would almost hypnotise you into thinking it all right. The Dortheimers were, I know, honestly convinced that I'd been at Covent Garden all the time. That I spent one interval with my cousin wouldn't strike them as suspicious. And she could always say she'd been with me there and that we hadn't left the place."

"Miss Marsh agreed to this—concealment?"

"Yes. Soon as I got the news, I got on to her and cautioned her for her life not to say anything about her excursion here last night. She'd been with me and I'd been with her during the last interval at Covent Garden. We'd walked in the street a little, that was all. She understood and she quite agreed."

He paused.

"I know it looks bad—coming out with this afterwards. But the story's true enough. I can give you the name and address of the man who let me have the cash on Geraldine's pearls this morning. And if you ask her, she'll confirm every word I've told you."

He sat back in his chair and looked at Japp.

Japp continued to look expressionless.

"You say you thought Jane Wilkinson had committed the murder, Lord Edgware?" he said.

"Well, wouldn't you have thought so? After the butler's story?"

"What about your wager with Miss Adams?"

"Wager with Miss Adams? With Carlotta Adams, do you mean? What has she got to do with it?"

"Do you deny that you offered her the sum of ten thousand dollars to impersonate Miss Jane Wilkinson at the house that night?"

Ronald stared.

"Offered her ten thousand dollars? Nonsense. Someone's been pulling your leg. I haven't got ten thousand dollars to offer. You've got hold of a mare's nest. Does *she* say so? Oh! dash it all—I forgot, she's dead, isn't she?"

"Yes," said Poirot quietly. "She is dead."

Ronald turned his eyes from one to the other of us. He had been debonair before. Now his face had whitened. His eyes looked frightened.

"I don't understand all this," he said. "It's true what I told you. I suppose you don't believe me—any of you."

And then, to my amazement, Poirot stepped forward.

"Yes," he said. "I believe you."

CHAPTER XXII

STRANGE BEHAVIOUR OF HERCULE POIROT

WE WERE in our rooms.

"What on earth——" I began.

Poirot stopped me with a gesture more extravagant than any gesture I had ever seen him make. Both arms whirled in the air.

"I implore of you, Hastings! Not now. Not now."

And upon that he seized his hat, clapped it on his head as though he had never heard of order and method, and rushed headlong from the room. He had not returned when, about an hour later, Japp appeared.

"Little man gone out?" he inquired.

I nodded.

Japp sank into a seat. He dabbed his forehead with a hand-kerchief. The day was warm.

"What the devil took him?" he inquired. "I can tell you, Captain Hastings, you could have knocked me down with a feather when he stepped up to the man and said: 'I believe you.' For all the world as though he were acting in a romantic melodrama. It beats me."

It beat me also, and I said so.

"And then he marches out of the house," said Japp. "What did he say about it to you?"

"Nothing," I replied.

"Nothing at all?"

"Absolutely nothing. When I was going to speak to him he waved me aside. I thought it best to leave him alone. When we got back here I started to question him. He waved his arms, seized his hat and rushed out again."

We looked at each other. Japp tapped his forehead significantly.

"Must be," he said.

For once I was disposed to agree. Japp had often suggested before that Poirot was what he called "touched." In those cases he had simply not understood what Poirot was driving at. Here, I was forced to confess, I could not understand Poirot's attitude. If not touched, he was, at anyrate, suspiciously changeable. Here was his own private theory triumphantly confirmed and straight away he went back on it.

It was enough to dismay and distress his warmest supporters. I shook my head in a discouraged fashion.

"He's always been what I call peculiar," said Japp. "Got his own particular angle of looking at things—and a very queer one it is. He's a kind of genius, I admit that. But they always say that geniuses are very near the border line and liable to slip over any minute. He's always been fond of having things difficult. A straightforward case is never good enough for him. No, it's got to be tortuous. He's got away from real life. He plays a game of his own. It's like an old lady playing at patience. If it doesn't come out, she cheats. Well, it's the other way round with him. If it's coming out too easily, he cheats to make it more difficult! That's the way I look at it."

I found it difficult to answer him. I was too perturbed and distressed to be able to think clearly. I, also, found Poirot's behaviour unaccountable. And since I was very attached to my strange little friend, it worried me more than I cared to express.

In the middle of a gloomy silence, Poirot walked into the room.

He was, I was thankful to see, quite calm now.

Very carefully he removed his hat, placed it with his stick on the table, and sat down in his accustomed chair.

"So you are here, my good Japp. I am glad. It was on my mind that I must see you as soon as possible."

Japp looked at him without replying. He saw that this was only the beginning. He waited for Poirot to explain himself.

This my friend did, speaking slowly and carefully.

"*Ecoutez*, Japp. We are wrong. We are all wrong. It is grievous to admit it, but we have made a mistake."

"That's all right," said Japp confidently.

"But it is not all right. It is deplorable. It grieves me to the heart."

"You needn't be grieved about that young man. He richly deserves all he gets."

"It is not he I am grieving about—it is you."

"Me? You needn't worry about me."

"But I do. See you, who was it set you on this course? It was Hercule Poirot. *Mais oui*, I set you on the trail. I direct your attention to Carlotta Adams, I mention to you the matter of the letter to America. Every step of the way it is I who point it!"

"I was bound to get there anyway," said Japp coldly. "You got a bit ahead of me, that's all."

"*Cela ce peut*. But it does not console me. If harm—if loss of prestige comes to you through listening to my little ideas —I shall blame myself bitterly."

Japp merely looked amused. I think he credited Poirot with motives that were none too pure. He fancied that Poirot grudged him the credit resulting from the successful elucidation of the affair.

"That's all right," he said. "I shan't forget to let it be known that I owe something to you over this business."

He winked at me.

"Oh! it is not that at all." Poirot clicked his tongue with impatience. "I want no credit. And what is more, I tell you there will be no credit. It is a fiasco that you prepare for yourself, and I, Hercule Poirot, am the cause."

Suddenly at Poirot's expression of extreme melancholy Japp shouted with laughter. Poirot looked affronted.

"Sorry, M. Poirot." He wiped his eyes. "But you did look for all the world like a dying duck in a thunderstorm. Now look here, let's forget all this. I'm willing to shoulder the credit or the blame of this affair. It will make a big noise— you're right there. Well, I'm going all out to get a conviction. It may be that a clever Counsel will get his lordship off—you never know with a jury. But even so, it won't do me any harm. It will be known that we caught the right man even if we couldn't get a conviction. And if, by any chance, the third housemaid has hysterics and owns up she did it—well, I'll take my medicine and I won't complain you led me up the garden. That's fair enough."

Poirot gazed at him mildly and sadly.

"You have the confidence—always the confidence! You never stop and say to yourself—Can it be so? You never doubt —or wonder. You never think: This is too easy!"

"You bet your life I don't. And that's just where, if you'll excuse me saying so, you go off the rails every time. Why shouldn't a thing be easy? What's the harm in a thing being easy?"

Poirot looked at him, sighed, half threw up his arms, then shook his head.

"*C'est fini!* I will say no more."

"Splendid," said Japp heartily. "Now let's get down to brass tacks. You'd like to hear what I've been doing?"

"Assuredly."

"Well, I saw the Honourable Geraldine, and her story tallied exactly with his lordship's. They may both be in it together, but I think not. It's my opinion he bluffed her—she's three parts sweet on him anyway. Took on terribly when she found he was arrested."

"Did she now? And the secretary—Miss Carroll?"

"Wasn't too surprised, I fancy. However, that's only my idea."

"What about the pearls?" I asked. "Was that part of the story true?"

"Absolutely. He raised the money on them early the following morning. But I don't think that touches the main argument. As I see it, the plan came into his head when he came across his cousin at the opera. It came to him in a flash. He was desperate—here was a way out. I fancy he'd been meditating something of the kind—that's why he had the key with him. I don't believe that story of suddenly coming across it. Well, as he talks to his cousin, he sees that by involving her he gains additional security for himself. He plays on her feelings, hints at the pearls, she plays up, and off they go. As soon as she's in the house he follows her in and goes along to the library. Maybe his lordship had dozed off in his chair. Anyway, in two seconds he's done the trick and he's out again. I don't fancy he meant the girl to catch him in the house. He counted on being found pacing up and down near the taxi. And I don't think the taxi-man was meant to see him go in. The impression was to be that he was walking up and down smoking whilst he waited for the girl. The taxi was facing the opposite direction, remember.

"Of course, the next morning, he has to pledge the pearls. He must still seem to be in need of the money. Then, when he hears of the crime, he frightens the girl into concealing their

visit to the house. They will say that they spent that interval
together at the Opera House."

"Then why did they not do so?" asked Poirot sharply.

Japp shrugged his shoulders.

"Changed his mind. Or judged that she wouldn't be able
to go through with it. She's a nervous type."

"Yes," said Poirot meditatively. "She is a nervous type."

After a minute or two, he said:

"It does not strike you that it would have been easier and
simpler for Captain Marsh to have left the opera during the
interval by himself. To have gone in quietly with his key,
killed his uncle, and returned to the opera—instead of having
a taxi outside and a nervous girl coming down the stairs any
minute who might lose her head and give him away."

Japp grinned.

"That's what you and I would have done. But then we're
a shade brighter than Captain Ronald Marsh."

"I am not so sure. He strikes me as intelligent."

"But not so intelligent as M. Hercule Poirot! Come, now,
I'm sure of that!" Japp laughed.

Poirot looked at him coldly.

"If he isn't guilty why did he persuade the Adams girl to
take on that stunt?" went on Japp. "There can be only one
reason for that stunt—to protect the real criminal."

"There I am of accord with you absolutely."

"Well, I'm glad we agree about something."

"It might be he who actually spoke to Miss Adams," mused
Poirot. "Whilst really—no, that is an imbecility."

Then, looking suddenly at Japp, he rapped out a quick
question.

"What is your theory as to her death?"

Japp cleared his throat.

"I'm inclined to believe—accident. A convenient accident
I admit. I can't see that he could have had anything to do
with it. His alibi is straight enough after the opera. He was
at Sobranis with the Dortheimers till after one o'clock. Long
before that she was in bed and asleep. No, I think that was
an instance of the infernal luck criminals sometimes have.
Otherwise, if that accident hadn't happened, I think he had
his plans for dealing with her. First, he'd put the fear of the
Lord into her—tell her she'd be arrested for murder if she

confessed the truth. And then he'd square her with a fresh lot of money."

"Does it strike you——" Poirot stared straight in front of him: "Does it strike you that Miss Adams would let another woman be hanged when she herself held evidence that would acquit her?"

"Jane Wilkinson wouldn't have been hanged. The Montagu Corner party evidence was too strong for that."

"*But the murderer did not know that.* He would have had to count on Jane Wilkinson being hanged and Carlotta Adams keeping silence."

"You love talking, don't you, M. Poirot? And you're positively convinced now that Ronald Marsh is a white-headed boy who can do no wrong. Do you believe that story of his about seeing a man sneak surreptitiously into the house?"

Poirot shrugged his shoulders.

"Do you know who he says he thought it was?"

"I could guess, perhaps."

"He says he thought it was the film star, Bryan Martin. What do you think of that? A man who'd never even met Lord Edgware."

"Then it would certainly be curious if one saw such a man entering that house with a key."

"Chah!" said Japp. A rich noise expressive of contempt. "And now I suppose it will surprise you to hear that Mr. Bryan Martin wasn't in London that night. He took a young lady to dine down at Molesey. They didn't get back to London till midnight."

"Ah!" said Poirot mildly. "No, I am not surprised. Was the young lady also a member of the profession?"

"No. Girl who keeps a hat shop. As a matter of fact, it was Miss Adams' friend, Miss Driver. I think you'll agree her testimony is past suspicion."

"I am not disputing it, my friend."

"In fact, you're done down and you know it, old boy," said Japp, laughing. "Cock and bull story trumped up on the moment, that's what it was. Nobody entered No. 17—and nobody entered either of the houses either side—so what does that show? That his lordship's a liar."

Poirot shook his head sadly.

Japp rose to his feet—his spirits restored.

"Come, now, we're right, you know."

"Who was D. Paris, November?"

Japp shrugged his shoulders.

"Ancient history, I imagine. Can't a girl have a souvenir six months ago without its having something to do with this crime? We must have a sense of proportion."

"Six months ago," murmured Poirot, a sudden light in his eyes. "*Dieu, que je suis bête!*"

"What's he saying?" inquired Japp of me.

"Listen." Poirot rose and tapped Japp on the chest. "Why does Miss Adams' maid not recognise that box? Why does Miss Driver not recognise it?"

"What do you mean?"

"Because the box was *new*! It had only just been given to her. Paris, November—that is all very well—doubtless that is the date of which the box is to be a *souvenir*. But it was given to her *now*, not *then*. It has just been bought! Only just been bought! Investigate that, I implore you, my good Japp. It is a chance, decidedly a chance. It was bought not here, but abroad. Probably Paris. If it had been bought here, some jeweller would have come forward. It has been photographed and described in the papers. Yes, yes, Paris. Possibly some other foreign town, but I think Paris. Find out, I implore you. Make the inquiries. I want—I so badly want—to know who is this mysterious D."

"It will do no harm," said Japp good-naturedly. "Can't say I'm very excited about it myself. But I'll do what I can. The more we know the better."

Nodding cheerfully to us he departed.

CHAPTER XXIII

THE LETTER

"AND NOW," said Poirot, "we will go out to lunch."

He put his hand through my arm. He was smiling at me.

"I have hope," he explained.

I was glad to see him restored to his old self, though I was none the less convinced myself of young Ronald's guilt. I fancied that Poirot himself had perhaps come round to this view, convinced by Japp's arguments. The search for the

urchaser of the box was, perhaps, a last sally to save his face.
We went amicably to lunch together.

Somewhat to my amusement at a table the other side of the
oom, I saw Bryan Martin and Jenny Driver lunching to-
ether. Remembering what Japp had said, I suspected a
ossible romance.

They saw us and Jenny waved a hand.

When we were sipping coffee, Jenny left her escort and
ame over to our table. She looked as vivid and dynamic as
ver.

" May I sit here and talk to you a minute, M. Poirot?"

" Assuredly, Mademoiselle. I am charmed to see you. Will
ot M. Martin join us also?"

" I told him not to. You see, I wanted to talk to you about
Carlotta."

" Yes, Mademoiselle?"

" You wanted to get a line on to some man friend of hers.
Isn't that so?"

" Yes, yes."

" Well, I've been thinking and thinking. Sometimes you
can't get at things straight away. To get them clear you've
got to think back—remember a lot of little words and phrases
that perhaps you didn't pay much attention to at the time.
Well, that's what I've been doing. Thinking and thinking—
and remembering just what she said. And I've come to a
certain conclusion."

" Yes, Mademoiselle?"

" I think the man that she cared about—or was beginning
to care about—was Ronald Marsh—you know, the one who
has just succeeded to the title."

" What makes you think it was he, Mademoiselle?"

" Well, for one thing, Carlotta was speaking in a general
sort of way one day. About a man having hard luck, and how
it might affect character. That a man might be a decent sort
really and yet go down the hill. More sinned against than sin-
ning—you know the idea. The first thing a woman kids herself with when she's getting soft about a man. I've heard the
old wheeze so often! Carlotta had plenty of sense, yet here
she was coming out with this stuff just like a complete ass who
knew nothing of life. 'Hello,' I said to myself. 'Something's
up.' She didn't mention a name—it was all general. But
almost immediately after that she began to speak of Ronald

Marsh and that she thought he'd been badly treated. She wa
very impersonal and offhand about it. I didn't connect th
two things at the time. But now—I wonder. It seems to m
that it was Ronald she meant. What do you think, M
Poirot?"

Her face looked earnestly up into his.

" I think, Mademoiselle, that you have perhaps given m
some very valuable information."

" Good." Jenny clapped her hands.

Poirot looked kindly at her.

"Perhaps you have not heard—the gentleman of whom
you speak, Ronald Marsh—Lord Edgware—has just been
arrested."

" Oh!" Her mouth flew open in surprise. " Then my b
of thinking comes rather late in the day."

"It is never too late," said Poirot. "Not with me, you
understand. Thank you, Mademoiselle."

She left us to return to Bryan Martin.

" There, Poirot," I said. " Surely that shakes your belief."

" No, Hastings. On the contrary—it strengthens it."

Despite that valiant assertion I believed myself that secretly
he had weakened.

During the days that followed he never once mentioned the
Edgware case. If I spoke of it, he answered monosyllabically
and without interest. In other words, he had washed his hands
of it. Whatever idea he had had lingering in his fantastic
brain, he had now been forced to admit himself that it had not
materialised—that his first conception of the case had been the
true one and that Ronald Marsh was only too truly accused
of the crime. Only, being Poirot, he could not admit openly
that such was the case! Therefore he pretended to have lost
interest.

Such, I say, was my interpretation of his attitude. It seemed
borne out by the facts. He took no faintest interest in the police
court proceedings, which in any case were purely formal. He
busied himself with other cases and, as I say, he displayed no
interest when the subject was mentioned.

It was nearly a fortnight later than the events mentioned in
my last chapter when I came to realise that my interpretation
of his attitude was entirely wrong.

It was breakfast time. The usual heavy pile of letters lay
by Poirot's plate. He sorted through them with nimble fingers.

Then he uttered a quick exclamation of pleasure and picked up a letter with an American stamp on it.

He opened it with his little letter-opener. I looked on with interest since he seemed so moved to pleasure about it. There was a letter and a fairly thick enclosure.

Poirot read the former through twice, then he looked up.

" Would you like to see this, Hastings?"

I took it from him. It ran as follows:

" Dear M. Poirot,—I was much touched by your kind— your very kind letter. I have been feeling so bewildered by everything. Apart from my terrible grief, I have been so affronted by the things that seem to have been hinted about Carlotta—the dearest, sweetest sister that a girl ever had. No, M. Poirot, she did *not* take drugs. I'm sure of it. She had a horror of that kind of thing. I've often heard her say so. If she played a part in that poor man's death, it was an entirely innocent one—but of course her letter to me proves that. I am sending you the actual letter itself since you ask me to do so. I hate parting with the last letter she ever wrote, but I know you will take care of it and let me have it back, and if it helps you to clear up some of the mystery about her death, as you say it may do—why, then, of course it must go to you.

You ask whether Carlotta mentioned any friend specially in her letters. She mentioned a great many people, of course, but nobody in a very outstanding way. Bryan Martin, whom we used to know years ago, a girl called Jenny Driver, and a Captain Ronald Marsh were, I think, the ones she saw most of.

I wish I could think of something to help you. You write so kindly and with such understanding, and you seem to realise what Carlotta and I were to each other.

Gratefully yours,

LUCIE ADAMS.

P.S.—An officer has just been here for the letter. I told him that I had already mailed it to you. This, of course, was not true, but I felt somehow or other that it was important you should see it first. It seems Scotland Yard need it as evidence, against the murderer. You will take it to them. But, oh! please be sure they let you have it back again some day. You see, it is Carlotta's last words to me."

"So you wrote yourself to her," I remarked as I laid the letter down. "Why did you do that, Poirot? And why did you ask for the original of Carlotta Adams' letter?"

He was bending over the enclosed sheets of the letter I mentioned.

"In verity I could not say, Hastings—unless it is that I hoped against hope that the original letter might in some way explain the inexplicable."

"I don't see how you can get away from the text of that letter. Carlotta Adams gave it herself to the maid to post. There was no hocus pocus about it. And certainly it reads as a perfectly genuine ordinary epistle."

Poirot sighed.

"I know. I know. And that is what makes it so difficult. Because, Hastings, as it stands, that letter is *impossible*."

"Nonsense."

"*Si, si*, it is so. See you, as I have reasoned it out, certain things *must* be—they follow each other with method and order in an understandable fashion. But then comes this letter. It does not accord. Who, then, is wrong? Hercule Poirot or the letter?"

"You don't think it possible that it could be Hercule Poirot?" I suggested as delicately as I was able.

Poirot threw me a glance of reproof.

"There are times when I have been in error—but this is not one of them. Clearly then, since the letter seems impossible, it *is* impossible. There is some fact about the letter which escapes us. I seek to discover what that fact is."

And thereupon he resumed his study of the letter in question, using a small pocket miscroscope.

As he finished perusing each page, he passed it across to me. I, certainly, could find nothing amiss. It was written in a firm fairly legible handwriting and it was word for word as it had been telegraphed across.

Poirot sighed deeply.

"There is no forgery of any kind here—no, it is all written in the same hand. And yet, since, as I say, it is impossible——"

He broke off. With an impatient gesture he demanded the sheets from me. I passed them over, and once again he went slowly through them.

Suddenly he uttered a cry.

I had left the breakfast table and was standing looking out of the window. At this sound, however, I turned sharply.

Poirot was literally quivering with excitement. His eyes were green like a cat's. His pointing finger trembled.

" See you, Hastings? Look here—quickly—come and look."

I ran to his side. Spread out before him was one of the middle sheets of the letter. I could see nothing unusual about it.

" See you not? All these other sheets they have the clean edge—they are single sheets. But this one—see—one side of it is ragged—it has been torn. Now do you see what I mean? *This was a double sheet*, and so, you comprehend, *one page of the letter is missing*."

I stared stupidly, no doubt.

" But how can it be? It makes sense."

" Yes, yes, it makes sense. That is where the cleverness of the idea comes in. Read—and you will see."

I think I cannot do better than to append a facsimile of the page in question.

" You see it now? " said Poirot. " The letter breaks off where she is talking of Captain Marsh. She is sorry for him, and then she says: ' He enjoyed my show very much.' Then on the new sheet she goes on: ' he said . . .' But, *mon ami*, a *page is missing*. The ' He ' of the new page may not be the ' he ' of the old page. *In fact it is not the he of the old page*. It is another man altogether who proposed that hoax. Observe, nowhere after that is the name mentioned. Ah! *c'est épatant!* Somehow or other our murderer gets hold of this letter. It gives him away. No doubt he thinks to suppress it altogether, and then—reading it over—he sees another way of dealing with it. Remove one page, and the letter is capable of being twisted into a damning accusation of another man—a man too who has a motive for Lord Edgware's death. Ah! it was a gift! The money, for the *confiture* as you say! He tears the sheet off and replaces the letter."

I looked at Poirot in some admiration. I was not perfectly convinced of the truth of his theory. It seemed to me highly possible that Carlotta had used an odd half sheet that was already torn. But Poirot was so transfigured with joy that I simply had not the heart to suggest this prosaic possibility. After all, he *might* be right.

> he said " I believe it
> would take in Lord
> Edgware himself. Look
> here, will you take some
> thing on for a bet?"
> I laughed said
> "How much?"
>   Lucie darling.
> the answer fairly took
> my breath away
>   Ten thousand dollars!

I did, however, venture to point out one or two difficulties
in the way of his theory.

"But how did the man, whoever he was, get hold of the
letter? Miss Adams took it straight from her handbag and gave
it herself to the maid to post. The maid told us so."

"Therefore we must assume one of two things. Either the
maid was lying, or else, during that evening, Carlotta Adams
met the murderer."

I nodded.

"It seems to me that that last possibility is the most likely one. We still do not know where Carlotta Adams was between the time she left her flat and nine o'clock when she left her suitcase at Euston station. During that time, I believe myself that she met the murderer in some appointed spot—they probably had some food together. He gave her some last instructions. What happened exactly in regard to the letter we do not know. One can make a guess. She may have been carrying it in her hand meaning to post it. She may have laid it down on the table in the restaurant. He sees the address and scents a possible danger. He may have picked it up adroitly, made an excuse for leaving the table, opened it, read it, torn out the sheet, and then either replaced it on the table, or perhaps given it to her as she left, telling her that she had dropped it without noticing. The exact way of it is not important—but two things do seem clear. That Carlotta Adams met the murderer that evening either before the murder of Lord Edgware, or afterwards (there was time after she left the Corner House for a brief interview). I have a fancy, though there I am perhaps wrong, that it was the murderer who gave her the gold box—it was possibly a sentimental memento of their first meeting. *If so, the murderer is D.*"

"I don't see the point of the gold box."

"Listen, Hastings, Carlotta Adams was not addicted to veronal. Lucie Adams says so, and I, too, believe it to be true. She was a clear-eyed healthy girl with no predilection for such things. None of her friends nor her maid recognised the box. Why, then, was it found in her possession after she died? To create the impression that she *did* take veronal and that she had taken it for a considerable time—that is to say at least six months. Let us say that she met the murderer after the murder if only for a few minutes. They had a drink together, Hastings, to celebrate the success of their plan. And in the girl's drink he put sufficient veronal to ensure that there should be no waking for her on the following morning."

"Horrible," I said with a shudder.

"Yes, it was not pretty," said Poirot dryly.

"Are you going to tell Japp all this?" I asked after a minute or two.

"Not at the moment. What have I got to tell? He would say, the excellent Japp, 'another nest of the mare! The girl wrote on an odd sheet of paper!' *C'est tout.*"

I looked guiltily at the ground.

"What can I say to that? Nothing. It is a thing that might have happened. I only know it did not happen because *it is necessary that it should not have happened*."

He paused. A dreamy expression stole across his face.

"Figure to yourself, Hastings, if only that man had had the order and the method, he would have cut that sheet not torn it. And we should have noticed nothing. But nothing!"

"So we deduce that he is a man of careless habits," I said, smiling.

"No, no. He might have been in a hurry. You observe it is very carelessly torn. Oh! assuredly he was pressed for time."

He paused and then said:

"One thing you do remark, I hope. This man—this D— he must have had a very good alibi for that evening."

"I can't see how he could have had any alibi at all if he spent his time first at Regent Gate doing a murder and then with Carlotta Adams."

"Precisely," said Poirot. "That is what I mean. He is badly in need of an alibi, so no doubt he prepared one. Another point: Does his name really begin with D? Or does D stand for some nickname by which he was known to her?"

He paused and then said softly:

"A man whose initial or whose nickname is D. We have got to find him, Hastings. Yes, we have got to find him."

CHAPTER XXIV

NEWS FROM PARIS

ON THE following day we had an unexpected visit.

Geraldine Marsh was announced.

I felt sorry for her as Poirot greeted her and set a chair for her. Her large dark eyes seemed wider and darker than ever. There were black circles round them as though she had not slept. Her face looked extraordinarily haggard and weary for one so young—little more, really, than a child.

"I have come to see you, M. Poirot, because I don't know how to go on any longer. I am so terribly worried and upset."

"Yes, Mademoiselle?"

His manner was gravely sympathetic.

"Ronald told me what you said to him that day. I mean that dreadful day when he was arrested." She shivered. "He told me that you came up to him suddenly, just when he had said that he supposed no one would believe him, and that you said to him: 'I believe you.' Is that true, M. Poirot?"

"It is true, Mademoiselle, that is what I said."

"I know, but I meant not was it true you said it, but were the words really true. I mean, *did* you believe his story?"

Terribly anxious she looked, leaning forward there, her hands clasped together.

"The words were true, Mademoiselle," said Poirot quietly. "I do not believe your cousin killed Lord Edgware."

"Oh!" The colour came into her face, her eyes opened big and wide. "Then you must think—that someone else did it!"

"*Evidément*, Mademoiselle." He smiled.

"I'm stupid. I say things badly. What I mean is—you think you know who that somebody is?"

She leaned forward eagerly.

"I have my little ideas, naturally—my suspicions, shall we say?"

"Won't you tell me? Please—please."

Poirot shook his head.

"It would be—perhaps—unfair."

"Then you *have* got a definite suspicion of somebody?"

Poirot merely shook his head non-committally.

"If only I knew a little more," pleaded the girl. "It would make it so much easier for me. And I might perhaps be able to help you. Yes, really I might be able to help you."

Her pleading was very disarming, but Poirot continued to shake his head.

"The Duchess of Merton is still convinced it was my stepmother," said the girl thoughtfully. She gave a slight questioning glance at Poirot.

He showed no reaction.

"But I hardly see how that can be."

"What is your opinion of her? Of your stepmother?"

"Well—I hardly know her. I was at school in Paris when my father married her. When I came home, she was quite kind. I mean, she just didn't notice I was there. I thought her very empty-headed and—well, mercenary."

Poirot nodded.

"You spoke of the Duchess of Merton. You have seen much of her?"

"Yes. She has been very kind to me. I have been with her a great deal during the last fortnight. It has been terrible —with all the talk, and the reporters, and Ronald in prison and everything." She shivered. "I feel I have no real friends. But the Duchess has been wonderful, and he has been nice too—her son, I mean."

"You like him?"

"He is shy, I think. Stiff and rather difficult to get on with. But his mother talks a lot about him, so that I feel I know him better than I really do."

"I see. Tell me, Mademoiselle, you are fond of your cousin?"

"Of Ronald? Of course. He—I haven't seen much of him the last two years—but before that he used to live in the house. I—I always thought he was wonderful. Always joking and thinking up mad things to do. Oh! in that gloomy house of ours it made all the difference."

Poirot nodded sympathetically, but he went on to make a remark that shocked me in its crudity.

"You do not want to see him—hanged, then?"

"No, no." The girl shivered violently. "Not that. Oh! if only it were her—my stepmother. It must be her. The Duchess says it must."

"Ah!" said Poirot. "If only Captain Marsh had stayed in the taxi—eh?"

"Yes—at least, what do you mean?" Her brow wrinkled. "I don't understand."

"If he had not followed that man into the house. Did you hear anyone come in, by the way?"

"No, I didn't hear anything."

"What did you do when you came into the house?"

"I ran straight upstairs—to fetch the pearls, you know."

"Of course. It took you some time to fetch them."

"Yes. I couldn't find the key of my jewel-case all at once."

"So often is that the case. The more in haste, the less the speed. It was some time before you came down, and then— you found your cousin in the hall?"

"Yes, coming from the library." She swallowed.

"I comprehend. It gave you quite the turn."

"Yes, it did." She looked grateful for his sympathetic tone. "It startled me, you see."

"Quite, quite."

"Ronnie just said: 'Hello, Dina, got them?' from behind me—and it made me jump."

"Yes," said Poirot gently. "As I said before it is a pity he did not stay outside. Then the taxi-driver would have been able to swear he never entered the house."

She nodded. Her tears began to fall, splashing unheeded on her lap. She got up. Poirot took her hand.

"You want me to save him for you—is that it?"

"Yes, yes—oh! please, yes. You don't know . . ."

She stood there striving to control herself, clenching her hands.

"Life has not been easy for you, Mademoiselle," said Poirot gently. "I appreciate that. No, it has not been easy. Hastings, will you get Mademoiselle a taxi?"

I went down with the girl and saw her into the taxi. She had composed herself by now and thanked me very prettily.

I found Poirot walking up and down the room, his brows knitted in thought. He looked unhappy.

I was glad when the telephone bell rang to distract him.

"Who is that? Oh! it is Japp. *Bonjour, mon ami.*"

"What's he got to say?" I asked, drawing nearer the telephone.

Finally, after various ejaculations, Poirot spoke.

"Yes, and who called for it? Do they know?"

Whatever the answer, it was not what he expected. His face dropped ludicrously.

"Are you sure?"

" . . . . "

"No, it is a little upsetting, that is all."

" . . . . "

"Yes, I must rearrange my ideas."

" . . . . "

"*Comment?*"

" . . . . "

"All the same, I was right about it. Yes, a detail, as you say."

" . . . . "

"No, I am still of the same opinion. I would pray of you to make still further inquiries of the restaurants in the neighbourhood of Regent Gate and Euston, Tottenham Court Road and perhaps Oxford Street."

" . . . . "

" Yes, a woman and a man. And also in the neighbourhood of the Strand just before midnight. *Comment?*"

" . . . . "

" But, yes, I know that Captain Marsh was with the Dortheimers. But there are other people in the world besides Captain Marsh."

" . . . . "

" To say I have the head of a pig is not pretty, *Tout de même*, oblige me in this matter, I pray of you."

" . . . . "

He replaced the receiver.

" Well?" I asked impatiently.

" Is it well? I wonder. Hastings, that gold box *was* bought in Paris. It was ordered by letter and it comes from a well-known Paris shop which specialises in such things. The letter was supposedly from a Lady Ackerley—Constance Ackerley the letter was signed. Naturally there is no such person. The letter was received two days before the murder. It ordered the initials of (presumably) the writer in rubies and the inscription inside. It was a rush order—to be called for the following day. That is, the day before the murder."

" And it was called for?"

" Yes, it was called for and paid for in notes."

" Who called for it?" I asked excitedly. I felt we were getting near to the truth.

" A woman called for it, Hastings."

" A woman?" I said, surprised.

" *Mais oui*. A woman—short, middle-aged and *wearing pince-nez*."

We looked at each other, completely baffled.

CHAPTER XXV

A LUNCHEON PARTY

It was, I think, on the day after that that we went to the Widburns' luncheon party at Claridge's.

Neither Poirot nor I were particularly anxious to go. It

was, as a matter of fact, about the sixth invitation we had received. Mrs. Widburn was a persistent woman and she liked celebrities. Undaunted by refusals, she finally offered such a choice of dates that capitulation was inevitable. Under those circumstances the sooner we went and got it over the better.

Poirot had been very uncommunicative ever since the news from Paris.

To my remarks on the subject he returned always the same answer.

"There is something here I do not comprehend."

And once or twice he murmured to himself.

"Pince-nez. Pince-nez in Paris. Pince-nez in Carlotta Adams' bag."

I really felt glad of the luncheon party as a means of distraction.

Young Donald Ross was there and came up and greeted me cheerily. There were more men than women and he was put next to me at table.

Jane Wilkinson sat almost opposite us, and next to her, between her and Mrs. Widburn, sat the young Duke of Merton.

I fancied—of course it may have been only my fancy—that he looked slightly ill at ease. The company in which he found himself was, so I should imagine, little to his liking. He was a strictly conservative and somewhat reactionary young man —the kind of character that seemed to have stepped out of the Middle Ages by some regrettable mistake. His infatuation for the extremely modern Jane Wilkinson was one of those anachronistic jokes that Nature so loves to play.

Seeing Jane's beauty and appreciating the charm that her exquisitely husky voice lent to the most trite utterances, I could hardly wonder at his capitulation. But one can get used to perfect beauty and an intoxicating voice! It crossed my mind that perhaps even now a ray of common-sense was dissipating the mists of intoxicated love. It was a chance remark —a rather humiliating *gaffe* on Jane's part that gave me that impression.

Somebody—I forget who—had uttered the phrase "judgment of Paris," and straight away Jane's delightful voice was uplifted.

"Paris?" she said. "Why, Paris doesn't cut any ice nowadays. It's London and New York that count."

As sometimes happens, the words fell in a momentary lull of

conversation. It was an awkward moment. On my right I
heard Donald Ross draw in his breath sharply. Mrs. Widburn
began to talk violently about Russian opera. Everyone hastily
said something to somebody else. Jane alone looked serenely
up and down the table without the least consciousness of
having said anything amiss.

It was then I noticed the Duke. His lips were drawn tightly
together, he had flushed, and it seemed to me as though he
drew slightly away from Jane. He must have had a foretaste
of the fact that for a man of his position to marry a Jane
Wilkinson might lead to some awkward contretemps.

As so often happens, I made the first remark that came into
my head to my left-hand neighbour, a stout titled lady who
arranged children's matinées. I remember that the remark in
question was: "Who is that extraordinary looking woman in
purple at the other end of the table?" It was, of course, the
lady's sister! Having stammered apologies, I turned and
chatted to Ross, who answered in monosyllables.

It was then, rebuffed on both sides, that I noticed Bryan
Martin. He must have come late for I had not seen him
before.

He was a little way farther down the table on my side and
was leaning forward and chatting with great animation to a
pretty blonde woman.

It was some time since I had seen him at close quarters, and
I was struck at once by the great improvement in his looks.
The haggard lines had almost disappeared. He looked younger
and in every way more fit. He was laughing and chaffing his
vis-à-vis and seemed in first-rate spirits.

I did not have time to observe him further, for at that
moment my stout neighbour forgave me and graciously permitted me to listen to a long monologue on the beauties of a
Children's Matinée which she was organising for Charity.

Poirot had to leave early as he had an appointment. He
was investigating the strange disappearance of an Ambassa-
dor's boots and had a rendezvous fixed for half-past two. He
charged me to make his adieus to Mrs. Widburn. While I was
waiting to do so—not an easy matter, for she was at the
moment closely surrounded by departing friends all breathing
out "Darlings" at a great rate—somebody touched me on
the shoulder.

It was young Ross.

" Isn't M. Poirot here? I wanted to speak to him."

I explained that Poirot had just departed.

Ross seemed taken aback. Looking more closely at him, I saw that something seemed to have upset him. He looked white and strained and he had a queer uncertain look in his eyes.

" Did you want to see him particularly?" I asked.

He answered slowly.

" I—don't know."

It was such a queer answer that I stared at him in surprise. He flushed.

" It sounds odd, I know. The truth is that something rather queer has happened. Something that I can't make out. I— I'd like M. Poirot's advice about it. Because, you see, I don't know what to do—I don't want to bother him, but——"

He looked so puzzled and unhappy that I hastened to reassure him.

" Poirot has gone to keep an appointment," I said. " But I know he means to be back at five o'clock. Why not ring him up then, or come and see him?"

" Thanks. Do you know, I think I will. Five o'clock?"

" Better ring up first," I said, " and make sure before coming round."

" All right. I will. Thanks, Hastings. You see, I think it might—just might—be very important."

I nodded and turned again to where Mrs. Widburn was dispensing honied words and limp handshakes.

My duty done, I was turning away when a hand was slipped through my arm.

" Don't cut me," said a merry voice.

It was Jenny Driver—looking extremely chic, by the way.

" Hello," I said. " Where have you sprung from?"

" I was lunching at the next table to you."

" I didn't see you. How is business?"

" Booming, thank you."

" The soup plates going well?"

" Soup plates, as you rudely call them, are going very well. When everybody has got thoroughly laden up with them, there's going to be dirty work done. Something like a blister with a feather attached is going to be worn bang in the middle of the forehead."

" Unscrupulous," I said.

" Not at all. Somebody must come to the rescue of the ostriches. They're all on the dole."

She laughed and moved away.

" Good-bye. I'm taking an afternoon off from business. Going for a spin in the country."

" And very nice too," I said approvingly. " It's stifling in London to-day."

I myself walked leisurely through the Park. I reached home about four o'clock. Poirot had not yet come in. It was twenty minutes to five when he returned. He was twinkling and clearly in a good humour.

" I see, Holmes," I remarked, " that you have tracked the Ambassadorial boots."

" It was a case of cocaine smuggling. Very ingenious. For the last hour I have been in a ladies' Beauty Parlour. There was a girl there with auburn hair who would have captured your susceptible heart at once."

Poirot always has the impression that I am particularly susceptible to auburn hair. I do not bother to argue about it.

The telephone rang.

" That's probably Donald Ross," I said as I went across to the instrument.

" Donald Ross?"

" Yes. The young man we met at Chiswick. He wants to see you about something."

I took down the receiver.

" Hello. Captain Hastings speaking."

It was Ross.

" Oh! is that you, Hastings? Has M. Poirot come in?"

" Yes, he's here now. Do you want to speak to him or are you coming round?"

" It's nothing much. I can tell him just as well over the telephone."

" Right. Hold on."

Poirot came forward and took the receiver. I was so close that I could hear, faintly, Ross's voice.

" Is that M. Poirot?" The voice sounded eager—excited.

" Yes, it is I."

" Look here, I don't want to bother you, but there's something that seems to me a bit odd. It's in connection with Lord Edgware's death."

I saw Poirot's figure go taut.

" Continue, continue."

" It may seem just nonsense to you——"

" No, no. Tell me, all the same."

" It was Paris set me off. You see——" Very faintly I heard a bell trilling.

" Half a second," said Ross.

There was the sound of the receiver being laid down.

We waited. Poirot at the mouthpiece. I was standing beside him.

I say—we waited. . . .

Two minutes passed—three minutes—four minutes—five minutes.

Poirot shifted his feet uneasily. He glanced up at the clock. Then he moved the hook up and down and spoke to the Exchange. He turned to me.

" The receiver is still off at the other end, but there is no reply. They cannot get an answer. Quick, Hastings, look up Ross's address in the telephone book. We must go there at once."

CHAPTER XXVI

PARIS?

A few minutes later we were jumping into a taxi.

Poirot's face was very grave.

" I am afraid, Hastings," he said. " I am afraid."

" You don't mean——" I said and stopped.

" We are up against somebody who has already struck twice—that person will not hesitate to strike again. He is twisting and turning like a rat, fighting for his life. Ross is a danger. Then Ross will be eliminated."

" Was what he had to tell so important?" I asked doubtfully. " He did not seem to think so."

" Then he was wrong. Evidently what he had to tell was of supreme importance."

" But how could anyone know?"

" He spoke to you, you say. There, at Claridge's. With people all round. Madness—utter madness. Ah! why did you not bring him back with you—guard him—let no one near him till I had heard what he had to say."

" I never thought—I never dreamt——" I stammered.

Poirot made a quick gesture.

" Do not blame yourself—how could you know? I—I would have known. The murderer, see you, Hastings, is as cunning as a tiger and as relentless. Ah! shall we never arrive?"

We were there at last. Ross lived in a maisonette on the first floor of a house in a big square in Kensington. A card stuck in a little slot by the door-bell gave us the information. The hall door was open. Inside was a big flight of stairs.

" So easy to come in. None to see," murmured Poirot as he sprang up the stairs.

On the first floor was a kind of partition and a narrow door with a Yale lock. Ross's card was stuck in the centre of the door.

We paused there. Everywhere there was dead silence.

I pushed the door—to my surprise it yielded.

We entered.

There was a narrow hall and an open door one side, another in front of us opening into what was evidently the sitting-room.

Into this sitting-room we went. It was the divided half of a big front drawing-room. It was cheaply but comfortably furnished and it was empty. On a small table was the telephone, the receiver stood down beside the instrument.

Poirot took a swift step forward, looked round, then shook his head.

" Not here. Come, Hastings."

We retraced our steps and, going out into the hall, we passed through the other door. The room was a tiny dining-room. At one side of the table, fallen sideways from a chair and sprawled across the table, was Ross.

Poirot bent over him.

He straightened up—his face was white.

" *He's dead. Stabbed at the base of the skull.*"

For long afterwards the events of that afternoon remained like a nightmare in my mind. I could not rid myself of a dreadful feeling of responsibility.

Much later, that evening, when we were alone together, I stammered out to Poirot my bitter self-reproachings. He responded quickly.

" No, no, do not blame yourself. How could you have suspected? The good God has not given you a suspicious nature to begin with."

"*You* would have suspected?"

"That is different. All my life, you see, I have tracked down murderers. I know how, each time, the impulse to kill becomes stronger, till, at last, for a trivial cause——" He broke off.

He had been very quiet ever since our ghastly discovery. All through the arrival of the police, the questioning of the other people in the house, the hundred and one details of the dreadful routine following upon a murder, Poirot had remained aloof—strangely quiet—a far-away speculative look in his eyes. Now, as he broke off his sentence, that same far-away speculative look returned.

"We have no time to waste in regrets, Hastings," he said quietly. "No time to say ' If '—The poor young man who is dead had something to tell us. And we know now that that something must have been of great importance—otherwise he would not have been killed. Since he can no longer tell us— we have got to guess. We have got to guess—with only one little clue to guide us."

"Paris," I said.

"Yes, Paris." He got up and began to stroll up and down.

"There have been several mentions of Paris in this business, but unluckily in different connections. There is the word Paris engraved in the gold box. Paris in November last. Miss Adams was there then—perhaps Ross was there also. Was there someone else there whom Ross knew? Whom he saw with Miss Adams under somewhat peculiar circumstances?"

"We can never know," I said.

"Yes, yes, we can know. We *shall* know! The power of the human brain, Hastings, is almost unlimited. What other mentions of Paris have we in connection with the case? There is the short woman with the pince-nez who called for the box at the jeweller's there. Was she known to Ross? The Duke of Merton was in Paris when the crime was committed. Paris, Paris, Paris. Lord Edgware was going to Paris—Ah! possibly we have something there. Was he killed to prevent him going to Paris?"

He sat down again, his brows drawn together. I could almost feel the waves of his furious concentration of thought.

"What happened at that luncheon?" he murmured,

"Some casual word or phrase must have shown to Donald Ross the significance of knowledge which was in his possession, but which up to then he had not known was significant. Was there some mention of France? Of Paris? Up your end of the table, I mean."

"The word Paris was mentioned but not in that connection."

I told him about Jane Wilkinson's "*gaffe*."

"That probably explains it," he said thoughtfully. "The word Paris would be sufficient—taken in conjunction with something else. But what was that something else? At what was Ross looking? Or of what had he been speaking when that word was uttered?"

"He'd been talking about Scottish superstitions."

"And his eyes were—where?"

"I'm not sure. I think he was looking up towards the head of the table where Mrs. Widburn was sitting."

"Who sat next to her?"

"The Duke of Merton, then Jane Wilkinson, then some fellow I didn't know."

"M. le Duc. It is possible that he was looking at M. le Duc when the word Paris was spoken. The Duke, remember, was in Paris or was supposed to be in Paris at the time of the crime. Suppose Ross suddenly remembered something which went to show that Merton was *not* in Paris."

"My dear Poirot!"

"Yes, you consider that an absurdity. So does everyone. Had M. le Duc a motive for the crime? Yes, a very strong one. But to suppose that he committed it—oh! absurd. He is so rich, of so assured a position, of such a well-known lofty character. No one will scrutinise his alibi too carefully. And yet to fake an alibi in a big hotel is not so difficult. To go across by the afternoon service—to return—it *could* be done. Tell me, Hastings, did Ross not say anything when the word Paris was mentioned? Did he show no emotion?"

"I do seem to remember that he drew in his breath rather sharply."

"And his manner when he spoke to you afterwards. Was it bewildered? Confused?"

"That absolutely describes it."

"*Précisément*. An idea has come to him. He thinks it preposterous! Absurd! And yet—he hesitates to voice it. First he will speak to me. But alas! when he has made up his mind, I am already departed."

"If he had only said a little more to me," I lamented.

"Yes. If only—— Who was near you at the time?"

"Well, everybody, more or less. They were saying good-bye to Mrs. Widburn. I didn't notice particularly."

Poirot got up again.

"Have I been all wrong?" he murmured as he began once more to pace the floor. "All the time, have I been wrong?"

I looked at him with sympathy. Exactly what the ideas were that passed through his head I did not know. "Close as an oyster," Japp had called him, and the Scotland Yard inspector's words were truly descriptive. I only know that now, at this moment, he was at war with himself.

"At anyrate," I said, "this murder cannot be put down to Ronald Marsh."

"It is a point in his favour," my friend said absent-mindedly. "But that does not concern us for the moment."

Abruptly, as before, he sat down.

"I cannot be entirely wrong. Hastings, do you remember that I once posed to myself five questions?"

"I seem to remember dimly something of the sort."

"They were: Why did Lord Edgware change his mind on the subject of divorce? What is the explanation of the letter he said he wrote to his wife and which she said she never got? Why was there that expression of rage on his face when we left his house that day? What were a pair of pince-nez doing in Carlotta Adams' handbag? Why did someone telephone to Lady Edgware at Chiswick and immediately ring off?"

"Yes, these were the questions," I said. "I remember now."

"Hastings, I have had in my mind all along a certain little idea. An idea as to who the man was—*the man behind*. Three of those questions I have answered—and the answers accord with my little idea. But two of the questions, Hastings, I cannot answer.

"You see what that means. Either I am wrong as to the person, *and it cannot be that person*. Or else the answer to the two questions that I cannot answer is there all the time. Which is it, Hastings? Which is it?"

Rising, he went to his desk, unlocked it and took out the letter Lucie Adams had sent him from America. He had asked

Japp to let him keep it a day or two and Japp had agreed. Poirot laid it on the table in front of him and pored over it.

The minutes went by. I yawned and picked up a book. I did not think that Poirot would get much result from his study. We had already gone over and over the letter. Granted that it was not Ronald Marsh who was referred to, there was nothing whatever to show who else it might be.

I turned the pages of my book. . . .

Possibly I dozed off. . . .

Suddenly Poirot uttered a low cry. I sat up abruptly.

He was looking at me with an indescribable expression, his eyes green and shining.

" Hastings, Hastings."

" Yes, what is it?"

" Do you remember I said to you that if the murderer had been a man of order and method he would have cut this page, not torn it?"

" Yes?"

" I was wrong. There is order and method throughout this crime. *The page had to be torn, not cut.* Look for yourself."

I looked.

" *Eh bien*, you see?"

I shook my head.

" You mean he was in a hurry?"

" Hurry or no hurry it would be the same thing. Do you not see, my friend? *The page had to be torn. . . .*"

I shook my head.

In a low voice Poirot said:

" I have been foolish. I have been blind. But *now—now—* we shall get on!"

CHAPTER XXVII

CONCERNING PINCE-NEZ

A MINUTE later his mood had changed. He sprang to his feet.

I also sprang to mine—completely uncomprehending but willing.

" We will take a taxi. It is only nine o'clock. Not too late to make a visit."

I hurried after him down the stairs.

" Whom are we going to visit? "

" We are going to Regent Gate."

I judged it wisest to hold my peace. Poirot, I saw, was not in the mood for being questioned. That he was greatly excited I could see. As we sat side by side in the taxi his fingers drummed on his knee with a nervous impatience most unlike his usual calm.

I went over in my mind every word of Carlotta Adams' letter to her sister. By this time I almost knew it by heart. I repeated again and again to myself Poirot's words about the torn page.

But it was no good. As far as I was concerned, Poirot's words simply did not make sense. Why had a page *got* to be torn. No, I could not see it.

A new butler opened the door to us at Regent Gate. Poirot asked for Miss Carroll, and as we followed the butler up the stairs I wondered for the fiftieth time where the former " Greek god " could be. So far the police had failed utterly to run him to earth. A sudden shiver passed over me as I reflected that perhaps he, too, was dead. . . .

The sight of Miss Carroll, brisk and neat and eminently sane, recalled me from these fantastic speculations. She was clearly very much surprised to see Poirot.

" I am glad to find you still here, Mademoiselle," said Poirot as he bowed over her hand. " I was afraid you might be no longer in the house."

" Geraldine would not hear of my leaving," said Miss Carroll. " She begged me to stay on. And really, at a time like this, the poor child needs someone. If she needs nothing else, she needs a buffer. And I can assure you, when need be, I make a very efficient buffer, M. Poirot."

Her mouth took on a grim line. I felt that she would have a short way with reporters or news hunters.

" Mademoiselle, you have always seemed to me the pattern of efficiency. The efficiency, I admire it very much. It is rare. Mademoiselle Marsh now, she has not got the practical mind."

" She's a dreamer," said Miss Carroll. " Completely impractical. Always has been. Lucky she hasn't got her living to get."

" Yes, indeed."

" But I don't suppose you came here to talk about people

being practical or impractical. What can I do for you, M. Poirot?"

I do not think Poirot quite liked to be recalled to the point in this fashion. He was somewhat addicted to the oblique approach. With Miss Carroll, however, such a thing was not practicable. She blinked at him suspiciously through her strong glasses.

"There are a few points on which I should like definite information. I know I can trust your memory, Miss Carroll."

"I wouldn't be much use as a secretary if you couldn't," said Miss Carroll grimly.

"Was Lord Edgware in Paris last November?"

"Yes."

"Can you tell me the date of his visit?"

"I shall have to look it up."

She rose, unlocked a drawer, took out a small bound book, turned the pages and finally announced:

"Lord Edgware went to Paris on November 3rd and returned on the 7th. He also went over on November 20th and returned on December 4th. Anything more?"

"Yes. For what purpose did he go?"

"On the first occasion he went to see some statuettes which he thought of purchasing and which were to be auctioned later. On the second occasion he had no definite purpose in view so far as I know."

"Did Mademoiselle Marsh accompany her father on either occasion?"

"She never accompanied her father on any occasion, M. Poirot. Lord Edgware would never have dreamed of such a thing. At that time she was at a convent in Paris, but I do not think her father went to see her or took her out—at least it would surprise me very much if he had."

"You yourself did not accompany him?"

"No."

She looked at him curiously and then said abruptly:

"Why are you asking me these questions, M. Poirot? What is the point of them?"

Poirot did not reply to this question. Instead he said:

"Miss Marsh is very fond of her cousin, is she not?"

"Really, M. Poirot, I don't see what that has got to do with you."

"She came to see me the other day! You knew that?"

"No, I did not." She seemed startled. "What did she say?"

"She told me—though not in actual words—that she was very fond of her cousin."

"Well, then, why ask me?"

"Because I seek your opinion."

This time Miss Carroll decided to answer.

"Much too fond of him in my opinion. Always has been."

"You do not like the present Lord Edgware?"

"I don't say that. I've no use for him, that's all. He's not serious. I don't deny he's got a pleasant way with him. He can talk you round. But I'd rather see Geraldine getting interested in someone with a little more backbone."

"Such as the Duke of Merton?"

"I don't know the Duke. At anyrate, he seems to take the duties of his position seriously. But he's running after that woman—that precious Jane Wilkinson."

"His mother——"

"Oh! I dare say his mother would prefer him to marry Geraldine. But what can mothers do? Sons never want to marry the girls their mothers want them to marry."

"Do you think that Miss Marsh's cousin cares for her?"

"Doesn't matter whether he does or doesn't in the position he's in."

"You think, then, that he will be condemned?"

"No, I don't. I don't think he did it."

"But he might be condemned all the same?"

Miss Carroll did not reply.

"I must not detain you." Poirot rose. "By the way, did you know Carlotta Adams?"

"I saw her act. Very clever."

"Yes, she was clever." He seemed lost in meditation. "Ah! I have put down my gloves."

Reaching forward to get them from the table where he had laid them, his cuff caught the chain of Miss Carroll's pince-nez and jerked them off. Poirot retrieved them and the gloves which he had dropped, uttering confused apologies.

"I must apologise also once more for disturbing you," he ended. "But I fancied there might be some clue in a dispute Lord Edgware had with someone last year. Hence my questions about Paris. A forlorn hope, I fear, but Mademoiselle seemed so very positive it was not her cousin who committed

the crime. Remarkably positive she was. Well, good-night
Mademoiselle, and a thousand pardons for disturbing you.'

We had reached the door when Miss Carroll's voice recalled
us.

" M. Poirot, these aren't my glasses. I can't see through
them."

"*Comment?*" Poirot stared at her in amazement. Then
his face broke up into smiles.

" Imbecile that I am! My own glasses fell out of my pocket
as I stooped to get the gloves and pick up yours. I have mixed
the two pairs. They look very alike, you see."

An exchange was made, with smiles on both sides, and we
took our departure.

" Poirot," I said when we were outside. " You don't wear
glasses."

He beamed at me.

" Penetrating! How quickly you see the point."

" Those were the pince-nez found in Carlotta Adams' hand
bag?"

" Correct."

" Why did you think they might be Miss Carroll's?"

Poirot shrugged his shoulders.

" She is the only person connected with the case who wears
glasses."

" However, they are not hers," I said thoughtfully.

" So she affirms."

" You suspicious old devil."

" Not at all, not at all. Probably she spoke the truth. I
think she did speak the truth. Otherwise I doubt if she would
have noticed the substitution. I did it very adroitly, my
friend."

We were strolling through the streets more or less at random.
I suggested a taxi, but Poirot shook his head.

" I have need to think, my friend. Walking aids me."

I said no more. The night was a close one and I was in no
hurry to return home.

" Were your questions about Paris mere camouflage?"
asked curiously.

" Not entirely."

" We still haven't solved the mystery of the initial D,"
said thoughtfully. " It's odd that nobody to do with the case
has an initial D—either surname or Christian name—except—

h! yes, that's odd—except Donald Ross himself. And he's dead."

"Yes," said Poirot in a sombre voice. "He is dead."

I remembered another evening when three of us had walked at night. Remembered something else, too, and drew my breath in sharply.

"By Jove, Poirot," I said. "Do you remember?"

"Remember what, my friend?"

"What Ross said about thirteen at table. *And he was the first to get up.*"

Poirot did not answer. I felt a little uncomfortable as one always does when superstition is proved justified.

"It is queer," I said in a low voice. "You must admit it is queer."

"Eh?"

"I said it was queer—about Ross and thirteen. Poirot, what are you thinking about?"

To my utter amazement and, I must admit, somewhat to my disgust, Poirot began suddenly to shake with laughter. He shook and he shook. Something was evidently causing him the most exquisite mirth.

"What the devil are you laughing at?" I said sharply.

"Oh! Oh! Oh!" gasped Poirot. "It is nothing. It is that I think of a riddle I heard the other day. I will tell it to you. What is it that has two legs, feathers, and barks like a dog?"

"A chicken, of course," I said wearily. "I knew that in the nursery."

"You are too well informed, Hastings. You should say, 'I do not know.' And then me, I say, 'A chicken,' and then you say, 'But a chicken does not bark like a dog,' and I say, 'Ah! I put that in to make it more difficult.' Supposing, Hastings, that there we have the explanation of the letter D?"

"What nonsense!"

"Yes, to most people, but to a certain type of mind. Oh! if I had only someone I could ask . . ."

We were passing a big cinema. People were streaming out of it discussing their own affairs, their servants, their friends of the opposite sex, and just occasionally, the picture they had just seen.

With a group of them we crossed the Euston Road.

"I loved it," a girl was sighing. "I think Bryan Martin's just wonderful. I never miss any picture he's in. The way he rode down that cliff and got there in time with the papers."

Her escort was less enthusiastic.

"Idiotic story. If they'd just had the sense to ask Ellis right away, which anyone with sense would have done——"

The rest was lost. Reaching the pavement I turned back to see Poirot standing in the middle of the road with buses bearing down on him from either side. Instinctively I put my hands over my eyes. There was a jarring of brakes, and some rich bus driver language. In a dignified manner Poirot walked to the kerb. He looked like a man walking in his sleep.

"Poirot," I said, "were you mad?"

"No, *mon ami*. It was just that—something came to me. There, at that moment."

"A damned bad moment," I said. "And very nearly your last one."

"No matter. Ah, *mon ami*—I have been blind, deaf, insensible. Now I see the answers to all those questions—yes, all five of them. Yes—I see it all. . . . So simple, so childishly simple. . . ."

CHAPTER XXVIII

POIROT ASKS A FEW QUESTIONS

WE HAD a curious walk home.

Poirot was clearly following out some train of thought in his own mind. Occasionally he murmured a word under his breath. I heard one or two of them. Once he said, "Candles," and another time he said something that sounded like "*douzaine*." I suppose if I had been really bright I should have seen the line his thoughts were taking. It was really such a clear trail. However, at the time, it sounded to me mere gibberish.

No sooner were we at home than he flew to the telephone. He rang up the Savoy and asked to speak to Lady Edgware.

"Not a hope, old boy," I said with some amusement.

Poirot, as I have often told him, is one of the worst-informed men in the world.

"Don't you know?" I went on. "She's in a new play. She'll be at the theatre. It's only half-past ten."

Poirot paid no attention to me. He was speaking to the hotel lerk, who was evidently telling him exactly what I had just old him.

"Ah! is that so? I should like then to speak to Lady Edgware's maid."

In a few minutes the connection was made.

"Is that Lady Edgware's maid? This is M Poirot speaking. M. Hercule Poirot. You remember me, do you not?"

" . . . . "

"Très bien. Now, you understand, something of importance has arisen. I would like you to come and see me at once.

" . . . . "

"But yes, very important. I will give you the address. Listen carefully."

He repeated it twice, then hung up the receiver with a thoughtful face.

"What is the idea? ' I asked curiously. "Have you really got a piece of information?"

"No, Hastings, it is she who will give me the information."

"What information?"

"Information about a certain person.'

"Jane Wilkinson?"

"Oh! as to her, I have all the information I need. I know her back side before, as you say."

"Who, then?"

Poirot gave me one of his supremely irritating smiles and told me to wait and see.

He then busied himself in tidying up the room in a fussy manner.

Ten minutes later the maid arrived. She seemed a little nervous and uncertain. A small neat figure dressed in black, she peered about her doubtfully.

Poirot bustled forward.

"Ah! you have come. That is most kind. Sit here, will you not, Mademoiselle—Ellis, I think?"

"Yes, sir. Ellis."

She sat down on the chair Poirot had drawn forward for her.

She sat with her hands folded on her lap looking from one to the other of us. Her small bloodless face was quite composed and her thin lips were pinched together.

"To begin with, Miss Ellis, you have been with Lady Edgware how long?"

"Three years, sir."

"That is as I thought. You know her affairs well."

Ellis did not reply. She looked disapproving.

"What I mean is, you should have a good idea of who her enemies are likely to be."

Ellis compressed her lips more tightly.

"Most women have tried to do her a spiteful turn, sir. Yes, they've all been against her. Nasty jealousy."

"Her own sex did not like her?"

"No, sir. She's too good looking. And she always gets what she wants. There's a lot of nasty jealousy in the theatrical profession."

"What about men?"

Ellis allowed a sour smile to appear on her withered countenance.

"She can do what she likes with the gentlemen, sir, and that's a fact."

"I agree with you," said Poirot, smiling. "Yet, even allowing for that, I can imagine circumstances arising——" He broke off.

Then he said in a different voice:

"You know Mr Bryan Martin, the film actor?"

"Oh! yes, sir."

"Very well?"

"Very well, indeed."

"I believe I am not mistaken in saying that a little less than a year ago Mr. Bryan Martin was very deeply in love with your mistress."

"Head over ears, sir. And it's 'is,' not 'was,' if you ask me."

"He believed at that time she would marry him—eh?"

"Yes, sir."

"Did she ever seriously consider marrying him?"

"She thought of it, sir. If she could have got her freedom from his lordship, I believe she would have married him."

"And then, I suppose, the Duke of Merton appeared on the scene?"

"Yes, sir. He was doing a tour through the States. Love at first sight it was with him.'

"And so good-bye to Bryan Martin's chances?"

Ellis nodded.

"Of course Mr. Martin made an enormous amount of

money," she explained. "But the Duke of Merton had position as well. And her ladyship is very keen on position. Married to the Duke, she'd have been one of the first ladies in the land."

The maid's voice held a smug complacency. It amused me.

"So Mr. Bryan Martin was—how do you say—turned down? Did he take it badly?"

"He carried on something awful, sir."

"Ah!"

"He threatened her with a revolver once. And the scenes he made. It frightened me, it did. He was drinking a lot, too. He went all to pieces."

"But in the end he calmed down."

"So it seemed, sir. But he still hung about. And I didn't like the look in his eye. I've warned her ladyship about it, but she only laughed. She's one who enjoys feeling her power, if you know what I mean."

"Yes," said Poirot thoughtfully. "I think I know what you mean."

"We've not seen so much of him just lately, sir. A good thing in my opinion. He's beginning to get over it, I hope."

"Perhaps."

Something in Poirot's utterance of the word seemed to strike her. She asked anxiously:

"You don't think she's in danger, sir?"

"Yes," said Poirot gravely. "I think she is in great danger. But she has brought it on herself."

His hand, running aimlessly along the mantelshelf, caught a vase of roses and it toppled over. The water fell on Ellis's face and head. I had seldom known Poirot clumsy, and I could deduce from it that he was in a great state of mental perturbation. He was very upset—rushed for a towel—tenderly assisted the maid to dry her face and neck and was profuse in apologies.

Finally a treasury note changed hands and he escorted her towards the door, thanking her for her goodness in coming.

"But it is still early," he said, glancing at the clock. "You will be back before your mistress returns."

"Oh! that is quite all right, sir. She is going out to supper, I think, and anyway, she never expects me to sit up for her unless she says so special."

Suddenly Poirot flew off at a tangent.

"Mademoiselle, pardon me, but you are limping."

"That's nothing, sir. My feet are a little painful."

"The corns?" murmured Poirot in the confidential voice of one sufferer to another.

Corns, apparently, it was. Poirot expatiated upon a certain remedy which, according to him, worked wonders.

Finally Ellis departed.

I was full of curiosity.

"Well, Poirot?" I said. "Well?"

He smiled at my eagerness.

"Nothing more this evening, my friend. To-morrow morning, early, we will ring up Japp. We will ask him to come round. We will also ring up Mr. Bryan Martin. I think he will be able to tell us something interesting. Also, I wish to pay him a debt that I owe him."

"Really?"

I looked at Poirot sideways. He was smiling to himself in a curious way.

"At anyrate," I said, "you can't suspect *him* of killing Lord Edgware. Especially after what we've heard to-night. That would be playing Jane's game with a vengeance. To kill off the husband so as to let the lady marry someone else is a little too disinterested for any man."

"What profound judgment!"

"Now don't be sarcastic," I said with some annoyance. "And what on earth are you fiddling with all the time?"

Poirot held the object in question up.

"With the pince-nez of the good Ellis, my friend. She left them behind."

"Nonsense! She had them on her nose when she went out."

He shook his head gently.

"Wrong! Absolutely wrong! What she had on, my dear Hastings, were the pair of pince-nez we found in Carlotta Adams' handbag."

I gasped.

CHAPTER XXIX

T FELL to me to ring up Inspector Japp the following morning. His voice sounded rather depressed.

"Oh! it's you, Captain Hastings. Well, what's in the wind now?"

I gave him Poirot's message.

"Come round at eleven? Well, I dare say I could. He's not got anything to help us over young Ross's death, has he? I don't mind confessing that we could do with something. There's not a clue of any kind. Most mysterious business."

"I think he's got something for you," I said non-committally. "He seems very pleased with himself at all events."

"That's more than I am, I can tell you. All right, Captain Hastings. I'll be there."

My next task was to ring up Bryan Martin. To him I said what I had been told to say: That Poirot had discovered something rather interesting which he thought Mr. Martin would like to hear. When asked what it was, I said that I had no idea. Poirot had not confided in me. There was a pause.

"All right," said Bryan at last. "I'll come."

He rang off.

Presently, somewhat to my surprise, Poirot rang up Jenny Driver and asked her, also, to be present.

He was quiet and rather grave. I asked him no questions.

Bryan Martin was the first to arrive. He looked in good health and spirits, but—or it might have been my fancy—a shade uneasy. Jenny Driver arrived almost immediately afterwards. She seemed surprised to see Bryan, and he seemed to share her surprise.

Poirot brought forward two chairs and urged them to sit down. He glanced at his watch.

"Inspector Japp will be here in one moment, I expect."

"Inspector Japp?" Bryan seemed startled.

"Yes—I have asked him to come here—informally—as a friend."

" I see."

He relapsed into silence. Jenny gave a quick glance at him then glanced away. She seemed rather preoccupied about something this morning.

A moment later Japp entered the room.

He was, I think, a trifle surprised to find Bryan Martin and Jenny Driver there, but he made no sign. He greeted Poirot with his usual jocularity.

" Well, M. Poirot, what's it all about? You've got some wonderful theory or other, I suppose."

Poirot beamed at him.

" No, no—nothing wonderful. Just a little story quite simple —so simple that I am ashamed not to have seen it at once. I want, if you permit, to take you with me through the case from the beginning."

Japp sighed and looked at his watch.

" If you won't be more than an hour——" he said.

" Reassure yourself," said Poirot. " It will not take as long as that. See here, you want to know, do you not, who it was killed Lord Edgware, who it was killed Miss Adams, who it was killed Donald Ross?"

" I'd like to know the last," said Japp cautiously.

" Listen to me and you shall know everything. See, I am going to be humble." (Not likely! I thought unbelievingly.) " I am going to show you every step of the way—I am going to reveal how I was hoodwinked, how I displayed the gross imbecility, how it needed the conversation of my friend Hastings and a chance remark by a total stranger to put me on the right track."

He paused and then, clearing his throat, he began to speak in what I called his " lecture " voice.

" I will begin at the supper party at the Savoy. Lady Edgware accosted me and asked for a private interview. She wanted to get rid of her husband. At the close of our interview she said—somewhat unwisely, I thought—that she might have to go round in a taxi and kill him herself. Those words were heard by Mr. Bryan Martin, who came in at that moment."

He wheeled round.

" Eh? That is so, is it not?"

" We all heard," said the actor. " The Widburns, Marsh, Carlotta—all of us."

"Oh! I agree. I agree perfectly. *Eh bien*, I did not have chance to forget those words of Lady Edgware's. Mr. Bryan Martin called on the following morning for the express purpose of driving those words home."

"Not at all," cried Bryan Martin angrily. "I came——"

Poirot held up a hand.

"You came, ostensibly, to tell me a cock-and-bull story about being shadowed. A tale that a child might have seen through. You probably took it from an out-of-date film. A girl whose consent you had to obtain—a man whom you recognised by a gold tooth. *Mon ami*, no *young* man would have a gold tooth—it is not done in these days—and especially in America. The gold tooth it is a hopelessly old-fashioned piece of dentistry. Oh! it was all of a piece—absurd! Having told your cock-and-bull story you get down to the real purpose of your visit—to poison my mind against Lady Edgware. To put it clearly, you prepare the ground for the moment when she murders her husband."

"I don't know what you're talking about," muttered Bryan Martin. His face was deathly pale.

"You ridicule the idea that he will agree to a divorce! You think I am going to see him the following day, but actually the appointment is changed. I go to see him that morning and he *does* agree to a divorce. Any motive for a crime on Lady Edgware's part is gone. Moreover, he tells me that he has already written to Lady Edgware to that effect.

"But Lady Edgware declares that she never got that letter. Either she lies, her husband lies, or somebody has suppressed it—who?

"Now I ask myself *why* does M. Bryan Martin give himself the trouble to come and tell me all these lies? What inner power drives him on. And I form the idea, Monsieur, that you have been frantically in love with that lady. Lord Edgware says that his wife told him she wanted to marry an actor. Well, supposing that is so, but that the lady changes her mind. By the time Lord Edgware's letter agreeing to the divorce arrives, it is someone else she wants to marry—not you! There would be a reason, then, for you suppressing that letter."

"I never——"

"Presently you shall say all you want to say. Now you will attend to me.

"What, then, would be your frame of mind—you, a spoilt

idol who has never known a rebuff? As I see it, a kind of baffled fury, a desire to do Lady Edgware as much harm as possible. And what greater harm could you do her than to have her accused—perhaps hanged—for murder."

" Good lord! " said Japp.

Poirot turned to him.

" But yes, that was the little idea that began to shape itself in my mind. Several things came to support it. Carlotta Adams had two principal men friends—Captain Marsh and Bryan Martin. It was possible, then, that Bryan Martin, a rich man, was the one who suggested the hoax and offered her ten thousand dollars to carry it through. It has seemed to me unlikely all along that Miss Adams could ever have believed Ronald Marsh would have the ten thousand dollars to give her. She knew him to be extremely hard up. Bryan Martin was a far more likely solution."

" I didn't—I tell you I didn't——" came hoarsely from the film actor's lips.

" When the substance of Miss Adams' letter to her sister was wired from Washington—oh! *la, la!* I was very upset. It seemed that my reasoning was wholly wrong. But later I made a discovery. The actual letter itself was sent to me and instead of being continuous, a sheet of the letter was missing. So ' he ' might refer to someone who was not Captain Marsh.

" There was one more piece of evidence. Captain Marsh, when he was arrested, distinctly stated that he thought he saw Bryan Martin enter the house. Coming from an accused man that carried no weight. Also M. Martin had an alibi. That naturally! It was to be expected. If M. Martin did the murder to have an alibi was absolutely necessary.

" That alibi was vouched for by one person only—Miss Driver."

" What about it? " said the girl sharply.

" Nothing, Mademoiselle," said Poirot, smiling. " Except that that same day I noticed you lunching with M. Martin and that you presently took the trouble to come over and try to make me believe that your friend Miss Adams was specially interested in Ronald Marsh—not, as I was sure was the case—in Bryan Martin."

" Not a bit of it," said the film star stoutly.

" You may have been unaware of it, Monsieur," said Poirot quietly, " but I think it was true. It explains, as nothing else

ould, her feeling of dislike towards Lady Edgware. That dislike was on your behalf. You had told her all about your
rebuff, had you not?"

"Well—yes—I felt I must talk to someone and she——"

"Was sympathetic. Yes, she was sympathetic, I noticed it
myself. *Eh bien*, what happens next? Ronald Marsh, he is
arrested. Immediately your spirits improve. Any anxiety you
may have had is over. Although your plan has miscarried
owing to Lady Edgware's change of mind about going to a
party at the last minute, yet somebody else has become the
scapegoat and relieved you of all anxiety on your own account.
And then—at a luncheon party—you hear Donald Ross, that
pleasant, but rather stupid young man, say something to
Hastings that seems to show that you are not so safe after all."

"It isn't true," the actor howled. The perspiration was
running down his face. His eyes looked wild with terror. "I
tell you I heard nothing—nothing—I did nothing."

Then, I think, came the greatest shock of the morning.

"That is quite true," said Poirot quietly. "And I hope
you have now been sufficiently punished for coming to me—
me, Hercule Poirot, with a cock-and-bull story."

We all gasped. Poirot continued dreamily.

"You see—I am showing you all my mistakes. There were
five questions I had asked myself. Hastings knows them. The
answer to three of them fitted in very well. Who had suppressed that letter? Clearly Bryan Martin answered that question very well. Another question was what had induced Lord
Edgware suddenly to change his mind and agree to a divorce?
Well, I had an idea as to that. Either he wanted to marry
again—but I could find no evidence pointing to that—or else
some kind of blackmail was involved. Lord Edgware was a
man of peculiar tastes. It was possible that facts about him
had come to light which, while not entitling his wife to an
English divorce, might yet be used by her as a lever coupled
with the threat of publicity. I think that is what happened.
Lord Edgware did not want an open scandal attached to his
name. He gave in, though his fury at having to do so was
expressed in the murderous look on his face when he thought
himself unobserved. It also explains the suspicious quickness
with which he said, 'Not because of anything in the letter,'
before I had even suggested that that might be the case.

"Two questions remained. The question of an odd pair of

pince-nez in Miss Adams' bag which did not belong to her. And the question of why Lady Edgware was rung up on the telephone whilst she was at dinner at Chiswick. In no way could I fit in M. Bryan Martin with either of those questions.

" So I was forced to the conclusion that either I was wrong about Mr. Martin, or wrong about the questions. In despair I once again read that letter of Miss Adams' through very carefully. And I found something! Yes, I found something!

" See for yourselves. Here it is. You see the sheet is torn? Unevenly, as often happens. Supposing now that before the 'h' at the top there was an 's'...

" Ah! you have it! You see. Not *he*—but *she*! It was a *woman* who suggested this hoax to Carlotta Adams.

" Well, I made a list of all the women who had been even remotely connected with the case. Besides Jane Wilkinson, there were four—Geraldine Marsh, Miss Carroll, Miss Driver and the Duchess of Merton.

" Of those four, the one that interested me most was Miss Carroll. She wore glasses, she was in the house that night, she had already been inaccurate in her evidence owing to her desire to incriminate Lady Edgware, and she was also a woman of great efficiency and nerve who could have carried out such a crime. The motive was more obscure—but after all, she had worked with Lord Edgware some years and some motive might exist of which we were totally unaware.

" I also felt that I could not quite dismiss Geraldine Marsh from the case. She hated her father—she had told me so. She was a neurotic, highly-strung type. Suppose when she went into the house that night she had deliberately stabbed her father and then coolly proceeded upstairs to fetch the pearls. Imagine her agony when she found that her cousin whom she loved devotedly had not remained outside in the taxi but had entered the house!

" Her agitated manner could be well explained on these lines. It could equally well be explained by her own innocence, but by her fear that her cousin really had done the crime. There was another small point. The gold box found in Miss Adams' bag had the initial D in it. I had heard Geraldine addressed by her cousin as 'Dina.' Also, she was in a pensionnat in Paris last November and might possibly have met Carlotta Adams in Paris.

" You may think it fantastic to add the Duchess of Merton

o the list. But she had called upon me and I recognised in her
a fanatical type. The love of her whole life was centred on her
son, and she might have worked herself up to contrive a plot
to destroy the woman who was about to ruin her son's life.

" Then there was Miss Jenny Driver——"

He paused, looking at Jenny. She looked back at him, an
impudent head on one side.

" And what have you got on me?" she asked.

" Nothing, Mademoiselle, except that you were a friend of
Bryan Martin's—and that your surname begins with D."

" That's not very much."

" There's one thing more. You have the brains and the
nerve to commit such a crime. I doubt if anyone else had."

The girl lit a cigarette.

" Continue," she said cheerfully.

" Was M. Martin's alibi genuine or was it not? That was
what I had to decide. If it was, who was it Ronald Marsh had
seen go into the house? And suddenly I remembered something. The good-looking butler at Regent Gate bore a very
marked resemblance to M. Martin. It was he whom Captain
Marsh had seen. And I formed a theory as to that. It is my
idea that he discovered his master killed. Beside his master
was an envelope containing French banknotes to the value of a
hundred pounds. He took these notes, slipped out of the
house, left them in safe keeping with some rascally friend and
returned, letting himself in with Lord Edgware's key. He let
the crime be discovered by the housemaid on the following
morning. He felt in no danger himself, as he was quite convinced that Lady Edgware had done the murder, and the notes
were out of the house and already changed before their loss
was noticed. However, when Lady Edgware had an alibi and
Scotland Yard began investigating his antecedents, he got the
wind up and decamped."

Japp nodded approvingly.

" I still have the question of the pince-nez to settle. If Miss
Carroll was the owner then the case seemed settled. She could
have suppressed the letter, and in arranging details with Carlotta Adams, or in meeting her on the evening of the murder,
the pince-nez might have inadvertently found their way into
Carlotta Adams' bag.

" But the pince-nez were apparently nothing to do with
Miss Carroll. I was walking home with Hastings here, some-

what depressed, trying to arrange things in my mind with order and method. And then the miracle happened!

" First Hastings spoke of things in a certain order. He mentioned Donald Ross having been one of thirteen at table at Sir Montagua Corner's and having been the first to get up. I was following out a train of thought of my own and did not pay much attention. It just flashed through my mind that, strictly speaking, that was not true. He may have got up first at the end of the dinner, but actually Lady Edgware had been the first to get up since she was called to the telephone. Thinking of her, a certain riddle occurred to me—a riddle that I fancied accorded well with her somewhat childish mentality. I told it to Hastings. He was, like Queen Victoria, not amused. I next fell to wondering who I could ask for details about M. Martin's feeling for Jane Wilkinson. She herself would not tell me, I knew. And then a passer-by, as we were all crossing the road, uttered a simple sentence.

" He said to his girl companion that somebody or other ' should have asked Ellis.' And immediately the whole thing came to me in a flash! "

He looked round.

" Yes, yes, the pince-nez, the telephone call, the short woman who called for the gold box in Paris. *Ellis*, of course, Jane Wilkinson's maid. I followed every step of it—the candles—the dim light—Mrs. Van Dusen—everything. I *knew!* "

CHAPTER XXX

THE STORY

HE LOOKED round at us.

" Come, my friends," he said gently. " Let me tell you the real story of what happened that night.

" Carlotta Adams leaves her flat at seven o'clock. From there she takes a taxi and goes to the Piccadilly Palace."

" What? " I exclaimed.

" To the Piccadilly Palace. Earlier in the day she has taken a room there as Mrs. Van Dusen. She wears a pair of strong glasses which, as we all know, alters the appearance very much. As I say, she books a room, saying that she is going by the night boat train to Liverpool and that her luggage has gone on. At eight-thirty Lady Edgware arrives and asks for her. She is shown up to her room. There they change clothes. Dressed in a fair wig, a white taffeta dress and ermine wrap, *Carlotta Adams and not Jane Wilkinson leaves the hotel and drives to Chiswick*. Yes, yes, it is perfectly possible. I have been to the house in the evening. The dinner table is lit only with candles, the lamps are dim, no one there knows Jane Wilkinson very well. There is the golden hair, the well-known husky voice and manner. Oh! it was quite easy. And if it had not been successful—if someone had spotted the fake—well, that was all arranged for, too. Lady Edgware, wearing a dark wig, Carlotta's clothes and the pince-nez, pays her bill, has her suitcase put on a taxi and drives to Euston. She removes the dark wig in the lavatory, she puts her suitcase in the cloak-room. Before going to Regent Gate she rings up Chiswick and asks to speak to Lady Edgware. This has been arranged between them. If all has gone well and Carlotta has not been spotted, she is to answer simply—' that's right.' I need hardly say Miss Adams was ignorant of the real reason for the telephone call. Having heard the words, Lady Edgware goes ahead. She goes to Regent Gate, asks for Lord Edgware, proclaims her individuality, and goes into the library. *And commits the first murder*. Of course she did not know that Miss Carroll was watching her from above. As far as she is aware it will be the butler's word (and he has never seen her, remember—and also she wears a hat which shields her from his gaze) against the word of twelve well-known and distinguished people.

" She leaves the house, returns to Euston, changes from fair to dark again and picks up her suitcase. She has now to put in time till Carlotta Adams returns from Chiswick. They have agreed as to the approximate time. She goes to the Corner House, occasionally glancing at her watch, for the time passes slowly. Then she prepares for the second murder. She puts the small gold box she has ordered from Paris in Carlotta Adams' bag which, of course, she is carrying. Perhaps it is then she finds the letter. Perhaps it was earlier. Anyway, as soon as she sees the address, she scents danger. She opens it —her suspicions are justified.

" Perhaps her first impulse is to destroy the letter altogether. But she soon sees a better way. By removing one page of the letter it reads like an accusation of Ronald Marsh—a man who had a powerful motive for the crime. Even if Ronald has an alibi, it will still read as an accusation of a man so long as she tears off the s of ' she.' So that is what she does, then replaces it in the envelope and the envelope back in the bag.

" Then, the time having come, she walks in the direction of the Savoy Hotel. As soon as she sees the car pass, with (presumably) herself inside, she quickens her pace, enters at the same time and goes straight up the stairs. She is inconspicuously dressed in black. It is unlikely that anyone will notice her.

" Upstairs she goes to her room. Carlotta Adams has just reached it. The maid has been told to go to bed—a perfectly usual proceeding. They again change clothes and then, I fancy, Lady Edgware suggests a little drink—to celebrate. In that drink is the veronal. She congratulates her victim, says she will send her the cheque to-morrow. Carlotta Adams goes home. She is very sleepy—tries to ring up a friend—possibly M. Martin or Captain Marsh, for both have Victoria numbers —but gives it up. She is too tired. The veronal is beginning to work. She goes to bed—*and she never wakes again*. The second crime has been carried through successfully.

" Now for the third crime. It is at a luncheon party. Sir Montagu Corner makes a reference to a conversation he had with Lady Edgware on the night of the murder. That is easy. But Nemesis comes upon her later. There is a mention of the ' judgment of Paris,' and she takes Paris to be the only Paris she knows—the Paris of fashion and frills!

" But opposite her is sitting a young man who was at that dinner at Chiswick—a young man who heard the Lady Edgware of that night discussing Homer and Greek civilisation generally. Carlotta Adams was a cultured well-read girl. He cannot understand. He stares. And suddenly it comes to him. *This is not the same woman.* He is terribly upset. He is not sure of himself. He must have advice. He thinks of me. He speaks to Hastings.

" But the lady overheard him. She is quick enough and shrewd enough to realise that in some way or other she has given herself away. She hears Hastings say that I will not be in till five. At twenty to five she goes to Ross's maisonette. He opens the door, is very surprised to see her, but it does not occur to him to be afraid. A strong able-bodied young man is not afraid of a woman. He goes with her into the dining-room. She pours out some story to him. Perhaps she goes on her knees and flings her arms round his neck. And then, swift and sure, she strikes—as before. Perhaps he gives a choked cry—no more. He, too, is silenced."

There was a silence. Then Japp spoke hoarsely,

"You mean—she did it all the time?"

Poirot bowed his head.

"But why, if he was willing to give her a divorce?"

"Because the Duke of Merton is a pillar of the Anglo-Catholics. Because he would not dream of marrying a woman whose husband was alive. He is a young man of fanatical principles. As a widow, she was pretty certain to be able to marry him. Doubtless she had tentatively suggested divorce, but he had not risen to the bait."

"Then why send you to Lord Edgware?"

"Ah! parbleu." Poirot, from having been very correct and English, suddenly relapsed into his natural self. "To pull the cotton-wool over my eyes! To make me a witness to the fact that there was no motive for the murder! Yes, she dared to make me, Hercule Poirot, her cat's-paw! Ma foi, she suc-ceeded, too! Oh! that strange brain, childlike and cunning. She can act! How well she acted surprise at being told of the letter her husband had written her which she swore she had never received. Did she feel the slightest pang of remorse for any of her three crimes? I can swear she did not."

"I told you what she was like," cried Bryan Martin. "I told you. I knew she was going to kill him. I felt it. And I was afraid that somehow she'd get away with it. She's clever —devilish clever in a kind of half-wit way. And I wanted her to suffer. I wanted her to suffer. I wanted her to hang for it."

His face was scarlet. His voice came thickly.

"Now, now," said Jenny Driver.

She spoke exactly as I have heard nursemaids speak to a small child in the park.

"And the gold box with the initial D, and Paris November inside?" said Japp.

"She ordered that by letter and sent Ellis, her maid, to fetch it. Naturally Ellis just called for a parcel which she paid for. She had no idea what was inside. Also, Lady Edgware borrowed a pair of Ellis's pince-nez to help in the Van Dusen

impersonation. She forgot about them and left them in
Carlotta Adams' handbag—her one mistake.

"Oh! it came to me—it all came to me as I stood in the
middle of the road. It was not polite what the bus driver said
to me, but it was worth it. Ellis! Ellis's pince-nez. Ellis
calling for the box in Paris. Ellis and therefore Jane Wilkinson.
Very possibly she borrowed something else from Ellis besides
des pince-nez."

"What?"

"A corn knife. . . ?"

I shivered.

There was a momentary silence.

Then Japp said with a strange reliance in the answer:

"M. Poirot. Is this *true*?"

"It is true, *mon ami*."

Then Bryan Martin spoke, and his words were, I thought,
very typical of him.

"But look here," he said peevishly. "What about *me*?
Why bring *me* here to-day? Why nearly frighten me to
death?"

Poirot looked at him coldly.

"To punish you, Monsieur, for being impertinent! How
dare you try and make the games with Hercule Poirot?"

And then Jenny Driver laughed. She laughed and laughed.

"Serve you right, Bryan," she said at last.

She turned to Poirot.

"I'm glad as I can be that it wasn't Ronnie Marsh," she
said. "I've always liked him. And I'm glad, glad, *glad* that
Carlotta's death won't go unpunished! As for Bryan here,
well, I'll tell you something, M. Poirot. I'm going to marry
him. And if he thinks he can get divorced and married every
two or three years in the approved Hollywood fashion, well,
he never made a bigger mistake in his life. He's going to marry
me and stick to me."

Poirot looked at her—looked at her determined chin—and at
her flaming hair.

"It is very possible, Mademoiselle," he said, "that that
may be so. I said that you had sufficient nerve for anything.
Even to marry a film 'star.'"

CHAPTER XXXI

A HUMAN DOCUMENT

A DAY or two after that I was suddenly recalled to the Argentine. So it happened that I never saw Jane Wilkinson again and only read in the paper of her trial and condemnation. Unexpectedly, at least unexpectedly to me, she went completely to pieces when charged with the truth. So long as she was able to be proud of her cleverness and act her part she made no mistakes, but once her self-confidence failed her, owing to someone having found her out, she was as incapable as a child would be of keeping up a deception. Cross-examined, she went completely to pieces.

So, as I said before, that luncheon party was the last time I saw Jane Wilkinson. But when I think of her, I always see her the same way—standing in her room at the Savoy trying on expensive black clothes with a serious absorbed face. I am convinced that that was no pose. She was being completely natural. Her plan had succeeded and therefore she had no further qualms and doubts. Neither do I think that she ever suffered one pang of remorse for the three crimes she had committed.

I reproduce here a document which she had directed was to be sent to Poirot after her death. It is, I think, typical of that very lovely and completely conscienceless lady.

" DEAR M. POIROT,—I have been thinking things over and I feel that I should like to write this for you. I know that you sometimes publish reports of your cases. I don't really think that you've ever published a document by the person themselves. I feel, too, that I would like everyone to know just exactly how I did it all. I still think it was all very well planned. If it hadn't been for you everything would have been quite all right. I've felt rather bitter about that, but I suppose you couldn't help it. I'm sure, if I send you this, you'll give it plenty of prominence. You will, won't you? I should like to be remembered. And I do think I am really a unique person. Everybody here seems to think so,

189

"It began in America when I got to know Merton. I saw at once that if only I were a widow he would marry me. Unfortunately, he has got a queer sort of prejudice against divorce. I tried to overcome it but it was no good, and I had to be careful, because he was a very kinky sort of person.

"I soon realised that my husband simply had got to die, but I didn't know how to set about it. You can manage things like that ever so much better in the States. I thought and I thought —but I couldn't see how to arrange it. And then, suddenly, I saw Carlotta Adams do her imitation of me and at once I began to see a way. With her help I could get an alibi. That same evening I saw you, and it suddenly struck me that it would be a good idea to send you to my husband to ask him for a divorce. At the same time I would go about talking of killing my husband, because I've always noticed that if you speak the truth in a rather silly way nobody believes you. I've often done it over contracts. And it's also a good thing to seem stupider than you are. At my second meeting with Carlotta Adams I broached the idea. I said it was a bet, and she fell for it at once. She was to pretend to be me at some party and if she got away with it she was to have ten thousand dollars. She was very enthusiastic and several of the ideas were hers— about changing clothes and all that. You see, we couldn't do it here because of Ellis and we couldn't do it at her place because of her maid. She, of course, didn't see why we couldn't. It was a little awkward. I just said ' No.' She thought me a little stupid about it, but she gave in and we thought of the hotel plan. I took a pair of Ellis's pince-nez.

"Of course I realised quite soon that she would have to be got out of the way too. It was a pity, but after all, those imitations of hers really were very impertinent. If mine hadn't happened to suit me I'd have been angry about it. I had some veronal myself, though I hardly ever take it, so that was quite easy. And then I had quite a brainwave. You see, it would be so much better if it could seem that she was in the habit of taking it. I ordered a box—the duplicate of one I'd been given and I had her initials put on it and an inscription inside. I thought if I put some odd initial and Paris, November, inside it, it would make it all much more difficult. I wrote for the box from the Ritz when I was in there lunching one day. And I sent Ellis over to fetch it. She didn't know what it was, of course.

" Everything went off quite well on the night. I took one of Ellis's corn knives, while she was over in Paris, because it was nice and sharp. She never noticed because I put it back afterwards. It was a doctor in San Francisco who showed me just where to stick it in. He'd been talking about lumbar and cistern punctures, and he said one had to be very careful, otherwise one went through the cistertia magna and into the medulla oblongata where all the vital nerve centres are, and that that would cause immediate death. I made him show me the exact place several times. I thought it might perhaps come in useful one day. I told him I wanted to use the idea in a film.

" It was very dishonourable of Carlotta Adams to write to her sister. She'd promised me to tell nobody. I do think it was clever of me to see what a good thing it would be to tear off that one page and leave he instead of she. I thought of that all by myself. I think I'm more proud of that than anything else. Everyone always says I haven't got brains—but I think it needed real brains to think of that.

" I'd thought things out very carefully and I did exactly what I'd planned when the Scotland Yard man came. I rather enjoyed that part of it. I had thought, perhaps, that he'd really arrest me. 1 felt quite safe, because they'd have to believe all those people at the dinner and I didn't see how they could find out about me and Carlotta changing clothes.

" After that 1 felt so happy and contented. My luck had held and I really felt everything was going to go right. The old Duchess was beastly to me, but Merton was sweet. He wanted to marry me as soon as possible and hadn't the least suspicion.

" I don't think I've ever been so happy as I was those few weeks. My husband's nephew being arrested made me feel just as safe as anything. And I was more proud of myself than ever for having thought of tearing that page out of Carlotta Adams' letter.

" The Donald Ross business was just sheer bad luck. I'm not quite sure now just how it was he spotted me. Something about Paris being a person and not a place. Even now I don't know who Paris was—and I think it's a silly name for a man anyway.

" It's curious how, when luck starts going against you, it keeps on going. I had to do something about Donald Ross quickly, and that did go all right. It mightn't have, because I hadn't time to be clever or think of making an alibi. I did think I was safe after that.

"Of course Ellis told me you had sent for her and questioned her, but I gathered it was all something to do with Bryan Martin. I couldn't think what you were driving at. You didn't ask her whether she had called for the parcel in Paris. I suppose you thought if she repeated that to me I should smell a rat. As it was, it came as a complete surprise. I couldn't believe it. It was just uncanny the way you seemed to know everything I'd done.

"I just felt it was no good. You can't fight against luck. It *was* bad luck, wasn't it? I wonder if you are ever sorry for what you did. After all, I only wanted to be happy in my own way. And if it hadn't been for me you would never have had anything to do with the case. I never thought you'd be so horribly clever. You didn't look clever.

"It's funny, but I haven't lost my looks a bit. In spite of all that dreadful trial and the horrid things that man on the other side said to me, and the way he battered me with questions.

"I look much paler and thinner, but it suits me somehow. They all say I'm wonderfully brave. They don't hang you in public any more, do they? I think that's a pity.

"I'm sure there's never been a murderess like me before.

"I suppose I must say good-bye now. It's very queer. I don't seem to realise things a bit. I'm going to see the chaplain to-morrow.

"Yours forgivingly (because I must forgive my enemies, mustn't I?),

JANE WILKINSON.

"P.S.—Do you think they will put me in Madame Tussauds?"

THE END